Monster Burger

24/7 Demon Mart Book 2

by D.M. Guay

ISBN: 9798648301498

Cover by James at Goonwrite.com

This book is a work of fiction. Any similarity between the characters and situations within its pages and real places or persons, living or dead, is unintentional and coincidental.

Dear Mom,
Thanks for watching bad horror movies with me when I was a kid. This book probably wouldn't be here if we'd changed the channel.

CONTENTS

MONSTER BURGER
24/7 DEMON MART 2
THIS ONE HAS ZOMBIES IN IT

Lying there, trapped underneath a four hundred pound man who'd clamped his teeth around my elbow like an alligator, I made a decision: I was not going to give up. Sure. It seemed hopeless. I had a dozen people chewing on my legs, trying to eat me, and a dozen more waiting behind them to slurp up the scraps, but there was still hope, right? I was going to fight. I had no other choice. I had to save DeeDee—and the world—or die trying.

CHAPTER 1

It was midnight, and Demon Mart was unusually quiet. No demons. No monsters. No customers. It was quite pleasant, actually. The fluorescent lights flickered a warmer hue, and the magical chanting Muzak charm was set to a disco funk beat. I kind of dug it. It was sexy.

I bumped my hips to the music as I restocked the rubbers in aisle four. I grabbed a handful of small, square condom boxes out of the stock tub. The packages were black with a cartoon logo: A chubby winking white dude with two thumbs up. "Fat Dude Gets Lucky" brand, "Ribbed for the pleasure of anyone who'll touch him."

Huh. You ever heard of these? Yeah. Me either.

I held up the box and ran it down the line of hangers, trying to figure out where it was supposed to go. Maximum Big Boy? Nope. Ultra Thin Joy Rides? Nope. Bucking Bronco Bare Skins? Nope. Rapture Ridge Pleasure pack? Uh, no. Ecstasy Ultra Ribbed? No again. Triple Velvet Lady Slayer? Geesh. I had no idea there were so many kinds of rubbers.

"Why would you? You don't have enough sex," angel eight ball said as he settled in on a nearby shelf by knocking bottles of lube away.

"Shut up."

"Come on. We both know you're a swipe left."

I scanned the condom display again, then examined the box of "Fat Dude Gets Lucky." Well, there wasn't a spot for it. The order must be messed up. Maybe we got them by mistake.

"There's no mistake." DeeDee stood at the end of the aisle. She was radiant tonight, a goddess among women, which meant she pretty much looked exactly the same way she did every night. She'd dyed her hair a sultry deep burgundy. Her black liquid eyeliner curved to a dangerous point at the end of her gray eyes. "I ordered those custom made, just for you. Stud."

She winked at me.

Gulp. "What?" The word barely squeaked out. Because dude. All my blood had rushed south. There wasn't enough left in my head to think of a word, let alone speak one.

"You heard me." DeeDee sashayed toward me, hips swinging, eyes locked on mine. "This is long overdue."

She grabbed the hem of her Siouxsie and The Banshees T-shirt and pulled it up and off as she walked. It fluttered to the floor.

Oh. My. God. Boobs. And not just any boobs. DeeDee's boobs. They were radiant beasts, luscious confections wrapped in a delicate black lace wrapper.

Woah boy. Full on wood.

"Why don't you open that box," she purred. "And we'll take that bad boy for a spin."

She grabbed me by the T-shirt, pulled me close to her and kissed me. With tongue. She felt so good. Curvy and warm, her hand sliding down down down. This was better than Christmas. Usually the only hands in my pants were mine.

Her hair tickled my face. I breathed deep. *Mmmmm.* She smelled like sugar. No maple. Maple sugar? Weird choice, but whatever. I'm into it.

"Wake up, honey," DeeDee whispered in my ear.

She gave it a little nibble, then licked it. Her tongue felt rough, like sandpaper, but I didn't mind. She just needed a sip of Snapple or something to moisten that up. Her fingers fumbled with the button of my cargo shorts.

Oh yes. This is happening. This is finally happening!

She said, "Rise and shine. It's time to get up."

Oh, I was up all right.

"Holy cow. Please stop," Angel eight ball said. "This is a total shit show."

"Shu uuuuup." It's hard to enunciate with a hot chick's tongue in your mouth.

DeeDee stopped kissing me and tilted her head back. So naturally, I totally motor-boated her flawless breasts. I mean, I really sunk my face in there. Deep. She moaned in ecstasy. "Uuuuuuuuuuuuuh. Aaaaaaaaaaar. Uuuuuuuuuuuuuuuuuuh."

That's right, girl. You love it.

She growled—ooh, she must really love it—then she bit the top of my head.

Ow! Holy crap, that hurt.

Weird, right? But I shrugged it off. Because boobs. And, because whatever DeeDee was into, I would be into. Guys like me can't be picky.

She bit me again, and this time it really hurt. Like next level agony. My hair suddenly felt very wet.

"Ouch! Stop!" I pulled back. When I saw her face, I froze. "Holy shit. Are you all right?"

No, she was not. Definitely not. Nope.

Blood dripped from her mouth. Her skin had turned pale green, and her eyes were milky white. She looked like the cleaning crew. Oh God. They got her. She must have been bitten. She must have turned.

My hand shot to the top of my head. When I pulled my fingers back, they were red. With blood. She bit *me*!

She spit a chunk of me out of her mouth and smiled, flashing her rotten black teeth. Dear God. What did they do to DeeDee? Why didn't I save her? I should have saved her!

She lunged at me and growled, "Honey? Do you want a doughnut?"

Um, that was a weird thing for a zombie to say, right?

"Wow. Your brain is a mess. I think you might have PTSD." Angel eight ball said. "But seriously. We're done here."

He flew off the shelf and smacked into my nuts. Hard.

"Ooooow!" I howled, because dude. Nuts!

I bent in half, holding my aching crotch, and my nose landed directly in a box of fresh doughnuts. Doughnuts? "NOOOOOOOOO! Get them away from meeeeeee. They're cursed!"

I punched the box. Glazed loops flew up through the air, flipping end over end, sprinkles hanging on for dear life. They splatted onto the floor, icing side down. Cream filling and jelly splurped all over the rug. Wait. The rug?

"Oh my gosh!" My Mom squeaked.

I blinked hard and looked around. Oh. I was in my room, sitting up in bed, holding my nuts. Angel eight ball was in my lap. *Dude! Not cool! Do you know how much that hurts?*

"No, I don't actually. But you're welcome." Angel eight ball's triangle slid side to side, like he was shaking his head at me. "Look."

His triangle flashed a drawing of a finger pointing straight at my cat, Gertrude, spread eagle on my pillow, leg up, licking her butt.

Aw, man. That wasn't DeeDee's sandpaper tongue nibbling my ear, was it? She didn't smell like maple either. That was doughnut frosting. And the dirty talk? Holy hell. That was my Mom, wasn't it? Wow. Immediate chainsaw to the morning wood. Total deforestation.

"Geesh, honey." My Mom stood next to the bed looking flustered, surveying the sad sprinkly mess on the carpet. "What's gotten into you? Since when do you hate doughnuts?"

She definitely did not want an honest answer to that question.

Oh, wait. Maybe she did. Because she stood there staring at me, waiting.

"What was all that punching about anyway? Bad dream?" Mom's voice curled up extra tight at the end. Her eyebrows squinched together, forming a deep wrinkle eleven between her eyes.

Uh oh. I knew that look. Those were her worried eyebrows.

"Is there something on your mind? Anything you want to talk about?"

And boom. Called it. Here. Let me translate the secret language of Mom for you: "Something on *your* mind" meant "something on *her* mind." Trust me. She didn't tiptoe around my room with doughnuts unless she was luring me into some sort of trap.

Mom knelt down and scooped doughnut shrapnel from the floor into the box. "Good thing all the fancy ones are downstairs. You better hurry. Your Dad's been hovering over the box for an hour. I told him he had to wait until you woke up so we could eat together as a family. I can't hold him off much longer."

Oh God. Stone cold dread blurbled in my belly. Doughnuts plus something on her mind, plus family meal equaled not good for Lloyd. Not good at all. I was a dead man.

"Yeah. You're totally screwed," angel eight ball said. "If Jennifer Wallace declares a family meal on a non-holiday, you're in for it. Even angels are quaking in their socks right now. What did you do this time?"

Nothing? My mind buzzed, trying to identify any new screw ups, but for once, I couldn't think of any. We'd already had the big talks:

1: When are you gonna get a job, Lloyd? Adults have jobs, and you're a legal adult.

2. How are you going to pay your student loans? They're coming due. (See 1. Job.)

3. When are you going back to college? Most good jobs require degrees. You want to have a good job, don't you?

Groan. My head hurt just thinking about those conversations. So painful. What could I possibly be in trouble for anyway? I had finished two out of three!

"You're a minimally employed community college dropout. Gee whiz. What could they possibly be concerned about? Any parent would be over the moon." Angel eight ball rolled his triangle at me. "If they ask about school, you should tell them you've earned an honorary doctorate in Pornhub. Seriously. You surf so much porn. So so soooo much porn. I bet your search history has herpes."

"Shut up!" I snapped. "Be quiet and let me think!"

"Excuse you, Mister?" Mom dug her fists into her hips.

Oops. That was out loud.

"Sorry Mom. Not you." I plastered on a fake smile and shook eight ball really hard. Really, really hard. *You made me look like a jerk!*

His triangle seemed impervious to my rage. "Don't blame the messenger. I'm only reading the room here. Now get up. Pull this Mom Band-Aid off already. We've got work to do. Jesus was serious about the cardio."

I flung my legs over the side of the bed and angel eight ball rolled off my lap, onto the carpet, and right into my Mom's foot. She stopped picking sprinkles out of the shag. "Oh. Is this the same one you had when you were little? I thought you lost it!" Mom picked up the eight ball and shook it. "What is my baby up to these days? Is he being a good boy?"

The triangle turned and said, "Don't count on it."

Worst guardian angel ever.

"Here. Let me put that away." I snatched the ball out of her hand and tossed it into the closet. It landed in a box of old video games and dirty socks. Yeah yeah. I was still working on that cleanliness and godliness thing. Don't judge me. It'd only been twenty-four hours since I saved the world. You're welcome.

Mom followed me downstairs. When we stepped into the kitchen, Dad had a ring of white cream around his mouth, and his cheeks were puffed up like a hamster's.

"Really honey? You couldn't wait five more minutes?" Mom huffed.

"Sowwwy." A wall of doughnut mush churned between his lips.

Dude. I feel ya. If I'd been left alone with a box of fancies at any point in history before this weekend, I woulda cleared it in five minutes flat. But I was a changed man. After what I'd seen, I'd never eat a doughnut ever again.

"Sit down, honey," Mom said to me.

I could see all traces of hope and joy drain out of my Dad as he spotted the box of ruined doughnuts coated in carpet, dust and lint in her hand. "Wha happun...?"

"Nothing." Mom sighed, dropped the box into the garbage can, then turned to us. "Now. Let's get to it."

A green light flashed behind her. It grew into a swirling misty portal, about as big around as a soda can, hanging in midair above the garbage. *AHHH! HELL BEAST! ATTACK! ATTACK!*

My muscles clenched up so tight, so fast, I could have shit a diamond. I grabbed the closest weapon, which turned out to be a fork. A set of antennae emerged from the vortex, two legs, then two more. A second later, a cockroach swan dived out of the portal and straight into the discarded doughnut box. It locked eyes with me, then winked as it landed on the powdery remains of a raspberry jelly filled.

Kevin. What the hell was he doing here?

"Nice to see you too, kid," he said. "I need somewhere to hang out until the store reopens. My roommates are the worst. Unbearable. DeeDee didn't have any good snacks. Nothing but vegetables. Blech. Do I look like a rabbit? I see you've got the good stuff."

He took a bite out of the doughnut and groaned as he chewed. "Mmmmmmmm. That's what I'm talking about. Fuck carrots." He closed his eyes and swayed joyfully. "Hold up. What's that?"

He picked something out of his...*teeth?* Do roaches have teeth*?* "These doughnuts are a little linty. Whatevs."

He shrugged and kept on eating. The tiny green portal zipped up and disappeared behind him.

Mom, oblivious to the wayward roach, brought a gallon of milk and the tray of remaining fancy doughnuts to the table and said, "Uuuuuuuuuuuuuh."

You heard that, right? No. Mom was not a zombie. (As soon as she made that noise, I double checked.) This was worse. This, my friend, was THE SIGH. The "It's sooooooo hard being your mom" sigh, dipped in disappointment like a strawberry in dark chocolate.

Mom put our doughnuts on actual plates and gave us paper towels for napkins, like we were uppity civilized people. I don't know what you do at your house, but this was weird for us. Our meal times were more like stand around the kitchen island, shoving food in as fast as possible, crumbs flying, sticky fingers wiped on sweatpants like apocalypse survivors. The Wallaces were microwave stalkers, not sit down fancy people. Paper towel napkins and doughnuts on actual plates? I was in deep. Either this is the speech about finishing college or my parents were getting divorced.

"So, Lloyd—" Mom said, words short and clipped.

Ugh. Brace yourself. Here it comes.

"We need to talk about your job."

Glug-gurg. That was me nearly choking on a mouthful of milk while trying really hard to keep it from panic-shooting out of my nostrils.

My job?

My heart thumped. I definitely did not want to talk about my job. Nope. Didn't even want to think about it. Not now, not ever. Never again. Nope. Nope. Nope.

"Tell me everything you do there, and I mean everything." She stared me right in the eyes, squinting, as if using some sort of magic X-Ray vision to scan my thoughts.

"Well, Mom, I guard the border between hell and earth. Yesterday, I saved the earth from an angry demon octopus with plans for world domination. You're welcome. Oh, and zombies are real, so start stockpiling food, guns, and lumber to cover the windows. Just in case. The world could go full Resident Evil any minute. Be prepared."

Mom stared at me. Waiting. Because I did *not* say any of that out loud. Sure, I said it in my head (part of it in a British accent, because that makes everything sound better) but come on. I kept my lips zipped. I couldn't tell her that! I wasn't a total moron.

"You sure fooled me." Kevin stood in my lap, with four arms on his hips—carapace? Whatever.—coated head-to-toe in powdered sugar. "Point me to the liquor cabinet, kid. While we were saving the world, my dickhead roommates drank my stash dry. Every last drop, the bastards. Uncle Kev's thirsty. It's five o'clock somewhere, am I right?"

He held up a hand—well, technically, all he had were feet—expecting a high five.

What? No! Not now.

But he didn't listen. He gawked at my Mom's legs under the table instead. "Hubba. Hubba. Check out those gams. Hello! MILF alert!"

Shut up. That's my Mom! I flicked him off my lap. I heard a faint "aaaaaaah" as he fell to the floor. *Thunk.*

"Well, Lloyd?" Mom asked.

"Uh. What was that? Sorry, I got distracted."

"Tell me about your job, honey."

She looked at me, still waiting. *Think, Lloyd. Think!*

But let's be real here. Thinking wasn't my strong suit, so I didn't say anything. I stared at her, wide-eyed, frying in my own stress juice like a strip of Lloyd bacon. I didn't want to lie to my Mom. I wanted her to be proud of me. But I couldn't tell her about Demon Mart. No way. She was better off not knowing.

It didn't matter anyway because I planned to quit. I wasn't stepping foot in the 24/7 Demon Mart ever again. I'll just tell her that. No lying involved. I opened my mouth, and something hit my foot. I could feel Mom's eyes boring into my skull as she watched me look down. It was angel eight ball. Phew! Here to rescue me. *Quick. What do I tell Mom?*

"You're not quitting. You're going back to work. You made a pact with God."

Throw me a rope here. I'm drowning. Help!

"Sorry. I'm not here to handle your mom. I'm here to help you ditch your sad dad bod and live up to your ultimate potential," he said. "So chop chop. Move this along so we can get to the cardio."

Gah. The stupid jerk was useless. I stomped down hard on the ball. "I'm done with you. Shut up and get out of here. Shoo!"

"You're out of line, young man," Dad said.

"What?" I looked up. My parents stared at me, jaws dropped in shock. Well, crap. I'd said that out loud, didn't I? "I'm sorry. I wasn't talking to you."

I scanned the floor. Angel was gone.

Mom looked down and around, too. "Then who are you talking to? Gertrude is deaf, and you shouldn't scream at her like that. She's old."

Gertrude was in fact old. And deaf. And blind. And lost a front leg and had a wiggly, fur-covered stump in its place. She weighed north of twenty pounds and had defied all odds by living to nineteen. She was basically a big round gray beach ball with one remaining tooth that frequently mistook Mom's knitting basket for the litter box.

"Well, honey, since you're not answering me, I'll cut right to it." Mom rubbed her temples.

Here it comes. Bomb drop in three...two...one...

"Your father and I appreciate that you paid us back for the exterminator and tuition, and that you insured your car," she said. "But we don't understand how you came up with so much money in such a short time. You couldn't possibly have earned that much working for a few weeks at a corner store."

"Seriously, dipshit?" Kevin stood on my plate, sucking the cream filling out of the little hole in the end of my maple-iced fancy doughnut. He stopped long enough to shoot me some stink eye. "You did *not* tell your Mom about your bonus, did you?"

I said nothing. He shook his head. "Great. You did, didn't you? What is this, amateur hour? Demon Mart is like Fight Club. Rule number one: Don't talk about it. The less your family knows, the better. Don't be a dumbass. What if she gets curious and comes to the store? She could step right into a demon's mouth. Or worse. You sure don't want her around Morty!"

Oh. I hadn't thought of that. Kevin was right.

"Damn straight," he said. Then, he eyeballed my dad. "I don't get it. Your mom's a babe. Why'd she marry that dweeb? Oh well. Even nerds get lucky sometimes. Guess there's hope for you after all, kid."

Shut up, Kevin.

"Here's the deal, Lloyd." Mom snapped me back to. "Your father and I want you to make good decisions. We hope you haven't resorted to anything dangerous or illegal. Money isn't worth it. It's time to get serious and think about your future."

CHAPTER 2

A few minutes later, I sprinted out the front door, car keys in hand, twenty-dollar bill in my pocket, barking something about "running errands" back at my parents.

Thing was, Mom was preaching to the converted. Money was NOT worth it. That's why I was never stepping foot in Demon Mart ever again. I tried to say as much without saying too much, but boy, that was way harder than it sounded when you couldn't tell your parents the truth.

And do not even think about giving me a lecture on "honesty being the best policy." What would I say? That I battled thousand-eyed beasts from the coldest depths of hell for cash? The beer cave was the portal to hell? Devils, zombies, and two-story tall jelly centipedes were real? If I said any part of that out loud, my Mom would deliver me like a pizza to a shrink's office in thirty minutes or less. Guaranteed.

Besides, normal people were better off not knowing. It didn't make life easier or happier. Ask me how I know.

I had no choice but to rustle up an excuse and skedaddle. You know how moms are. Once they get their hands on you, they twist you like a wet towel until they wring every last drop of truth out of you.

The plan? Eat my feelings. Immediately. Now that doughnuts were off limits forever, I had one option: A Number Seven Monster Burger Combo, extra onions, extra salt, no mayo. It was a king's feast of red meat and grease. Just thinking about it melted my anxiety away. Mmmmm. Mmmmm. Mmmmm.

My stomach rumbled. I opened my car door, itching to hit the drive thru. Angel eight ball rolled out from under my front tire, triangle side up. "Your mom thinks you're dealing drugs."

"What? No way."

"Yes. She does. When I rolled through the kitchen last night, I caught her desperation Googling 'top ten signs your child's on drugs.' Remember when she caught you and Big Dan smoking weed in the basement? She hasn't forgotten. Trust me."

"How did you know about that?"

His triangle traced the top arch of the liquid window.

"Did you just eye roll me?"

"I know everything about you. Duh. But seriously, that tear-streaked rage lecture she gave the two of you about how all drugs are laced with LSD melamine fentanyl PCP baby laxatives? Epic. It's all we talked about at the Thirsty Halo that night. Boy, when your mom sees a catchy news headline, she really runs with it."

"What does that even mean?"

"The Thirsty Halo is an angel bar," he said. "We like to drink too, you know. Unfortunately, all we can get is communion wine. It's not great, but God loves it, so—"

"Jesus. Shut up!" I snipped. "She does not think I'm dealing drugs."

"First, leave the J man out of this, and second, yes, Lloyd. Yes, she does," angel said. "I'll bet you a bag of pizza rolls. They smell delicious. I really want to try one, but we can't get them up here. Your mom made some last night. When she was crying alone in the dark. Lit only by the sad glow of her laptop. While Googling 'Is my son a drug dealer?' Because she thinks you're a drug dealer. Wowza, you're up the creek. Hey. Wait a minute. Where are you going? What's the plan here?"

"Go away." I sniffled. Yeah, I cried a little, okay? My feelings were hurt. Mom really thought this about me? "I want to be alone."

"Sorry. You know the deal. We're stuck together until you've mastered the skills on your 'Capable Adult' checklist. Here. I'll mail you a copy. Wait. What's this?" The triangle turned, and I swear I heard a sound like papers shuffling. "*And* successfully completed a hero's journey? Hell's bells. This is a new work order!"

His triangle moved up and down like he was sizing me up. "Crap. We're gonna be together forever."

"No. We aren't." I kicked him under the car. I didn't care if he was an angel. I didn't need another person on my case right now.

I slid into the driver's seat, buckled up, and lay my head on the steering wheel for a hot minute. *Deep breaths. Deep breaths.*

Nope. Not helping. Still stressed out.

What if eight ball was right?

I'd only worked at Demon Mart for a few weeks. And for all Mom knew, the job paid minimum wage. No wonder she was suspicious. She didn't know Faust had paid all my debts, nearly ten grand worth, as a reward for defeating a horde of angry hell beasts. I had waltzed right in the door and immediately showed Mom all of my receipts, all my zero balances. I gave her every cent I owed her—all of it—right then. Because I was riding the high. I'd finally done something right for once in my life.

I only wanted Mom to be proud of me.

It's just like Pastor Woodruff always said, "Pride goeth before a fall." Or was it, "the devil's hands slide straight to the genitals?" Probably both.

Either way, I screwed up. I didn't think it through. If I'd been smart, I would have showed her one receipt, one paid bill at a time, slowly over a few months. But no. Apparently, I was just smart enough to save the world and just dumb enough to blow up my own life.

Click.

What the...? I looked over. Angel eight ball had somehow buckled himself into the passenger seat, triangle facing me. "So you messed up. So she thinks you're dealing drugs because there's no way a guy like you could legally earn that much money so quickly."

"Did you just call me a loser? I'm not a loser." *Am I? Don't answer.*

"Face facts: You're a loser on paper, Lloyd, not deep down. My job is to help you align what's on the inside with what's on the outside," angel said. "And, apparently, help you become a hero. In the real world, not just in Diablo 3. Holy moly. This deal is getting worse all the time. Honestly, I don't know how we're gonna pull this off."

"I don't even know what that means!"

He triangle eye rolled me again. "You don't have to. Just trust me. I won't lead you astray. Well, not on purpose. Just get out of the car. You're riding your bike to Monster Burger."

"What? No."

"Seriously. Take the bike. I'll give you a free pass on the fast food because you saved the world yesterday, but only if you work out."

"No way. The car's fixed. I'm driving." This was America, dammit. Driving everywhere, even up the block, was our God-given natural right. Plus, I was lazy.

I swear I heard angel eight ball sigh. "A deal's a deal. You promised the Big Guy you'd do cardio if you survived, and you survived, so now you do cardio."

"I can't deal with this right now." I yanked that angel straight out of his seat belt, rolled down my window, and threw him out. He arced through the air, and I heard him curse when he landed in the prickly branches of the evergreen bush by the garage. *Ha. Take that.*

Hey. Don't judge me. I didn't care if he was an angel. I didn't even care about the cardio. I just needed a break. I deserved to enjoy the day. I mean, look around. The sky's sunny and crayon blue, not a cloud in sight. Red and orange leaves were raked in heaps on lawns, and Thanksgiving pumpkins were piled up on porches. If it weren't for me, we'd all be ass-deep in gigantic hell fish babies and thirty-foot-tall man-eating spiders right now. You're welcome. Now let me drive my fat ass across town, eat three thousand calories worth of cheeseburgers and fries, and celebrate in fucking peace.

I kicked the car into reverse and backed down the driveway.

Crack. Angel eight ball hit the windshield, triangle pressed against the glass. "HIT THE BRAKES! NOW!"

"No."

"DO IT NOW OR GERTRUDE DIES!"

What? Shit! I hit the brakes. The car screeched to a stop.

Thunk.

My eyes shot to the side mirror. There was a ball of gray fur by the back tire. *No. No no no no no no no! Gertrude!*

Tears flew. Like projectiles. Seriously. They shot horizontally straight out of my eyes and rained down on the steering wheel. I'd had Gertrude my whole life. She couldn't die now, not like this, not after all we'd been through. It wasn't fair!

I put the car in park and was about to open the door when Gertrude staggered out from behind the tire, clearly annoyed. She stopped and looked around with her blind, milky eyes. The corners of her mouth crinkled down, like she wanted to say, "watch where you're going!" but couldn't see who she was supposed to yell at. Then she hobbled across the lawn, moving her fur stump like it still had a leg on it. She waddled straight to the flower bed, squatted over one of Mom's pink mums, and showered the flowers with pee. *Phew.* Gertrude was okay!

"Thanks for the heads up," I said to eight ball. "I owe you one."

And I immediately regretted saying that.

"That was no accident," angel said. "That was a warning shot from God."

"No way. God wouldn't hurt Gertrude. That's just mean. She's innocent."

"If you think He won't kill a cat to make a point, you haven't read the Old Testament lately." The triangle bobbed. "We've got an entire nature preserve up here for all the animals Noah couldn't fit on the ark."

"You're bluffing."

"I wish. Ride the bike, for the cat's sake. Please."

"No," I said. "You're full of it."

"Fine. I can't make you, but heed my warning: You made a deal with God. Don't defy Him. It won't end well. Oh, and the roach needs a ride."

Angel eight ball rolled across the windshield and plopped off the side of the car. Just as I heard the thump on the concrete, I saw Kevin scuttling across the porch, fast as the wind.

"Wait for me!" he yelled. "Your Mom tried to spray me with Kill

'Em Dead. Take me with you. I don't want to die!"

"Fine." No use fighting it, right?

He crawled in the driver's side window, then scuttled across the dash. Blech. I didn't think I'd ever get used to that, because even though he was sentient and talking, ew roach.

He settled on the red fuzzy dice hanging from my rear-view mirror. "Ooh. Plush! Where ya headed, kid?"

"Monster Burger."

"Awesome. Can we swing by the liquor store after? Your Mom caught me before I got the cork out of the Maker's Mark. That shit's hard to open without thumbs. I miss thumbs."

Thumbs? I looked at him. He looked at me.

"What?" He snipped.

"Nothing."

I put the car in reverse, but didn't lift my foot off the brake until I spotted Gertrude on the porch, beached like a whale in the patio chair, soaking in a sunbeam. I backed out, turned around, and headed up toward the street. We hadn't even made it out of Hummingbird Court when the sunny bright sky suddenly filled with swirling, angry, black clouds.

"Weird," Kevin said. "It's not supposed to rain today."

"It's cool. It'll be fine." It was just a coincidence, angel eight ball being a dick to make a point.

I hung a left onto the street and immediately hit a wall of pouring rain. It came down so hard and heavy it sounded like pebbles hitting the windshield. I kicked the wipers into high gear, but they couldn't keep up. Water sloshed and flew. The windshield fogged up solid white. I dialed up the defrost and wiped my hand across the glass to clear it. I still couldn't see, but I wasn't about to stop or turn back. Stubborn? Yeah. But if I didn't call angel eight ball's bluff, I'd never hear the end of it. I had to take a stand. This was my moment.

Seriously, though. That angel was giving it to me good. The sky was so dark it looked like midnight. I couldn't see houses or trees or porch pumpkins. Nothing, not even parked cars in the street. But I kept driving, slow enough a snail could outrun me. Kevin held tight to the fuzzy dice. I white-knuckled the steering wheel as I inched up the street.

CRACK! The sky flashed and a zigzag of blinding white cut through the darkness. *CRACK!* Lightning hit right outside the car, so close the sound and light were simultaneous.

"Who did you piss off?" Kevin's voice shook. "Turn back."

"No." Okay, yes. We should stop. The bumper of a parked car appeared inches away. I swerved.

"Holeeeeee sheeeeeeet!" Kevin screamed. "Look out!"

Yeah. He's right. Totes not safe, but I couldn't let the angel win. It was about the principle at this point. If I quit now that snarky little triangle would own me forever.

"Hold up. Are you risking our lives in a celestial grudge match?"

Dammit, Kevin. Stop zoning in on my brain waves. "I'm not stopping."

Sure, I was holding onto the wheel so tight it was about to snap in half, and Kevin could have gotten out and walked faster than the car. But nope. Not stopping. Can't make me.

"Pull over. Let me out. I'm not dying again."

"Suck it up," I growled. "You're a roach. You're impossible to kill."

Flash. Crack.

Lightning nearly hit the hood.

"You can't win," Kevin said.

"You don't know anything."

"Guys like you don't challenge God and win," he said. "You're not Hercules. You're the fat kid who still lives at home with his parents and gets winded walking *down* the stairs for a midnight snack. Seriously. Who gets out of breath going *down* stairs? But if you insist, fine, kid. Sure. Carry on. I'm sure this'll all work out great for you."

"Shut up!" Now I really wasn't turning back, because I had two jerks to prove wrong.

The car inched forward. Angel eight ball dialed up the rain so high, it sounded like my windshield was under Niagara Falls.

Chink. Chink. Chink. Chink. Little white balls hit the glass. Hail? Seriously? Jerk. I doubled down. Nope. Gonna get my burger. I won't let him win.

"Look around, kid," Kevin said. "You've lost."

"Get out of my head."

"I wish. It's not great in there." Kevin had moved from the fuzzy dice to the passenger seat, where he was now buckled in and clinging to the seat belt for dear life. "Stop already. Please."

"No. That dickhead angel can suck it!"

So, of course, that's when the sky flashed white, then black, then white again like the dance floor at a cheap European discotheque. Lightning zig zagged across the pitch black sky.

"Stop already, dipshit!"

"No!" Come on. I couldn't give up now. Right?

A flash of yellow—headlights—emerged from the darkness. A horn honked. I jerked the wheel. The car skidded and dovetailed.

"Aaaaaaaaaaaaahhhhhh!" For the record, that was Kevin screaming.

Clunk. Crunk. We hit the curb. The passenger side front tire went up and over.

Pop. Pop. Ffffffffffff.

Aw, man. Don't tell me. That was the sound of my brand new tires dying, wasn't it?

The headlights passed by. They were attached to a large pickup truck. Expletives poured from the driver's side window.

"Fine. You win!" I yelled at no one and everyone.

I turned off the car. All of a sudden, the sky cleared, and the sun returned in all its blazing glory. It's like someone had flipped a switch.

"Take the hint, kid. I didn't come this far to let your dumb ass kill me again."

"What? Shut up. You didn't have to come with me, you know."

"Faust only gave me so many portals. Look at these legs. I can't walk to the liquor store. It'd take weeks!" Yes, he was wiggling all six of his legs, just to emphasize his point.

I looked around. The neighborhood was bright, sunny. The sky was clear, cloudless and blue. The ground was dry, like it'd never rained at all. This had to be a joke.

I started the car again. The sky immediately went black, and the rain turned on like a spigot.

I turned the car off and took the keys out. Bright sun, clear sky. I put the keys in and started the car. Lightning, black sky, torrential rain. I turned the car on and off again. And again, just to be sure. Each time, the same result. Car on: Pouring rain, howling wind, utter darkness. Turn off the car: Sunny sky. You have got to be kidding me. *Fine.* I admitted defeat.

I stepped out of the car and stomped around to the sidewalk. Two completely blown-out tires. The rubber was shredded. The hood had dozens of tiny dents in it from all the hail. Fuck me. The devil had just helped me fix this car, and heaven had busted it up again.

And the rest of the neighborhood? Like nothing happened. Kids rode bikes with their friends. Fat grandmas pulled weeds in the flower beds. That storm appeared to be a punishment tailor-made only for me.

Kevin slipped through the crack in the passenger door, jumped onto the grass and kissed it. "Land! We're safe on dry land! Thank you, Jesus!" Then he looked at the sky and pointed to me. "I'm not with this guy."

"You're the worst. Do you know that?"

He shrugged. "Duh."

Angel eight ball was waiting for me in the driveway when I walked up. All that white-knuckled driving had landed me less than two blocks from home.

"You're a total jerk," I said. "Did you really have to blow out my brand new tires? I just got that stupid car running again. I saved the earth, and that's how you thank me?"

"Don't blame me. That was Him." The triangle turned, flashing a finger pointing up. "I told you to ride your bike. I warned you."

"Why would God go through all that for a bike ride?" Boom. Answer that. The big man surely had more important things to do.

"Look. This isn't about a bike ride. It's about keeping promises. It's the principle."

"I didn't make any promises."

The triangle turned. "Yes, you did. When those beasts attacked, you prayed to God. In exchange for His help, you promised you would do whatever He asked of you, including squats and cardio."

"No, I did not."

The triangle flipped, and once again I swear I heard the sound of paper rustling. "And I quote: 'If you get me through this, I promise I will get my life together. I'll do whatever you ask, whatever it takes. Pinkie swear.' And don't forget: 'If I live through this, I am definitely doing more cardio. I swear.' Your own words. Clearly, you are contractually obligated to ride your bike. Just do it. Trust me. You don't want to see what happens when God gets really angry."

CHAPTER 3

I admitted defeat. Sure, it took God slashing two of my tires, threatening to kill my cat, and nearly slicing me in half with lightning, but I knew when to quit. So here I was, twenty minutes later, zooming across town on my Huffy, pedaling as fast as a fat guy can, panting and out of breath, sweat flying. Dude. This was not by choice. I would have loved to leisurely ride to Monster Burger, but do you think the man upstairs cut me some slack? Hell no. Every time I slowed down, a dark cloud formed three feet above my head and thunder rumbled. So I pedaled, fast and furious, because I did not want to play "What Would Jesus Do?" when all that stood between me and the wrath of God was a cheap plastic bike helmet.

At least Kevin was having fun. He hung out of my hoodie pocket, wind ruffling his antennae, yelling "ha ha ha! Faster, kid!" and "weeeeeeeeeee!" the entire way.

This was not fun for me. For lots of reasons, but mostly the primal need to avoid Demon Mart at all costs. I couldn't deal. No one in their right mind would go anywhere near there. Would you go back to your neighborhood beer cave if a colossal spider popped out from behind the Pabst and tried to eat you? No. You wouldn't. You'd find some place else to buy beer.

Maybe angel eight ball was right. Maybe I did have PTSD. I took the long way to Monster Burger because the thought of riding past Demon Mart made me break out in a cold sweat. I couldn't completely avoid it. The restaurant was catercorner across the intersection. But, I did cut through a couple of alleys then loop around the backside of Doc's pawn shop by Henrietta's store. The display of life-sized plastic Marys in the window of the Jesus Saves Discount Religious Supplies was a marginally less disturbing view.

I put my hand up to block any accidental, peripheral glimpse of the Demon Mart as I pedaled into the Monster Burger lot. I parked my bike in the wide swath of perfectly manicured green grass under Frankenstein's left neck bolt. Did I mention the Monster Burger sign was a neon green Frankenstein's monster biting into a neon yellow bun with a red ketchup splurp in the middle? A light-up whiteboard underneath had movable type advertising the daily specials.

Mr. Jimmy, the restaurant's elderly owner, stood near the top of a wobbly ladder rearranging the letters. Honestly, I didn't know why he bothered. The restaurant rarely had any customers. The drive-thru never had a line, and the parking lot was always empty. God only knew why. The burgers were amazing.

"Well, it must be my lucky day. A customer! How's my Number One fan?" Jimmy waved to me, his salt-white comb-over flapping up in the wind. His hair was like a tumbleweed, so thin and aloof it looked wholly unrooted to his totally bald, shiny scalp.

Mr. Jimmy held a big letter C printed on a clear plastic rectangle. He was posting a special that likely involved chicken. Or hillbillies. Hard to tell, because all that was on the board so far was "hick." In Ohio, this could go either way.

"How you doing, son? I heard you're working over at the Dairy Mart," he said. "Don't know what you boys were up to the other night, but Mr. Faust came by and said you'd be closed for renovations. Must be serious, because that store has never closed once in the sixty years we've been here. Looks like it's coming along, though. I'll tell ya. That crew never stops, works day and night. They never get tired. Boy, if I had a crew like that, there'd be no stopping me! I can't wait 'til it's finished so I can see what the ole devil did with the place."

Um, yeah. This conversation made me a little uncomfortable. Was it just me or did it kinda sound like Mr. Jimmy was in on it? I didn't dare ask. Kevin's "Fight Club" rule, remember? So, I smiled and nodded, and said "yeah" and "me, too," on cue, all the while trying *not* to look across the intersection.

I totally failed. I couldn't *not* look. It's like talking to someone with a gigantic volcano zit, topped with an oozing pus whitehead, right in the middle of their forehead. You look at that zit, no matter how hard you try not to look at that zit. Because you *have* to look, because it's right there, screaming at you. Demon Mart was that big pus-filled zit. So I looked, and what I saw was, well, normal.

The hole in the roof had been repaired. The shattered glass had been replaced, and the stickers advertising beer and hot dog specials reapplied in neat lines along squeaky clean new windows. The building was nearly perfect, unruffled. Even the Temptations Tavern next door had a fresh coat of paint. The type below the neon 24/7 Dairy Mart sign said, "Pardon our progress. Closed for renovations. Reopening Monday."

That was tomorrow. And I was on the schedule. Gulp. Was it getting hot in here? Are you sweating bullets? No? Just me?

Caution tape and panels of chain-link fence blocked off the parking lot. A couple of plain white contractor vans with ladders on top, along with pallets of bricks and concrete block, sat around the building. Two dozen men in tan coveralls painted the outside with rollers on sticks. It looked like a normal construction site.

Until I looked away. For a split second, the scene morphed like a hologram in my peripheral vision. The sunburned and tanned faces of the workmen slid away, replaced by gray skin, blue lips. Pink flesh turned rotten. *Oh God.* I should have known. The tan coveralls. It was a zombie crew. Outside, in broad daylight, where everyone could see them, like it was nothing.

I instantly felt ice cold. Dear God. What was stopping them from wandering off and starting the zombie apocalypse? Some "Do Not Enter" tape? I felt the sudden urge to call in the National Guard. Or the Umbrella Corporation? Wait. No. They were the bad guys, right? Who were you supposed to call to stop the zombie apocalypse again? Think, Lloyd. Think!

"Relax, kid. As long as the collars are on, it's fine. It alters their brainwaves. Keeps all the grrrr and the brain-eating in check." Kevin sat on my shoulder watching the crew. "Not that you have anything to worry about. They'll never come after you."

"How do you know that?" I looked at him.

He looked at me. "Because you don't have any brains."

"Ha ha. Very funny."

Kevin stared at the zombies for a minute, then shivered. "Poor bastards. If it comes down to it, I'll never let you go zombie, kid. I'll pop you right in the brain. I'll kill you *dead* dead. Just promise you'll do the same for me. Squish me real good so I can't come back."

"What? No!" I couldn't kill someone, even if he was a roach.

"Oh, excuse me, snowflake. I thought we were on the same page." Kevin folded his arms and turned away from me. "That's what pals are supposed to do for each other in the zombie apocalypse."

Wait. We're pals now?

"Apparently not. It's cool. Go ahead. Go full zombie. See if I care."

I could tell by his tone that he did care.

"No, I don't," Kevin snipped. "Can we go in already? I'm starving. Order me a Number Two, and double monster size it. No salt. It gives me diarrhea."

"Enjoy your food, boys!" Jimmy said, then turned back to the sign.

Wait a minute. Did he say "boys?" Did he know about Kevin?

I was about to ask him, when something small, a bird maybe, fluttered in a circle around him. He swatted at it. "Shoo! Go away. Shoo! Stupid buggers."

The ladder wobbled. He grabbed the sign. "Oof, steady there. Phew. Okay. It's okay. Now where was I? Oh, yes..."

"Get moving, kid," Kevin snipped. "I'm so hungry you're starting to look like a chicken leg."

I shook off my suspicions and stepped inside. The dining room was the same neon yellow as the bun on the sign. It was empty, a ghost town. There was no line, as usual.

"There's two things you can count on in the world. One: Monster Burger will always be dead," Kevin said. "And two: Earl will always be stuck in 1984. Poor bastard."

"Says the guy who's obsessed with Ronnie James Dio."

"Hmph." Kevin crossed his arms and looked away. Again. I was not winning any Kevin points today.

But Kevin wasn't wrong. Earl stood behind the counter, waiting to take our order. He wore a tracksuit with a stripe running down the arms and legs, a color-coordinated sweatband and a pair of mesh, fingerless driving gloves. He always looked like he'd just stepped off the set of Breakin' 2: Electric Boogaloo. Always. He wasn't doing it to be ironic. He was just stuck in 1984.

Earl was a little older than my Mom, with dyed black hair and a mustache that lay over his top lip like a fat black banana slug. His body was rounded and soft like an eclair. He was also the one and only employee of Monster Burger. He was the cashier, the fry cook, and the drive-thru order taker. Probably not too difficult, considering Monster Burger never had customers. He did all of this while moonwalking and robot-dancing between stations. Go Turbo, go. Indeed.

"Hey! Number seven extra salt, extra onions, no mayo! My main man!" Earl said as he popped and locked to the store's synthesizer beat-box soundtrack. "The usual?"

"Jesus. How often do you eat here?" Kevin looked me up and down. "Never mind It's obvious."

"Are you calling me fat?"

"Yeah. And you don't look like the kind of fat guy who shares, so don't forget to order my food."

"The usual. But can you add a Number Two, double monster size, too? No salt?" Yuck. Who eats fries with no salt? Oh, that's right, the roach with the old man digestive issues.

Kevin flipped me the bird. Four times. I think. Roaches don't really have middle fingers, but he held up four little legs at me like he did.

"Woah there. Mixing it up, huh? Keeping me on my toes. Owww-ah!" Right then, Earl arched his back and went up on the very tip-toes of his white Adidas like he was a ballet dancer. "All right."

The register beeped as Earl—moving like a robot, naturally—typed in the order. "The weirdest thing happened today, Number Seven," Earl said. "I swear I saw Ed McMahon steal a piece of lettuce then fly right out the window."

Uh, what? You heard that right?

"He was naked. He had wings, and he was this tall." Earl held his fingers about six inches apart.

"This dude is bat shit crazy," Kevin said. "Is it safe to have him near food?"

"Did I ever tell you about that time I auditioned for Star Search? Junior dance competition."

"Well, shit. Here we go again. This guy is obsessed!" Kevin said.

Yes. Yes, he was. I'd heard some version of this story at least a hundred times. Although, this was the first time it involved Ed McMahon naked with wings.

"Star Search woulda changed my life," Earl put his arms down at his side and did a full spin. "That'll be thirteen twenty three."

I handed him my twenty. He gave me my change, then electric slid to the fryer to drop a basket of fries. "Always fresh for you, my man. I didn't make the cut because Ed McMahon didn't like me. The producers said it was because I couldn't caterpillar, but I can and I did. I'll prove it. Hold on."

Earl had the burgers, fresh off the grill, finished by the time the timer on the deep fryer chimed. He lifted the fries, grabbed a gigantic round salt shaker and said, "extra salt, for my main man."

"Wait! No salt on half."

Earl scooped Kevin's sad saltless fries into a separate sleeve, then liberally shook the shaker over mine. He bagged everything up, then came out from behind the counter. "Food's ready, but before you go, it's caterpillar time."

He dropped to the floor and undulated across the tile, his spine whipping and rolling him back and forth.

"Huh. He really can do the caterpillar," Kevin said. "Earl's got some abs under all that dough. Who knew? What about you, kid? You got any abs under there?"

Kevin pulled on my shirt collar and looked down in.

"Get out." I smacked his hand away.

"Didn't think so," he said.

Earl hopped up, spun around, then he handed us two paper bags filled with french-fried, all-beef deliciousness. I praised his caterpillar, then made a hasty exit. I knew better than to stick around. Earl could talk about his near-miss at Star Search—for which he squarely blamed Ed McMahon—all day if you let him.

I scanned the receipt as I pushed the door open with my butt. "You owe me seven fifty."

"Uh, this one's on you, bub," Kevin said.

"That wasn't the deal," I said. "I know you've got cash. You have a job!"

"Yeah. I have money. In a bank. Where am I supposed to keep cash or cards? This suit doesn't come with pockets." Kevin rolled his arms up and down his tiny brown roach body for emphasis.

Gah! I had the distinct feeling Kevin wouldn't pay me back. DeeDee probably kicked him out for freeloading.

"Hey. She did not kick me out. I left because she didn't have any good snacks."

"Yeah right." But the second I stepped outside, I no longer cared about the money. I dropped the receipt and the food. The bags thumped to the sidewalk.

"Seriously, butterfingers? Half my fries are on the sidewalk! Fine. You made your point, stingy pants. I'll Venmo you when I get home."

"Kevin." My voice shook.

"What?"

"Look." I was shaking all over now.

"What's gotten into you?"

I pointed.

"Oh. Shit."

Mr. Jimmy lay motionless on the ground. The bottom half of his body lay in the patch of soft green grass under the Monster Burger sign. Unfortunately, the top half had splattered across the asphalt entrance to the drive-thru lane. And I mean splattered. Blood everywhere. The ladder lay on top of him. One of the wooden rungs had snapped in two. Mr. Jimmy must have fallen. Judging from the unholy angle of his neck, he was clearly dead. He was still clutching the plastic letter C in his hand.

I looked up at the sign. The daily special read, "hick sandwich, $3."

CHAPTER 4

Every time I closed my eyes, I relived the moment Earl fell to his knees, tears flying, fists punching the sky, screaming "Nooooo! I'll get you Ed McMahon!" before collapsing in a heap of tears on Mr. Jimmy's body. I couldn't stop thinking about it, or about the squad coming and taking the old man's body away. Poor Earl. Poor Mr. Jimmy.

I couldn't deal with it, so I did what I always did when life was overwhelming. I shut myself in my room and alternated between hiding under the covers, sleeping, and binge-playing Call of Duty: Black Ops 3 with Big Dan. (Dude. Zombies were real. Fuck Diablo 3. I was training for the apocalypse now.) We played online only. Because I wasn't leaving the house. Ever again. Nope. No way. The world was too dangerous and too scary.

I was once again enjoying the lying in bed portion of my avoidance strategy when angel eight ball rolled into my forehead. "You're late." His arrow pointed at the alarm clock.

10:25. At night. Monday night. A chill ran through me. I was supposed to be at work right now. "No. I'm not." I was never going back there. No way. I was not gonna get eaten by monsters. I threw angel eight ball on the floor, rolled over and hid under my blanket.

I pulled the comforter over my head, and something growled. I was assaulted by a horrific smell, like rotten tuna that had been left out in the blazing hot sun for ten days, then sprayed with thirty gallons of spring-scented air freshener. "Aaaaaah!"

Yes, I screamed. Angel eight ball put a monster in my bed!

I lifted the covers and kicked my legs, ready to fight. A gray ball emerged from the dark depths. Gertrude! Phew. She hobbled and grunted as she waddled toward me. She thrust her dry pink nose in close to mine, stuck her stinky tongue out and tried to lick me.

"Noooooooooo!" I raised my arm as a shield.

Dude. I had a firm no licking policy. Cat tongue is kitty toilet paper. Cats don't take showers or use soap. I didn't want that on my face. Did you? But Gertrude was determined. She tapped my cheek with her cat-box fake-fresh-scent paw as I tried to Karate block her every move. "Blech. Stop it!"

Frustrated by my spurns, she walked past my head, turned around and attempted to sit her butt hole on my cheek. "Gack! Did that stupid angel put you up to this?"

I pushed her, but she didn't go away. Sure, she lifted her butt, but it just hovered there. She waved it around, avoiding my shoos, trying and trying again to sit her pink puckery behind on my forehead. Here's the thing about Gertrude: Like any old person, she feels entitled to do whatever she wants. Unfortunately, she wants to drag her dirty pink anus across any surface that strikes her fancy, whether it's my face or Dad's tweed recliner in the den.

She was about to drag it across my nose when I finally managed to roll her fat body off me. She lost her balance, and was so round that when she fell, she kept right on rolling, straight off the side of the bed.

Thud.

"Meeeew."

"Sorry, Gertrude."

I heard the *shw shw* of furry cat stub rubbing against the carpet as she tried to right herself. Before I could retreat underneath the covers again, a small circle of green light appeared above my head. Kevin leaped out, landed directly on my nose, and punched me in the eye.

"Ow!"

"Get up, kid. You're late."

"Get off!" I swatted him, and he thunked into the unopened combo meal on my nightstand. I hadn't eaten it. Mr. Jimmy's death had ruined my appetite.

"It's not my fault you're late. A well check is Demon Mart standard procedure. For all we knew, you were dead and the cat ate your face. I mean, look at that thing." Kevin pointed at Gertrude, still on the carpet, too fat to roll over. "Definitely a face eater. What are y'all feeding it? Is everything in this house fat?"

He eyeballed me.

"Shut up, Kevin."

"Whatever." He crawled straight into the Monster Burger bag and reemerged with a chunk of cheeseburger. "You didn't eat this? Are you nuts? This was your last chance! Monster Burger's out of business without Jimmy. No one's gonna buy a restaurant with no customers."

He shoved the entire chunk in his mouth. "Mmmm. Dewishuuush."

"Go away."

"Sure thing, kid." The green vortex opened next to him. "Get up, buttercup. Be at work in fifteen minutes, or I'm writing you up. We all know you didn't quit, because no one showed up to replace you. So stop playing with yourself and get dressed."

He stepped into the portal, thought better of it, and backed out. He grabbed a corner of my Monster Burger bag and pulled it into the vortex behind him. He and yesterday's lunch disappeared.

I don't know if you remember, but Demon Mart is awash in magic spells. One spell dictates that when you quit, the poor sucker destined to replace you shows up when you leave. So don't worry about Kevin. I wasn't leaving him in a lurch. My replacement would be along any minute now, because I was definitely one hundred percent never going back there.

I fluffed my pillows, laid back down and tried to sleep.

Thwap. Crack.

My bed shook. Uh, what was that?

Crack.

My room flashed like Dr. Frankenstein's lab. White light feathered across the ceiling. Gertrude hissed.

Eight ball rolled out from under my pillow, triangle up. "Go to work."

"You can't make me. It isn't fair! I saved the world already. Isn't that enough?"

"Apparently not, or else I wouldn't have a new work order for a hero's journey."

"What does that even mean? What else is there to do?"

"Look, you saved the world. Then you went right back to living with Mom, playing video games 24/7. Nothing changed. Your heroic moment didn't sink in. You didn't learn anything. It didn't add direction and purpose to your life, so now we have to do it all over again," he said. "Beowulf didn't slay Grendel so he could spend fifty years playing Fallout 4 in his mom's basement."

And yes, that was a lot of text to fit on such a small triangle. I had to squint. It was like two point type. "Wait. Who did what?"

"It was a literary reference. I keep forgetting you dropped out of college." He triangle eye rolled me. "Doesn't matter. Get up, get dressed, get to work. It's time to hero up. Slay some demons, woo the princess, yada yada. Get ready to fairy tale the shit out of your life. You know the drill."

"What?" I had no idea what he was talking about. "No. I'm not going back there!"

Crack. Fwap. Lightning hit the window outside.

"Aaaaah! Make it stop!" I white knuckle death squeezed my blanket and pulled it up around me.

"I'm only the messenger, remember? Seriously. Angel literally means messenger." The triangle turned. "I can't make it stop. YOU have to make it stop."

Crack. Fwap. Crack.

Lightning. Lots of it. So close it was almost on top of me. I was so scared, I made this high-pitched *eeeeeeeeeeeeeep* noise that I didn't even know humans could make. It was definitely not a noise that screamed bravery or self respect. I mean, come on. This is me we're talking about here. I didn't magically transform overnight.

"Get up. Time for work."

"I ca-a-a-an't."

Zzzzp. Lightning skipped across the ceiling, short circuiting the fan. Yet I still couldn't bear the thought of stepping foot in that store.

"No." I whimpered. "I'm not going."

Why sugar coat it? Struck by lightning would be better, right?

"Fine," angel eight ball huffed. "Remember I told you so."

Crack crack. Flash. *Crack.* Flash. *Reeee eeeee.*

I held even tighter to my blanket as lightning and wind whipped the giant oak tree by my window. I would have peed my pajamas, if I weren't so terrified. Yep. This whole showing God I could stand my ground thing? Nailing it!

Crack. Crack. Crash!

A tree branch broke through my window and hit the floor hard. Glass and bark flew in all directions.

"MEEEOOOOOOO!" Gertrude screamed, then went silent.

"Gertrude?"

She didn't answer.

In the darkness, I could see the outline of her fat, round body crunched in half beneath the branch. Her tongue hung limp from her mouth, her blind eyes frozen in terror, looking right at me. Her mouth curled up, as if to say, "How many times did I let your dickhead friends yank me around by the tail so you could look cool, huh? How could you do this to meeeeeee?"

"No! Gertrude! Take it back, and I'll go! I'll go. I promise! Don't hurt Gertrude!"

"Oh, good. That's settled then," angel eight ball said.

My bedroom went completely dark, then the light flipped on. And the room was perfect. Well, messy and twenty-one-year-old man disgusting yes, but the window wasn't broken. The tree was outside where it belonged. And Gertrude was alive, licking the few parts of her fat belly she could actually reach as she lay on the carpet next to the bed. Alive.

Oh thank, God. Thank you. Thank you!

Angel eight ball jiggled in my lap. "Now get up. You're late."

I did not hesitate. I threw on my Pumas and was outside in the driveway in under five minutes, car keys in hand. Shit. My car was two blocks away with two shredded tires. This sucked. I didn't want to ride my bike.

Lightning flashed overhead. "Fine. I'll ride my stupid bike!"

Yes, I yelled at the sky like a lunatic. But boy, did I ride. I pedaled, hard and fast, brrr freezing down to my core, because autumn nights in Ohio are really, really cold. But I pedaled, and I didn't turn back, even though I wanted to. I was driven by the vision of poor dead Gertrude on my bedroom floor. And the fear of getting struck with lightning or turned to a pillar of salt like some poor sucker in the Old Testament.

Man. God could really be a meany pants. Wait. Could He read my thoughts? Shit! Oh...uh...sorry. Forget I said that. I didn't mean it. Actually, I totally did, but—oh crap. La la la la la. Nothing to see here!

I coasted into the Demon Mart parking lot, and suddenly the freezing fall air was no match for the icy cold doom bubbling inside me. The happy naivety of believing monsters only existed in the movies? Gone forever. That was the hardest part of the job. Monsters were real. Hell was real. And once you knew that, it changed everything.

My guts churned when I saw the neon 24/7 Demon Mart sign flickering in ominous blood red. The movable type said, "Grand reopening. Gate open midnight to dawn. Rules strictly enforced. Professions of eternal, undying love strictly prohibited."

Well, that last line was clearly a jab at Tristan, who's bid to win over DeeDee had accidentally thrown the hell gate wide open and summoned an angler fish of doom. Have I mentioned how much I hate hipsters?

I leaned my Huffy against the signpost. I didn't bother to lock it because anyone dumb enough to steal it would be carried away by a humongous demon bird. And, you know, if it were stolen, maybe angel would let me drive the car.

Angel eight ball hit my foot. Triangle up, of course. Always an opinion. "No bike = walk. Or jog, preferably. Cardio!"

Jerk. I kicked him away. He cursed as he rolled across the lot into a couple of bushes.

I fished my name tag out of my pocket. That's when I noticed I had run out of the house so fast, I was still in the clothes I'd slept in. A green T-shirt with two thumbs pointing up that said "This Guy Needs a Beer," paired with my—Seriously, God? Why?—Christmas pajama pants. The red and white striped ones with gingerbread men tap dancing with candy canes. My cheeks flushed hot. Mom always bought me the worst pajamas. It's like she wanted me to be four years old forever, only with a job and my own apartment.

I took a deep breath, straightened my name tag, and reminded myself that I only had to stay alive until God decided I could quit. Whenever that might be. Maybe if I did what angel eight ball told me to, that would be soon. But right now, I had no choice but to be brave. Fake it 'til you make it, right? For Gertrude.

I mustered a tiny shred of courage, stepped in the front door, and was immediately smacked in the face by a naked man.

CHAPTER 5

A tiny one. I meant a tiny *man*. Get your mind out of the gutter.

He was buck naked and about the size of a Star Wars action figure. He moved like a hummingbird, hovering in front of me, held aloft by fast buzzing wings. He had a beer gut and skinny legs, so his body kinda looked like a potato with two toothpicks sticking out of it, and his wrinkly skin was so pale it was almost blue like a raw shrimp. His hair was pure white, and the curtains matched the drapes, if you get my drift. What. The. Hell.

I had a lot of questions, but the most immediate was, "where are your pants?" Did he really need to have his little dinger hanging out there for the whole world to see?

The tiny naked grandpa gave me a pointed look, then said something in a high, fast voice. He jabbed his finger at my nose, then pointed at his not-so-private parts like he was lecturing me for looking.

"Uh." I was actually staring at a hairy brown mole next to his belly button. He should definitely get that looked at. I tried to keep my eyes up, but dude, it was so hard. I mean difficult. *Gah!*

"Well, this is getting weird." Kevin sat on my shoulder, holding a spray can that was bigger than he was. "Kill him already. It's us or them. Too late."

The flying, bare-ass grandpa charged. He poked me right in the eye. "Ow!"

I fwapped at him, but my vision had gone blurry, so he managed to zip out of the way. I swung again, and he zipped the other way. Man, he was fast for a fat guy.

"Unlike you," Kevin said. "Jealous?"

"Shut up."

The naked grandpa spat some words at me and flipped me the bird. Seriously?

"Jesus, kid. You're worthless. Take two steps left."

I did. Kevin squirted his spray can at a different little naked dude, who was buzzing in circles around us. Jesus! How many tiny naked guys were in here?

This one was young and fit, with milky skin covered in freckles, big green kitten eyes, and fiery red hair. He landed on my cheek, sunk his nails into my skin and scratched. "Eeeoow!!"

Kevin sprayed me right in the face. "Aack! Is that poison?"

"Relax. It's Pixie Rid. It won't hurt you."

The spray smelled like lemons to me, but it seemed to hurt the tiny guy. He let go of me, screeched, and rubbed his skin like he'd been sprayed with acid. He fluttered to the floor and rolled around on the linoleum.

"Get him. Quick! Before he get in the walls. No mercy! The damned things are like roaches."

I looked at Kevin. He looked at me. "Not me. Regular roaches. Duh. Step on him."

I lifted my foot, but hesitated. This was basically a tiny human. Wasn't this, like, murder? I tapped the little dude with my foot, and he yelped. No. No way. I couldn't squish him. It didn't feel right.

"What are you waiting for? Pixies are total assholes!" Kevin yelled. "Kill him!"

"You know the rules. We aren't allowed to kill them." DeeDee walked up. "The store is certified cruelty free, remember?"

"Not on my watch. Stupid hippies," Kevin snipped. "Kill 'em, kid."

I didn't. Mostly because the world melted away, leaving only me and DeeDee behind. She was flawless and beautiful, head to toe in black. The diamond in her septum ring sparkled under the fluorescent lights. She'd dyed her hair a deep burgundy, just like in my dream. Except she wasn't a zombie, which was nice. Being close to her made my insides tingle.

DeeDee stared at me for a minute. She smiled, then her perfectly tweezed eyebrows shot up. "What are you wearing? You look like a Christmas elf who's pledging a fraternity."

My cheeks flushed hot. Yes. Yes. I did.

DeeDee shrugged, then wrapped her arms around me and squeezed me tight. Oh God. She was so warm and soft and smelled so good. Tropical, like pineapples and coconuts.

"I missed you, Lloyd. I'm so happy you're here. I was afraid you weren't coming back. Silly, right? I knew I could count on you. You're my hero!" She winked and pinched my cheek.

Well, tonight was looking up. I tingled all over, just from the touch of her. Especially down south. Ahem. Until she handed me a big pink flyswatter.

"We have a pixie problem. Use this to keep them in the air. If they're on the ground too long, they build nests and have babies. We don't want that. We're nearly at infestation level already," she said. "They probably snuck in during construction. We have to flush them out. Check between the slushy machines. They like to hide there. It's warm."

"Disgusting things," Kevin said. "Step to it, kid. We gotta get 'em before they start humping. That's some gnarly shit. Trust me."

"Keep them in the air until I find the net," DeeDee said. "The construction crew shuffled all the tools around. I can't find anything. Nothing is where it belongs."

Just then, something streaked past her face. She raised her hand to grab it but missed. It landed in her hair and starting pulling. She tried to smack it off, but it was tangled up and hanging on for dear life. "Stupid thing. Let go!"

She dropped a few F bombs as she wrestled with a tiny naked lady. Oh geesh. It had boobs. Tiny perky boobs.

"What are you, desperate? Mind outta the gutter, kid." Kevin pinched my ear.

"Ow!"

"You heard the lady. Get moving."

Fine. I inched down the row of slushy machines. Huh. There were more flavors, more machines. Hades Honeydew? Salvation Strawberry? *Mmm. Yes, please!* No. Wait. Scratch that. I didn't need any more reasons to stick around, no matter how delicious they might be. Well, one sip couldn't hurt. If I was gonna be killed by a bunch of tiny naked redheads, I may as well have a taste. I leaned in and nearly had my mouth under a nozzle when Kevin punched me. Right on the spot where that pixie had bitten me. "Eowch! Cut it out!"

"Focus!" Kevin snipped. "And use a cup. This isn't your mom's milk jug. But I'll tell ya, I'd like to get my hands on her jugs. Heh heh."

OMG. You are not talking about my mom right now.

Kevin was about to say something but was interrupted by the *thunk voooooooorp* sound of the tiny lady pixie DeeDee pulled out of her hair hitting the window then sliding down the glass.

"Disgusting." DeeDee smoothed out her hair. "Remember, Lloyd. Keep them flying."

I moved down the row, clutching my pink fly swatter like it was a baseball bat. Kevin's spray can rattled as he shook it, mixing up the brew for another round.

"There, kid. Get 'em!" Kevin pointed at the Rapture Raspberry.

Two of them—young ones, judging by the red hair—were on the lever. And well, I'll just come straight out and say it. They were doing *it*, and not in a way that could be mistaken for making sweet love. They were really giving it to each other. Hair pulling. Biting. Grunting like rabid wild boars hopped up on boner pills.

"Hurry up with the net!" Kevin yelled. "They're mating!"

"I'm hurrying!" DeeDee rifled through the safe.

Kevin poked my neck. "What are you waiting for, kid? Nail 'em."

Uh, they didn't need me to nail them. They had that covered. I swatted down hard on them and accidentally tripped the lever. The two lovebirds fell off, and a bit of violet slushy splurped out, landing on top of them as they fell to the floor. They cursed and yelled in teeny, fast voices nearly too high-pitched for human ears.

Sssssss ssssssss ssssssssssss. Kevin laid hard on the Pixie Rid. "Swat, kid. Swat!"

Sssssss ssssssss ssssssssssss.

I was about to go for the slushy-covered love birds writhing on the linoleum, but that wasn't who Kevin was spraying. A swarm of about twenty tiny naked people had surrounded us, led by the fat grandpa. They were all stark naked, wings flapping. Red hair, perky boobs, teeny weenies, and pubes free for the world to see. Woah boy. This was one smartphone video away from its own tab on Pornhub.

They growled, fists up. Kevin's cloud of lemon spray kept them at arm's length, coughing and buzzing. "That's right, ya dumb shits!" Kevin screamed. "Go on. Get out! Little bastards. Kid, corral them to the door!"

I swung my pink flyswatter around and around like a baton twirler in a Fourth of July parade. The pixies flitted and looped in the air. They were fast, a blur of orange, whirring like dragonflies. I swung, Kevin sprayed. We didn't land any hits, but did a respectable job of inching them closer to the front door.

Sssssss. Sssssssssssssssssssssss.

Fwwwwwwwwww. Plllllllllllp. Pppp. Ppp.

Until Kevin's Pixie Rid spray fizzled out. "Shit," he said.

The teeny furious nudists were all over us in a split second. They attacked. One punched me in the eye. One bit my cheek. One bit the end of my nose, and another one stood on the top of my head trying to yank my hair out.

"Aaaaaaah!" I screamed and wailed and swung my fist and that flyswatter around, but I didn't manage to hit a single one. These jerks were fast and wily. Desperate, I sunk my face into my armpit and used my bicep like a windshield wiper to scrape them all off.

"You're a shit shot, kid." Kevin dropped the empty can of Pixie Rid and held onto my shirt for dear life, as I ducked and dodged and stumbled and swung. "And bicep? Heh heh. Where?"

"Shut up!"

"You're snippy lately. What's your problem?"

A tiny man flew down and punched me right on the nose. "THIS JOB IS MY PROBLEM!" And, yes, I all-caps screamed it like an angry old man sending an email from an AOL.com address.

I felt another hard pinch on my cheek and when my hand went to it, the naked grandpa was there, biting my face. I grabbed him and pulled, but the jerk didn't let go. "Eeeeoooooooooow!"

The cranky old coot held on for dear life with his teeth. It felt like he had fangs! I squeezed him, harder and tighter, his beer gut squishing between my fingers, until he squeaked and finally let go. He took part of my face with him. He looked me right in the eyes and spit out a bloody chunk of my cheek. I threw him straight at the floor and stepped on him. He zeeped like a squeaky dog toy.

"Told you they were dicks," Kevin said. "But no, you didn't listen."

"How did they get out of the gate? It's not midnight!"

Kevin stared at me, blinking, like he was trying to devise a scientific measure for exactly how stupid I was. "These jerks live on earth all the time. They're terrestrial. They don't need a stinkin' gate!"

"What? No way." One flew by and kicked me right in the eyeball. OW! "How do we get rid of them?"

I yanked a handful of them off my shirt.

Kevin put four of his hands—legs?—on his carapace and sighed. "Jesus, kid. You still haven't read your employee manual?"

"Shut up!"

That's when one of them kicked Kevin off my shoulder, and the two of them thudded to the floor. He and a tiny naked lady rolled around on the mat, wrestling. I won't lie. It was oddly satisfying to watch Kevin get his butt kicked. Except that he was technically on my side. And my boss.

"Lloyd, duck!" Before I knew what hit me, DeeDee pushed me out of the way. Naturally, I slipped and fell flat on my butt because yes, I'm that graceful.

"Roll over, kid, you're crushing me," Kevin said. I could feel him and the pixie wiggling around, stuck in the microfiber fleece of my jammy bottoms. I reached under my butt, grabbed the pixie and threw it.

DeeDee had a butterfly net. She did some sort of Chun-Li Street Fighter jump spin in the air.

Angel eight ball rolled out from behind the hot dog station. "Now that's cardio! You need sweet moves like that."

"Leave me alone!" I kicked eight ball across the store. If God expected me to do that, I was gonna be working here forever.

By the time DeeDee's first boot gracefully touched down on the floor, her net was filled with nearly two dozen tiny naked people. She landed on one knee, full on super hero stance. "Open the door."

I crawled to the door on hands and knees. Kevin wriggled, still stuck to my behind. I held the door open while DeeDee carried the net outside. She shook it, and the creatures squeaked and shrieked. "Listen up. Demon Mart is off limits. I don't want to see you in here again. Got it? There's a cemetery on the other side of Monster Burger. It's got plenty of nesting spots. Now go on. Get."

The swarm of naked tiny people flew up and away, their auburn hair —upstairs and down—red as a campfire in the neon glow of the sign. The grumpy grandpa with the big hairy mole turned around, looked straight at me, did that "I'm looking at you" thing with his fingers, then shot me not one, but both middle fingers before buzzing up up and away over the roof.

"Oh, it's on buddy. It's on!" Kevin, finally free of my jammies, flipped *four* birds back at the guy.

DeeDee stepped in and pulled the door shut behind her. "I really hate pixies. They're nothing like they are in the storybooks."

"Nothing ever is," Kevin said. "Now cue up the Zebra. It's time to rock."

"There's a zebra in here?" I asked.

"Really, dipshit?" Kevin huffed. "Zebra is the best eighties hair band you've never heard of—until tonight. You're welcome."

CHAPTER 6

DeeDee dropped the needle on the record player behind the counter. Yes. I said record player.

Faust had seriously upgraded the sound system. Stereo receiver. Record player. Tape deck. Streaming music. iPod. Eight-track player? Let's just say if music had ever been released in a format, we could play it. There was even a neatly arranged shelf loaded with albums, next to Kevin's brand new Zune.

The guitar plus synthesizer sound of Zebra—the band, not the striped African horse—poured from speakers in all corners of the store.

"You feel that bass?" Kevin air guitared while balancing precariously on the Purgatory Pineapple slushy nozzle. He sang along. Something about heads on the floor and wasting time? "Oooooooh yeah!"

"I'm sure they'll be a quiz later, so read over it." DeeDee handed me the album sleeve. A black-and-white photo of three dudes with epic 80s rock mullets grinned at me. "Guard it with your life. It's from Kevin's personal collection. He bought it new, the day it was released. To say he's attached to it is an understatement."

I flipped it over. 1983? I looked at Kevin. Bought it new? He was full of it. Roaches didn't live that long.

DeeDee rummaged through a small first aid kit, then dabbed an alcohol pad on my cheek. Ouch. I bit my lip and tried really hard not to flinch. As she swabbed, she whispered, "Don't let Kevin connect any rocks to the stereo. I'm pretty sure the guys in Zebra are still alive. If he summons them here like Dio, we'll be knee deep in guts."

Well. Okay, then.

One more sting of an alcohol pad and a flurry of Band-Aids, and DeeDee had me patched up. "Don't worry. Pixie bites heal quickly. The gate opens in thirty minutes. Are you ready?"

NO, I AM NOT READY! I WILL NEVER BE READY! AAAAAAAAAH!

Of course, I didn't say that out loud. I'm not that stupid. I kept my lips zipped and nodded because chicks didn't dig cowards. No need to clue her in.

"I'm amped to be back at work, aren't you? The real world is so boring compared to this."

I waited for the punchline, but she wasn't kidding. For a hot second, my faith that DeeDee and I were soul mates faltered. I liked boring. Yes. Boring was good. Boring was safe. I would like more boring in my life, please.

She winked at me and smiled. Then, she grabbed a pack of disinfectant wipes off the counter and walked them over to Kevin, who was still on the slushy nozzle, headbanging. I think. It was hard to tell because he didn't have any hair to swing around.

"Aw, man. I'm on poo duty? Damn pixies," he said. "Why can't the cleaning crew do it?"

"Sorry, Kev." DeeDee sat the wipes next to him. "Cleaning crew is level one and two only. You know that. A little pixie poop hardly qualifies. Besides, we need to use sparingly. We talked about this."

She pointed back at me on the sly.

"Yeah yeah. Our delicate flower," Kevin said.

I slumped. They were talking about me, weren't they? I was the delicate flower. So much for keeping up appearances.

DeeDee moved her wood stool to its usual spot by the beer cave door, then opened the weapons safe. "Geesh. What a mess. Well guys, let's hope the bad guys don't escape tonight. Nothing is where it's supposed to be. We don't even have a doughnut!"

She huffed as she moved things around in the safe, reorganizing. Kevin cursed under his breath as he scooped up pixie dookie with a wet wipe. Okay, then. We were really doing this, weren't we? The cazh, cool, back to work like this place wasn't dangerous and everything's fine thing? Was I the only one who cared that we could all die at any second? I closed my eyes. *All you have to do is stay alive, Lloyd. Stay alive until God lets you out of this.*

"Whatevs. We're all just trying to get through the day, kid," Kevin said.

Gah. Stop zoning in on my brain waves.

"Relax, will ya? Enjoy the music. Listen to that. Sing it, Randy!"

Relax? Nope. Not happening. I couldn't pinpoint it, but something was off. Something was out of sorts, even though the store looked pristine. All the rocks and jars of weird crap under the register had been labeled and organized. The bags of chips and candy were lined up perfectly. The white linoleum sparkled, impeccably clean. The fluorescent tube lights hummed in their fixtures. Bottles sparkled behind the cooler doors.

Weird, right? Because this place was in ruins two days ago.

Everything was new, including the creepy old book behind the counter. It was open to an illustration of two buck naked pixies, a weird gourd, and a hobbit hole in the fresh dirt over a grave. Huh. So that's how DeeDee knew to send them to the cemetery.

"Yeah, kid. There are these magic things called books. You should try reading one sometime." Kevin peeked out from between two slushy machines. "I've got a crazy idea. Start with your employee manual."

Shut up, Kevin.

Dude. My employee manual. Don't get me started. I'd stashed that book in the very bottom of my closet, under a pile of clothes and board games. I didn't dare leave it out. Do you want to know why? It snored. All night. It grunted and burped during the day, too. Would you read a book that snored and burped? No, you wouldn't. You'd poke it with a stick, maybe, but sit down and read it? Hell no! It could bite!

"Millennials," he huffed. "Not everything is on YouTube, you know."

Anyway, back to *this* book. I looked closely at the illustrations. The pixies had sharp little teeth, which explained the throbbing pain under all my Band-Aids. They were also naked, so that was a thing. The red ink coloring their flaming pubes practically lasered out my eyes.

"How about you quit looking at tits and do some work. Go put away the bum wad in aisle four." Kevin held his nose as he worked. "Ricky's too chicken to stay past dark. Now that the days are short, we gotta pick up his slack. Unless you want to trade jobs."

He held up a wet wipe streaked with pixie poo. Uh, yeah. That would be a no.

I shuffled off to aisle four. Sure enough, there was an open stock tub at the end, half-filled with single-wrapped toilet paper rolls. Mummy's Choice Ultra Mega Super Strong. Huh. Did you recognize that brand? Me either.

I stacked. And I stacked. It was a delightfully mindless job until I found an open Pringles can stuffed with shredded napkins hidden behind the plungers. It looked like a hamster's nest. I shook it, but I didn't hear a squeak. Okay. Nothing alive in there, so I jump shot it into the trash can at the end of the counter. It hit the side, but went in. Boom. Three points! Playing all that NBA Live finally paid off.

There was a single squeeze bottle of mayonnaise—blech—in the bottom of the stock tub. I walked it back to the grocery aisle and popped it on the shelf, then *bop*. Something hit me on the back of the head.

Aaaah! Monster! I fwapped, arms swinging, ready to fend it off. But there was nothing there. Except a single roll of toilet paper lying on the floor.

Uh. Okay? I picked it up, and another roll of toilet paper flew up over the aisle and bonked me right in the nose. Not hard, it just kind of blooped, but still. This one was unwrapped, and it had unrolled as it flew. Then a third roll arced gently over the aisle, unrolling as it went. I ducked. "Come on. I just stacked those. You're making a mess."

DeeDee and Kevin must be pranking me. A fourth roll flew over the aisle. It hit me square in the face. I was not amused. "Cut it out!"

Teeeeeeee heeeeee heeeee heeee.

Oh, great. Now they were laughing at me. Low blow.

Another roll flew over the aisle and bonked me on the top of the head. "That's it. Stop it! It's not funny!"

They didn't stop. Two rolls hit me smack in the forehead, thrown from different directions. I stumbled as I tried to swat them away, and fell backward right into the condiment shelf, sending bottles raining to the floor. And another roll hit me in the face. "Stop! Puh..lee.eee.eeeze."

I cried, okay? Don't judge. I was tightrope walking on spaghetti emotionally by just being here.

DeeDee stepped into the end of the aisle. She eyed the toilet paper rolls and jars scattered across the floor. "What are you doing? Are you crying?"

"It's not funny!" And yes. *Sniff. Sniff.*

"Huh." Her eyebrows wrinkled, like she was confused, as another roll arced over the aisle and hit me right in the temple.

"What's not funny?" Kevin scuttled up to DeeDee, dragging a half-filled garbage bag behind him. "What the hell? Look at this mess. You're cleaning this up, kid."

Another roll flew through the air.

I looked at them. They looked at me. Kevin didn't throw that toilet paper. Neither did DeeDee.

"Oh, I see. Ha ha. Very funny. It's Morty. No. Too early. It's Bubby, right? You guys put him up to this."

"Um, no. Bubby's on vacation," DeeDee said. "He's in Jamaica."

I froze in place. That means it's a—*gulp. Monster.* DeeDee's eyes were wide. She didn't move. Because all the toilet paper rolls in the aisle had risen up into the air and started to unroll. The loose paper trailed the linoleum like mummy wrappings. The irony.

"Lloyd," DeeDee whispered. "Come here. Slowly."

Gulp. I took one step. Then another. And that's when I realized the toilet paper rolls had me surrounded.

"Aw, shit. More of these assholes?" Kevin snipped.

What? Who? Never mind. The answer was right in front of my face. Literally. Clutching each toilet paper roll were two pixies. These ones looked rough and meaner than the last bunch. Streaked with dirt, red hair coated with mud, growling.

"Lloyd. Run!" DeeDee held her arms out, ready to catch me.

She didn't have to tell me twice. Unfortunately, the dirty pixies had other plans. I took one step, and the toilet paper rolls flew and looped and fluttered in circles around me. My heart kicked up.

"Help!" I squeaked. But no one answered. DeeDee and Kevin were too busy arguing.

"Yes, it's their fault. The construction crew shoulda sealed this place up!" Kevin yelled. "Get me the phone. I got a few choice words for Steve down at the plant."

The toilet rolls moved faster, closer, around and around. Suddenly, I couldn't move my arms.

Teeeeeeee heeeeee heeeee heeee.

Great. The pixies were laughing at me. I had to get outta here. Right now. *Run! Run!*

In my defense, I tried, but it wasn't easy. My foot moved maybe an inch before it caught on something. I looked down. Well, shit. They'd used that Mummy's Choice to wrap me up tight like a cheap Halloween mummy, from my elbows all the way down to my ankles. Gee, guys. Way to be literal.

I wanted to scream, but a pixie shoved a cardboard toilet paper tube in the second I opened my mouth. So I did what any man would do in this situation: I took the biggest, fastest steps a man wrapped in three miles of Mummy's Choice could take. I waddled. That worked fine until my foot hit something slippery and went right out from under me. I went airborne for a second, then my back hit the floor.

Ooooooooooooooooow. That hurt. So bad. Like a high dive belly flop onto concrete.

"Do you like mayonnaise, kid?" Kevin asked.

"Mmmmum." Gah. *Ppppt. Ppppt.* I spit the toilet paper tube out of my mouth. Was he seriously asking me that now? Dude, monster alert! Hello! "I hate mayo!"

"You're really gonna hate it after this."

Pixies hovered in the air above me, holding tight to a squeeze bottle of Miracle Whip. Upside down. Open. Aimed right at me.

"What did I ever do to you?"

A man pixie held up a bit of red paper with a yellow P on it. A piece of a Pringles wrapper. Then, he flipped me the bird, and the rest of the little naked jerks squeezed.

Splllllllllllllllllllrp. Splllllllllllllllllllrp. Pffffffffffft.

They squirted that bottle—all of it—directly in my face. Globs of sticky mayo goop plopped and oozed, completely filling my open screaming mouth. Mayo pooled in my eye sockets and sucked up into my nostrils. *Can't breathe!* Dear God. Drowning in mayo. WHY?

I spit and wheezed and tried to flop away like a fish on a boat deck. But these jerks could fly, so they just zipped back and forth, following me, squirting stuff in my face. I tried to swat them away, but that toilet paper really was Ultra Mega Super Strong. I couldn't break free. I was a wiggling, helpless lump on the floor.

Most of the mayo did fling off my eyes, though. When I opened them, I saw a blurry vision of two pixies flying at me with tiny orange cones. Wait. Were those Bugles? What were they gonna do with those?

Hold up. Don't tell me. Yep. They jabbed me right in the eyes with the pointy ends. *Ouch! Wait. Holy crap, it burns! It burns! Aaaaaaah!* Those weren't ordinary Bugles. They were the Hot Buffalo Bugles! "Ooooooooooooow! Help meeee! My eyes!"

"America's #1 Finger Hat," my butt!

I rolled side to side. It was my only defense. I had hoped that would keep them from squirting anything else in my face, but no. The Bugles were just the start. The pixies tore open a bag of flour and emptied it all over me. A few more fluttered into formation, armed with ketchup, mustard and spicy relish. They tittered and squeezed. *Plop. Plop. Splllllllllllllllp.*

Chunks hit my face. Jesus. How many things come in squeeze bottles?

"Lloyd," DeeDee said. "Hold on. We have a plan."

A plan? Take your time. I'm kidding. Get me the hell out of here. The pixies had found the Frank's Red Hot. This was not going to end well for me.

I heard a rustling sound, then a *zuuuuuuuuuuur. Crinkle. Crinkle.* Through my burning eyeballs I could see DeeDee moving in. Thank God. She's gonna save me! With a big piece of foil? Yeah. You heard me. She had her arms stretched all the way out, holding a five foot long stretch of aluminum foil.

This was the plan?

Nope. I'm out. I tried extra hard to lift my arms and pull my hands free, but the stupid stuff didn't break. Man, this toilet paper really was super strong!

Angel eight ball rolled onto my chest. "Geesh. You can't break wet toilet paper? You're in worse shape than I thought."

"Help me!"

"I'm not coming all the way down there for a few feral pixies."

Clunk. A can of Vienna sausage hit me right in the forehead. *Ooooooooow.*

"I'm sorry I threw away your Pringles!" I yipped. The pixies didn't notice my apology or care. They were too busy wrestling with the plastic shrink wrap around the Frank's Red Hot cap.

"What are you doing, Kevin? That's not the plan!" DeeDee yelled. Her words did not inspire confidence.

"We're out of Pixie Rid, so I improvised!" Kevin said. "Hey, kid. Duck!"

Dude. Was he blind? I was already on the floor, a helpless toilet paper mummy. I couldn't duck more. I tilted my head back so I could see him. He stood at the end of the aisle with a grill lighter and an aerosol can of cheap hair spray.

Click. Click. Click. A tiny blue flame flickered at the end of the grill lighter. He jumped onto the hair spray nozzle. "Eat this, pixie scum."

A fireball exploded like a flamethrower, shooting halfway down the aisle. The heat of it melted my eyebrows.

The pixies screeched and retreated, right into DeeDee's aluminum foil. They hit the wrap, and she closed it up tight around them, rolling each pixie in foil like a baseball stadium hot dog. They wiggled and hissed and punched. *Pop pop pop.*

Wow. I had to hand it to Kevin and DeeDee. That half-ass plan netted most of the pixies. A few scattered, flying up into a heat vent in the ceiling. They slid right through the grates like it was nothing.

DeeDee dropped to her knees and pulled the toilet paper off of me. I wiggled, and she tugged until I was finally free. I sat up and rubbed my eyes, because dude. I didn't know what those people put on those Bugles, but my eyeballs were on fire.

"Look at this mess," Kevin shook his head.

Aisle four was was wrecked. TP. Ketchup. Mustard. Broken bottles of hot sauce. Ripped open bags of flour.

"I vote cleaning crew," Kevin said. "Whatdaya say?"

"Nice try, Kev, but it's level one and two for a reason," DeeDee said. "They need something meatier to chew on. You know that."

"Fine," Kevin huffed. "You're up, kid. Get the mop."

CHAPTER 7

Nope. Can't do it. I'm out.

I did not get the mop. I stood up and walked straight out the front door.

"Where're you going?" Kevin called after me. "You know I'm too short to fill the mop bucket!"

Too bad. I quit. Zone in on that, Kevin.

I stepped out onto the sidewalk and woah. Jesus, it was freezing outside. The night air was cold. It didn't help that I was soaked straight through, head to toe, in condiments like a slutty cheeseburger. I could feel the relish chunks freezing to my skin.

I looked up at the sky. Black. Clear. I took a deep breath. *I'm sorry, God. I'm not your guy. I'm not brave.* There had to be someone better for this job than me. I scanned the street and the parking lot, hoping the spell would kick in and my replacement would show up. *Come on, guy. Or girl. Whoever you are. I'm ready. Any second now. Anyone? Anyone? Hello?*

Sigh. Oh well. I couldn't do it. I quit.

Something hit my foot. Ugh. It was angel eight ball. "Wow. Rough night, huh?"

"Ya think?" I'd been at work for an hour and had already been assaulted by miniature nudists. Twice. "Is God punishing me? What did I do to deserve this?"

"Probably nothing," he said. "Look at poor Job. He got a terrible deal and for what? A bet? Either way, God has a plan for you."

"You're lying. There is no plan."

"Oh, you're the expert now? The Bible says, 'No one can fathom the mysteries of God.' Well, okay. I can because I'm an angel, but you? Sorry. You have to roll with it. I wouldn't be here to enforce the plan if there was no plan."

"Right. So what's the plan then? I'll stay if you tell me why God wants me here."

"I can't tell you that," the triangle turned. I could swear I heard him huff. "God works in *mysterious* ways, remember?"

"You don't know, do you?"

"Yes, I do!" His triangle bobbed in the red liquid. "Well, I know part of it."

"Not good enough." I couldn't do this. God had the wrong guy. DeeDee needed someone brave. She deserved better than a chicken shit scaredy cat like me.

"I'm sorry, Gertrude." I felt like a dirt bag selling her out, but she was nineteen and not exactly the picture of health. She was in God's waiting room already. So with that, I ran as fast as I could toward my bike.

The sky immediately turned angry.

Kunk. Kunk. Kunk.

Golf ball sized hail rained down all around me, and the sky flashed, saturated with lightning. But I kept running, so hard my mayonnaise-soaked thighs burned from rubbing together. Man. What kind of fabric were these jammies made of? It was like boy scouts starting a fire down there.

Kunk. Kunk. Kunk.

Ouch. Hail. Right on the head.

Really baby Jesus? I went to church camp. I saved the world once. I paid my debts. That should be enough! What do you want from me? Why do you want me to work here? Give me a sign!

A bright white light appeared. *Jesus? Is that you?*

Errrrrrrrrrrrrrrrr.

A horn. Was it an angelic trumpet?

Scrrrrrrrrrrrrrrrr.

Huh. Jesus must be having a little trouble on the wet pavement.

Thump.

Something big hit me.

Owwwww.

Pain radiated up and down the entire right side of my body. The smell of burning rubber filled my nostrils, then I saw stars. Literally, because I was on my back looking up at the sky, aching all over, partway under the front bumper of the Dolly's Divine Delicacies delivery truck.

A shadow appeared above me. "Jesus?"

"Not last time I checked." Bob the Doughnut Guy leaned over me. "You all right, new kid? You're lucky to be alive. You ran right out in front of me. If I hadn't hit the brakes, you'd be mush. You could have died."

Angel eight ball lolled around by my head, waiting to get a word in.

Of course. He stopped, window facing me, and the triangle emerged. "That wasn't Jesus. That was headlights. The van was my idea. Sorry about that, but I had to intervene. We have to keep Gertrude alive. If she dies, He'll go after someone else. Maybe your parents. Or DeeDee. He always gets what He wants. Like it or not."

"Wow. You're a shitty guardian angel."

Dread percolated through me. There really was no way out of this, was there? I sat up. *Ouch.* My muscles were tight, cramped.

DeeDee ran up to me, wrapped her arms around me and squeezed me so tight I thought my head was gonna pop off. *Ouch.* But, *Mmmmm.* Her body was so soft and warm and comforting she was like a human wubby.

"Oh, Lloyd. I thought I'd lost you." She squeezed me for a long time. When she let go, her shirt was soaked in mayonnaise. Her eyes were wet and a little pink. "I'm so glad you're okay."

Oh shit. Was she crying? Over me?

Angel eight ball's triangle turned again."DeeDee and Lloyd, sittin' in Galilee. No. Wait. How does it go? DeeDee and Lloyd, sittin' in a tree. K-I-S-S—"

Shut up. I fwapped him away, and he rolled under the tire of the Dolly's delivery van. *Jerk.*

Bob the Doughnut guy stood up. "Did you hear that?"

He abruptly turned and walked behind the truck, following a sound only he had heard.

"You seriously let a few pixies scare you outta here, kid?" Kevin stood next to me, with two sets of legs on his hips. "After all we've been through?"

"Those pixies tried to kill me."

"With mayo? By making you delicious? Please." Kevin rubbed his belly. "Mmmm. Speaking of. I'm starving."

Just then, Bob the Doughnut guy's booming voice cut through the night. "You! Get outta here. Beat it. Scram!"

A very beefy man—he looked like a wad of raw dough that had been molded into the shape of a bodybuilder, then left out on the counter to rise for too long—sprinted out from behind the van, trotting across the lot fast as a gazelle. It took me a hot minute to realize it was the jogger who came in for a doughnut every night. He had really bulked up. Like really bulked up. He looked like two Lou Ferrignos stuffed into one track suit.

Bob the Doughnut Guy chased after him, his silver-streaked mullet in glorious 80s hair-bands waves flowing behind him. "I told ya, no more! That's the last doughnut you're ever gonna eat. You got me?"

Panting and out of breath, he gave up the chase after about ten steps and resorted to shaking his fist. "You get your cheat meal somewhere else from now on, you hear me? Freak!"

Then he said to us, "Don't sell that guy any more doughnuts, got it? He's cut off. Word from corporate is he's been buying chocolate devil's frosted from multiple stores. Eating ten a night! Look at him. He's pumped up like a beefcake gingerbread man. He's an addict. So don't sell him any more. Not a single one. He can't handle it. It's not safe."

Not safe? Well, that was the understatement of the century. None of the doughnuts were safe. Touching one chocolate devil's frosted made my hand blow up like a balloon and eating one made Kevin grow to twenty feet tall. How on earth did Dolly's even have a license to bake these things?

Right then, the sky rumbled and flashed green. DeeDee grabbed my arm and held tight as we all looked around.

"Fine! I'm going! I'm going!" I said to God. I started to stand up and thought better of it. Ouch. My all of me hurt.

Angel eight ball, somehow, was in my hand. And he was shaking. "I don't think that's for you." The triangle turned. An arrow appeared, pointing across the street.

I looked up and saw a green light crackle inside the clouds right above the Monster Burger. Then a spider web of lightning hit Frankenstein right on the bolt. Sparks flew, arcing through the sky like fireworks. Then the sign *zzzzrd zzzzrt* flickered and fizzled, flipping on. Frankenstein glowed over his pulsing neon bun, as if the lightning had brought the sign back to life.

"Well, that's creepy," Kevin said. "Its alive! Alive! Am I right? Heh heh."

No one laughed.

"Frankenstein? Anyone? No?" Kevin said. "Geesh. Tough crowd."

We were all too busy watching the white board flicker to life. It didn't say, "Hick Sandwich, $3," like it did when Mr. Jimmy died. It said, "Under New Management. Grand reopening tomorrow. New and Improved No. 1 Monster Burger Combo FREE ALL DAY! Dine in only."

Huh. Kevin was wrong. I guess someone would buy a restaurant with no customers.

"Come on. We better get inside," DeeDee helped me to my feet. "Let's get you cleaned up. Kevin. You're in charge of the gate."

Kevin didn't hear. He was too busy arguing with Bob the Doughnut Guy. "I draw the line at pumpkin spice. That shit ain't coming into my store."

He walked to the back of the pink van with a still-yelling Kevin perched on his shoulder. "The world doesn't need any more pumpkin spice, Bob. Pumpkin spice is killing my soul."

"Dolly's Divine Delicacies doesn't make just any old pumpkin spice," Bob the Doughnut Guy said as he opened the back door. "Besides, we have a contract. When Dolly says you need pumpkin spice, you get pumpkin spice. We ever lead you wrong before?"

Aw man. I sincerely hoped Kevin won this argument. If the glazed with pink frosting and sprinkles could crunch a giant hell spider down to nothing like an ice cube, I didn't want to see the pumpkin spice in action.

DeeDee propped me up and helped me limp—slowly—back inside. I was sore and stiff. Getting hit by a van didn't tickle, that's for sure. She led me through the stockroom door, into the hallway between Faust's deluxe man cave and the posh employee lounge. The lounge where Chef used to make me the best steaks ever. Poor Chef. When the hell beasts showed up, he was the only one of us who didn't make it out of that battle alive. Oh, wait. Chef hadn't really been alive in the first place, had he? He was a zom—nope. I couldn't say it. Couldn't say the z word.

"Are you okay? You look pale," DeeDee said.

Nope. Not okay.

We stopped in front of the built-in microwave looking box that Ricky had once used to fetch my employee manual from my house. It was clearly some sort of magic portal. She typed my home address, then "Lloyd's bedroom, second floor, clean clothes" into the panel. Light poured from the window and a few seconds later. *Ding.* She opened it, and my T-shirt and shorts were inside.

I'd like to say they were neat and folded and clean, but come on. I didn't live that life. They were crumpled up, worn at least once, but they weren't coated in mayonnaise, so yay! Until I opened the shirt. It said, "When I fart, you'll be the second to know." And it had a reasonably fresh nacho cheese stain on it.

Jesus. No wonder I can't get a date.

"Your shirts are so bad they're almost charming. Almost," she said. "You know, I planned to take you out shopping and for drinks yesterday, but you didn't return any of my calls or texts. Are you avoiding me?"

"Wha? No!" My cheeks flushed hot. So so so hot. While my heart sunk. Avoiding DeeDee? Never! *Tell her you love her so hard forever. Tell her, Lloyd! Speak!* But my lips flubbed there, bubbing open and closed like a suffocating fish.

It wasn't DeeDee. I just couldn't bear the thought of anything Demon Mart. Faust had given me a fancy new iPhone as part of my save-the-world bonus. I charged it, turned it on, and the first dozen messages that popped up? All updates from Faust about the store reopening. I couldn't deal. I'd turned it off and shut it in my sock drawer. I hadn't even seen DeeDee's texts. I wanted to tell her all of this, but my lips kept on flubbing and none of those words came out.

She smiled to fill the awkward silence, but it wasn't a real smile. It only curled in one corner, and her eyes stayed sad. DeeDee typed something in on the microwave box. It lit up, dinged, then she took out a black T-shirt. Neatly folded. It must be hers.

Then she took off her shirt.

Oh. Boy.

You heard that right. She pulled her mayonnaise-soaked T-shirt off. Right in front of me. I swear a 1970s disco porn soundtrack flipped on the second the cotton rose above her belly button. Boom chica bow ow. Time dialed down to slow motion as she lifted her T-shirt up, over her beautiful face, revealing a black lace bra holding her two milky, soft perfect...Oh dear Lord Jesus Christ, you made the perfect woman. My dream is coming true. The good parts!

They were like two perfect perky grapefruits in an underwire. Once the shirt came all the way off, she shook her head back and forth, and ran her fingers through her hair as the shirt fluttered to the floor.

Woah boy. Room spinning. Feeling dizzy. Every single drop of blood in my body had gone south. Ahem. I moved my crumpled clothes over my pants just to cover up anything that might, uh, pop up.

I could swear that DeeDee was bathed in a golden beam of angelic light sent straight down from heaven as she jiggled in slow motion, topless, and unfolded her new clean T-shirt. Boom chicka, hell yeah! And I mean that in the most "holy shit, I totally respect the fuck out of her because she's a bad ass and I love her for her mind, too, " way. Give me some credit. I'm not a total pig. But hot damn. I am only a man.

Thunk. Thunk. Thunk.

My heart raced. My eyes traced the soft line of her collar bone, the dizzying edge of the lacy strap on her shoulder, the wisp of hair touching her neck, the tall white chef's hat rising up as it moved closer to her. Wait what? Cue record scratch.

Thunk. Thunk. Thunk.

That was not the sound of my heart racing. That was the sound of heavy boots. A greenish gray face appeared over DeeDee's shoulder. Oh God. It was Chef. Zombie chef! Shouldn't he be dead? Like dead dead? He'd been snapped in half!

His head moved back and forth as he sniffed the air, his nose wiggling like a rabbit's. It's like he could smell us—warm, delicious, alive—and was honing in on us with his nose.

Thunk. Thunk. Thunk.

He was almost on her now. Oh shit. Was he gonna eat her? Was he moving in for the kill? This was just like my dream. I had to save her. I couldn't let her die. "DeeDee, run! Run! ZOMBIE!!!!" I screamed. "SAVE YOURSELF!"

Sadly, I only screamed it in my head, not out loud. My mouth opened, but no words came out. The sight of her boobs, combined with abject terror, had completely immobilized all of my higher brain functions. *Shit! Shit! No! Speak, dumbass. Speak!* But nothing. Well, now I knew why every dude in every single slasher movie stood there like a wide-eyed idiot while the killer cut up his naked girlfriend. No man could think straight with a hard on. There just wasn't enough blood in our brains. For real.

DeeDee pulled on her clean shirt, and must have caught a glimpse of Chef, because a second later she jump-spun toward him and had her fists up. "Oh. Chef. You scared me. How did you get out?"

She slumped, relaxed. Relaxed? Hello! ZOMBIE! RUN!

A bit of blood must have freed up, because I moved. Well, just enough to drop my clothes, stumble and fall on my butt. Again. Jesus. This was becoming my signature move.

DeeDee stepped to Chef, rolled down the collar of his crisp, clean white uniform, and checked that weird electric bondage collar he always wore. There was a tiny row of lights on it, all green. "Well, your collar's working. I'm not sure how you got out, though," she said. "Come on. Let's get you back in the kitchen. It's too hot out here. You've got to stay cool, or you'll rot."

She grabbed his shoulders and turned him back toward the lounge.

Thunk. Thunk. Thunk.

He tromped back down the hallway. That's when I figured out why he was so loud and how he was walking. He had a weird black exoskeleton support brace thing running from his chest all the way down to his feet. Man. They'd snapped him back together and put him in some sort of sci fi mech suit. Wait. Did that make him a super zombie boss? I'd played enough video games to know the bosses always get you in the end. Every. Single. Time.

And zombies are real, so I'm sure this will all end well. I felt the urgent need to put on clean clothes. I did not want to be covered in mayonnaise when the zombie apocalypse started. It's like a chicken nugget dipping itself in barbecue sauce. Why make yourself more delicious?

Yep. I could use one of those magic showers right about now. I gathered up my clothes and pushed the bathroom door open with my behind, as I scooped up the stray clean sock I'd dropped on the floor. *Brrr.* Man, it was cold in here.

The door thumped closed. I stood up, turned around and bumped straight into a man. "Oh, excuse me."

Wait. Why was there another guy in the bathroom? I looked up at him. And *plup.* That was the sound of my guts hitting the floor. Because, oh shit. Wrong door. This wasn't the bathroom. I had walked into some sort of cold storage locker. A dozen men in coveralls stood inside swaying. Their noses sniffed the air aggressively. It was the cleaning crew. The zombie cleaning crew. HERE? AAAAAAH!

This chicken nugget had landed right on the buffet line. I backed right into the door. It was ice cold. "HEEEEEEEEEELLLLLLLLLLLP!"

I screamed, loud and clear. In my head, at least. In the real world, all that came out was a squeak. Which was probably good, because, dude, you don't scream when you're surrounded by a zombie horde. I'd played enough Resident Evil to know that much.

The cleaning crew wore giant black Terminator sunglasses like Chef's, but I could tell they were looking at me, even under all that black plastic. Like looking looking. With piqued interest. Their lips curled back, exposing a dozen sets of rotten teeth. They were drooling.

Uuuuuuuuuuuuuuuuh. Aaaaaaaaaaaar. Uuuuuuuuuuuhhhh.

Uh oh. That was an excited moan, a "Hey guys, pizza's here!" kind of moan. They shuffled closer. I ran my hand along the door, fumbling, searching for a handle. But it was smooth. Nothing but metal. Oh God. I turned around. There wasn't a handle! NO HANDLE!

The cooler only opened from the outside! *Aaaaaaaah!!* I panicked and did the only thing I could think to do. I pounded on the door, hoping that DeeDee—anybody—was still out there and would hear me.

Uuuuuuuuuuuuuuuuh. Aaaaaaaaaaaar. Uuuuuuuuuuuhhhh.

"Help MEEEEEEEEEE!"

Pound. Pound. Pound. No one came. I was alone. I was screwed. The noise only gave the zombies a firm target.

Uuuuuuuuuuuuuuuuh. Aaaaaaaaaaaar. Uuuuuuuuuuuhhhh.

They moved in, pressing me against the door. I had nowhere to go.

Uuuuuuuuuuuuuuuuh. Aaaaaaaaaaaar. Uuuuuuuuuuuhhhh.

So this is it, huh? This is how I'm gonna go out? This was God's big plan? I slunk down to the floor and balled up, making my body as small as possible. I was surrounded.

Err Err Err Err Err.

I covered my ears. An alarm sounded, and yellow lights flashed.

Uuuuuh?

Yeah. You heard that. They moaned in a way that sounded more like a question. The zombies looked up at the light.

Clunk fwooooooooooo.

No, that was not a new martial art. That was the sound of the cooler door unlocking and all the air going out as it opened. I rolled backward right on out of the cooler into the hallway. The zombies shuffled out after me. I was too scared to do anything but scream.

"AAAAAAAAAAAAAAAAAAAAAAAHH!"

They were closing in. All of them. They moaned again, and my survival instinct flipped on. Finally! (Apparently, it was a late bloomer, like me.) I kicked up off the floor and ran faster than I ever had before. I pushed through the door out into the store, screaming, "Zombies! RUN!" as loud as I could.

I ran. I tripped. And I fell, smack on my face, right into a pile of something hot, steaming and wet. I flailed, trying to get up, still screaming "Zooooooooooombeeeeeeeeeeees!"

"Well, duh," Kevin stood on the counter carefully easing his Zebra album back into the sleeve. "Who else is gonna clean up this mess? Where you been? You missed all the action."

"What?" I rolled over. I was lying in a puddle of white slime. Wait. Was that mayonnaise? No. It was a chunk of what looked like ruffly jellyfish tentacles, thick and rubbery. "Jesus Christ!"

And boy did it stink. It smelled like thirty pissed-off skunks wrestling in a steaming pig pen. *Vlurp. Gonna barf.* I covered my mouth.

"Relax, kid. It isn't gonna hurt you," Kevin said. "The rest of him got away."

"What happened?" Wait. Scratch that. Didn't want to know.

Kevin decided to tell me anyway. "We opened the gate at midnight, and this poor sucker got sucked through. Routing error. He was just as surprised as we were. Then the portal closed up and accidentally cut off one of his legs. Well. Whatever this is. Poor dude. Long story short, gate malfunction. Wait 'til I get a hold of Steve. His half-ass gate repair almost cost me an album. The needle skipped and almost scratched it!"

I scurried out of that pile of ick ASAP. Good thing, too. The zombies descended on it like a fat kid on a Happy Meal. They chewed and groaned. *Mmmmmmm. Aaaaaaaa. Mmmmmmm. Myum. Myum. Myum.*

"Get over here before you're zombie lunch."

I didn't move. I was too scared.

"What's wrong with you?"

All I could do was point. Zombies. Come on. Did he need to ask?

"Relax. As long as the collars are on and the lights are green, they won't hurt you. You don't register as food. Don't put your fingers anywhere near their mouths, though. Better safe than sorry," Kevin said. "If they bite you, you're screwed. Unless you want to spend your afterlife working for the devil for free."

CHAPTER 8

"Get up, kid." Kevin leaned over the counter to look down at me. "We aren't paying you to hide in the corner."

Okay, yeah. So I'd spent the last forty-five minutes curled up on the floor behind the register. It was Tuesday, the gate opened in thirty minutes, and I hadn't quite recovered from last night. It was only a matter of time before a pixie or some other nasty horrible beast popped out of somewhere. I closed my eyes. *It's okay. You only have to stay alive until God lets you out of this. It's fine. It'll be fine.*

I had been pep talking myself nonstop ever since I came back to work. It didn't seem to be helping, because I couldn't understand what God wanted from me or why He wanted me to come back here. Did God want to kill me? Why would He want to kill me? Oh, man. I think I'm having my first existential crisis.

"Nah. You've either got PTSD, or you're a plain-vanilla chicken shit," Kevin said. "Don't overthink it. Now get up."

"No."

"Your loss, kid. You definitely want to see this. Hubba hubba." Kevin lifted an impossibly tiny pair of binoculars and trained them on the front window. "Hey, baby. Mmm. Come to papa. Man, she is stacked! Her tits are the size of Thanksgiving turkeys!"

I stood up and looked out the window. What? I'm a man. I have needs.

Kevin was scoping out the grand reopening of Monster Burger. Which, if I must say, was seriously grand. The place was absolutely packed. The drive-thru was closed, but there was a line of customers waiting to get in. The line spilled out the front door, snaked around the sign and all the way down the block. I didn't know how the new owners had done it, but they'd drawn the first crowd in Monster Burger history.

Kevin had his binoculars zoomed in on an incredibly busty woman in a low cut, flowing white dress standing on the curb. Her hair was black and ratted into a tall, thick beehive with a white stripe running up both sides. Her skin had been painted green, and she had a glowing bolt on each side of her neck. She held a sign that said, "FREE food today. So good it's scary."

"Mmm. I'm definitely gonna get some of that," Kevin said.

In your dreams. Chicks don't dig roaches.

"I meant the food, dumbass."

Great. He'd zoned in on my brainwaves again.

"Yeah. I did. And I'll have you know I was quite the ladies' man in my younger days. I had girls like that falling at my feet."

Surely, he meant girl roaches.

Kevin looked at me like I was the stupidest person on earth.

"What?"

He didn't answer. He resumed staring at the hot chick on the corner. And so did I. Kevin wasn't exaggerating. She was all woman and so top heavy I was surprised she could stand up.

"Wow. Nice cans." A voice came from behind us.

I whirled around, ready to fight. Never mind. It was Morty. He was dressed like a firefighter, in a tight white T-shirt, heavy tan pants held up by suspenders, and waterproof boots. "Move over and let me get a look at Frankenhooker."

Kevin handed him the teeny binoculars. Morty put them to his eyes and squinted. "Oowee. I like my ladies a little more lively. She's a dead lay, for sure, know what I mean?" He punched me in the shoulder. Ow. "So, chubs. A little voice told me your mom is a piece. A-1 MILF. Is she into firemen?"

My jaw dropped. I knew exactly what little voice. *Kevin. Stop ogling my Mom!*

"She's hot. Deal with it." Kevin shrugged. "Hold up. How did you get out, pervert? It's not midnight yet."

"The door was wide open," Morty said.

"Shit." Kevin rubbed his eyes like he suddenly had a headache. "And you came through anyway?"

"You know it. There are lonely ladies hungry for love next door, and I'm the meal. Why make 'em wait?"

"Real classy, Morty," Kevin said.

"Don't hate the player. Besides, I'm anxious to try these babies out. You like 'em?" Morty lifted his T-shirt to reveal a rippling eight pack of abs. Seriously. His stomach had segments like a Hershey bar. Human dudes couldn't compete with demon bods like that.

"Did you paint those on?" Kevin said.

"Sure did. There was a video tutorial on DemonTube. What do you think? A little contour to highlight my natural assets? It's the little touches that please the ladies. Speakin' of, where's my future ex-wife?"

He looked around.

"DeeDee's fixing Chef's baby gate. It's broken. He keeps wandering out of the kitchen. If you hadn't noticed, everything's busted around here," Kevin said. "Which reminds me, kid. Go guard the beer cave. If this jackass can get out, God only knows what's next."

My legs turned to Jello, barely able to hold my chunky midsection aloft. Beer cave? Me?

"Nut up, kid. Now, shoo! Before anything worse than Morty comes through. I gotta make a call." Kevin pushed the phone off the hook and started jumping up and down on the keys, dialing six six six.

Gulp. Terrified. But I did as I was told, because I really didn't want anything to sneak up on us. Be prepared, right? I walked straight to the safe. Man. Even with DeeDee's reorganizing, it was a mess in there. I grabbed a sword out of the jumble. My bad. It wasn't a sword. It was a giant hammer. I just couldn't see the top until I pulled it free of the mess. Oh well. It'll do.

I stepped up to the beer cave door, muscles tense. I could see an eerie light illuminating the craft beer. The blue glow of an open gate to hell. It flipped off. Then it flipped on. Then off again. Over and over, like a strobe light.

"The gate is blinking."

"Then go in there and see what's wrong!" Kevin stood on the telephone receiver. "Can't you see I'm busy, kid?"

In? There? Woah boy.

My hands tightened around the hammer. I honestly don't know how I did it, but my body somehow overcame every "Hell no!" circuit in my brain and stepped in. The edges of the gate expanded then receded, quickly, but not in a predictable rhythm. More like a short circuit, like some sort of glitch. The gate spread, the light pulsed, and then the edges suddenly shrank, as if the gate had flipped off.

Crunch. Something hissed. *Uh oh.* Something was here.

I took cover behind a stack of Milwaukee's Best.

I could tell the gate stayed small, because the light was dim, barely a glimmer of blue, but it was undulating. Moving. I peeked around to take a look, hammer held tight to my chest.

There was a dark shadow in the gate. It was stuck there, as if the gate had crunched down and trapped it. It lifted its head to reveal luscious red lips and cleavage. Yes. I said cleavage. So deep I could get lost in it. Holy cow. It was a woman!

She looked at me and said, "Can you give me a hand, cowboy? I'm late for work."

This wasn't just any woman. She was one of the succubus strippers that worked at the Sinbad's gentleman's club across the street. FYI the term 'gentleman' was a stretch. You'd know what I mean if you saw the place.

Anyway, she was stuck. Half of her body in and half of her body out of the gate. I dropped the hammer and ran to help her. She held out her delicate, manicured hands, and I pulled.

Eeehp. Eeeehp. Phew. I'm out of breath already!

Eeehp. Eeeehp. Man. She was really stuck in there.

That's when I noticed that one of her legs, up to the knee, was stuck, poking out the wrong way. The heel of her shoe was looking right at me. It was five feet away from the rest of her. Eek. She was bent like a pretzel. It didn't look like it tickled.

"Keep pulling," she said.

Eeehp. Eeeehp. Eeehp. Eeeehp. I pulled. She kicked. Her shoe moved up and down furiously. The gate suddenly flung wide open, engulfing the entire back wall of the beer cooler, mid-pull. She flew out of the gate and crashed into me with such force, the two of us slid across the icy steel floor and skidded to a stop when my head rammed hard into a stack of Bud Light 12-packs. Ow.

"My hero. How can I ever thank you?" She had landed on top of me. She smiled and ran a painted red fingernail down my cheek. Her body was soft, and her warm breath tickled my cheeks. She had me pinned. "I have a few ideas. Tell me. What's your fantasy?"

Woah boy. I'm pretty sure there are some pornos that start like this.

She put her head down and when she lifted it again, she had turned into the sign girl at Monster Burger. Big black beehive, green skin, glowing bolts, low cut dress. She ran her finger down my chest and moved in close like she was about to kiss me. She looked at me with white, milky eyes, and grinned. With rotten yellow teeth. "Mmm. So that's what you're into. Dangerous. Kinky," she purred. "I like it. I'm game if you are."

Nope. Not game. Definitely not game. Zombie! Zombie! "HELP! Aaah!"

"Too much, sweetheart? Let me try again." The zombie babe wiggled and transformed into DeeDee. She pressed her body into mine and grabbed my behind. I mean, she really had a death grip back there. One cheek in each hand, squeezing hard. I could feel her hot breath on my mouth. Oh Jesus. Hard on in three...two...one.

"Mmm. You're happy to see me. That's quite a hammer you're wielding."

And she didn't mean the wonky hammer I'd pulled out of the

weapons safe, you feel me? That was still on the floor by the Milwaukee's Best.

"Twila? Is that you?" DeeDee stepped into the beer cave. Uh oh. Busted. "You know the rules. Employees are off limits."

"Only if they say no," Twila purred as she slipped out of her DeeDee suit. She transformed into the curvalicious redhead stripper from Sinbad's. She licked her lips and said, "Are you telling me no, cowboy?"

Twila? Jesus. Even her name was hot. And trust me when I say it'd be hard to convince her that no means no. Because my tent was pitched. She licked my face. Oh boy. *Say no, Lloyd. Come on. You can do it. DeeDee is standing right there. You have to say no! Eyes on the prize.*

Twila and DeeDee both stared at me, waiting for an answer.

Logic alone wouldn't be enough to override my reptile brain, so I tried really hard to remember what Morty looked like in his regular skin. Red. Wings. Claw feet. Flying. Twila was not a human woman. She looked like Morty under all this. "No?"

I should have sounded more firm, but these were difficult circumstances.

"Sorry to hear it, cowboy. I will catch you next time," Twila said. Emphasis on catch. She slid off of me, smoothed out her dress, and swished her hair back. She waltzed over to DeeDee and said, "Saving him for yourself, hot stuff? I get it. The innocent ones are always the most fun to corrupt."

Twila blew me a kiss, then sashayed off, hips swinging.

DeeDee stared Twila down as she clip clopped away. "Kevin, how did these two get out before midnight?"

"Gate's busted," Kevin said.

"I thought it was just a routing error," she said.

"Apparently not," Kevin said. "Call Faust again."

"I did. Straight to voicemail. I asked Doc to have a look at the gate. He's coming tomorrow."

"We can't wait that long. I'm calling Steve down at the plant," Kevin said.

"Again?" DeeDee said.

"Look. His crew did a real number on us. He's gonna get a piece of my mind. Get over here. I'm gonna put it on speakerphone so you all can hear this."

"Oh boy. Here we go." DeeDee shook her head, then turned to me. "You might want to get up and um, pull yourself together."

She glanced at the tent pole in my pants, then stepped out of the beer cave. My cheeks flushed hot. Oh geesh. This is embarrassing. Twila had really laid my secrets bare, hadn't she? I stood up and tried to put on an air of dignity, which was difficult in a T-shirt that said "Guess what?" with an arrow pointing at a cartoon chicken butt. And mismatched socks. One green. One yellow. Shit. I really did need to get my life together, didn't I?

"Amen." Angel eight ball rolled out from behind the Heineken. "Let DeeDee take you shopping, though. I can't help you with fashion. We don't have regular clothes up here. No wing holes."

When I stepped out, Morty had just popped the top off a Colt 45 tallboy he'd filched from the reach-in refrigerator, and Twila looked right at me, peeled the wrapper off a Slim Jim Monster Meat Stick and sucked on it like a. Well. Ahem. Moving on.

DeeDee leaned against the doughnut case with her arms crossed, watching all of this unfold. She did not seem amused. I stood next to DeeDee. Safest place in the store. Trust me.

"Watch out," she said, eyeballing Twila and Morty. "They're extra hungry. They haven't been out for a few days."

Kevin not only put his call to Steve on speakerphone, he connected it to the intercom system so it could pour from every speaker in the store.

Brrring. Brrring. Brrring.

Voicemail. The message? "I knaw this is you, Kevin. Ya jagoff. I'm on a jahb, so yinz can stahp cawling me a hunderd times a day. Ahz not coming dahn dere. The store passed inspection, so the prahblem is on yer end. Find it and fix it yerself! This thing'll beep, but dahn't leave me another gahd dang message, ya idjit!"

"Uh..." I did not even know what I was hearing.

"Steve's from Pittsburgh. You get used to the accent." DeeDee whispered to me. She had her eyes on Twila, who had her eyes on me.

Kevin took a deep breath, ready to leave a mean message anyway.

Beep. Then a computerized female voice said: "This mailbox is full."

We all watched Kevin's mental fortitude visibly crack. His roach legs did little stompy roundhouse kicks. He kung pow chopped the phone clean off the counter. He stomped in circles, kicking and cursing.

"No good r*cking Fr$%cking Son of a B*%ch!" Kevin shook his...fists? Whatever was on the end of a roach leg. I swear I saw a black storm cloud of expletives swirling above him.

"Why is Kevin so mad at this Steve guy?"

"Steve is in charge of all the zombie crews in the Mid-Atlantic region. Construction, clean up, maintenance."

Gulp. How many crews was that? How many more zombies were there? Stop. Don't answer. I'd be awake doing zombie epidemic math all night. One bites one, two bites two, four bites four, until everyone's dead and me and Mom are surviving on sofa crumbs and nailing boards against the dining-room window to keep the zombies out.

"Kevin blames Steve for all the problems we've had since we reopened. He thinks they cut corners to get it done on time. It's never that simple around here, but he won't listen. To us, two days to rebuild this place seems like a rush job, but these people work on divine time. If God can make the world in seven days, and Jesus can come back from the dead in three, we should be able to reopen a corner store in a weekend, right?"

I nodded and tried my best to look astute, but WTF? Every time she opened her mouth, it was clear DeeDee thought about the world on an entirely different level than I did. She was way smarter than me. Like *way* way.

"Steve comes out once a month for zombie maintenance, and I doubt we'll see him before then. I told Kevin he's not going to make an extra trip. He's busy, and the plant's three hours away in Monroeville."

"Where?"

"Near Pittsburgh, where the whole zombie thing started. The plant has been there since the very first outbreak."

"What?" On earth was she talking about?

She looked at me. "You know. Monroeville? The outbreak at the mall? In 1978?"

My eyes went wide.

"It's in the employee manual. In the appendix? Dawn of the Dead was a documentary. George Romero didn't make that stuff up. All of our zombies came from the mall outbreak in 1978. The coolers keep them fresh. That plus a lot of embalming fluid. They look pretty good for how old they are."

Oh God. Room spinning. I bent over and put both hands on my knees. Dawn of the Dead. A documentary?

"Are you all right?" She put her hand on my back and rubbed it. "Don't worry. We've never had a zombie incident at this store. No escapes, no broken collars, not a single bite. See? She pointed to a small black sign bolted to the wall behind the Mountain Dew 2-liter tower that said: "This facility has been Z Accident free for 14,617 days."

An illustration of a zombie with a pompadour, smiling and giving us one rotten thumb up, was drawn on the bottom right corner. He had a speech bubble that said, "Don't get bit, and you'll be a hit!"

"What about the other stores?" I regretted asking it the second the words left my lips.

"Well, there was one incident in Louisville in 1985, but that wasn't one of our stores. It started in a medical supply warehouse. Long story."

CHAPTER 9

At midnight, Morty and Twila, the sexy hell pervs, left the store to sow their devilish oats across the neighborhood. DeeDee balanced precariously on her wood stool, nailing a rusty old horseshoe above the beer cave door. I stood next to her, ready to offer assistance. Which she didn't need. As usual. So really, I just stood there holding that long stupid hammer and drinking a slushy. A small one, not a Colossal Super Slurp. Angel eight ball smacked my hand away from the big cups and flashed something about Keto. Or Paleo. Whatever. The small cup was a compromise.

"There." DeeDee hammered the last nail into the horseshoe. "That should keep most of the bodiless entities inside the cooler if the gate malfunctions again."

Gulp. Bodiless entities? Can't deal. Must. Eat. Feelings.

I took a sip of my slushy. Oof. It was bitter, alcoholic—at least fifty percent cheap booze—and gritty. I picked a little black thing out of my teeth. Blech!

"How exactly does this work again?" I pointed to the horseshoe.

"Magical creatures hate iron."

"Cough. Bullshit. Cough." Kevin announced over the intercom. And yes, he did say "cough" as he faked his cough. "It didn't keep the pixies away. I can see one of them in the vents right now, flipping me the bird. Here you go, jerk. Here's two right back at you. I can do this all day!"

"Foil isn't made of iron, Kevin." DeeDee snipped. "We just have to figure out how to trap the stray pixies."

"Yeah, well until then, you clean up after them. I'm done. I caught 'em flying around the Combos bags, having a three-way in mid-flight. The pervs couldn't even land before they started porking! I am not wiping up pixie sex juice. No way. I draw the line."

"Did you find the switch yet, Kevin?" DeeDee sighed.

"I'm working on it. Geesh. Get off my back."

Let's just say Kevin had been in a mood since his call to Steve, and he was taking his frustration out on us. This had turned into quite the warm and welcoming work environment.

"Can you work faster? We don't want any normies in here."

"Oh, really? I didn't know that." Kevin totally did. "If you're so smart, why don't you do it?"

"Fine." DeeDee jumped off the stool and stomped over to Kevin, who was on the counter by the stereo trying to figure out how to flip on the Go Away charm.

In case you forgot, the Go Away charm kept humans out of the store and out of harm's way between midnight and dawn. Only truly desperate people could get through. Unfortunately, the charm—like the gate—was broken. That became abundantly clear last night when a handful of random humans wandered in to buy taquitos and Red Bull in the wee hours. To say we were on edge while they shopped would be a gross understatement. Every time they moved, we jumped. We waited for them to pull a gun or rob us or worse, but they didn't. Nothing. Because they weren't desperate. They were just normal people who really wanted a late-night snack.

 Before the renovation, the Go Away charm was a simple on and off, like a light switch. It had apparently been upgraded, replaced with a high-tech console with a dozen knobs and lights, all color coded. Only problem: No one could find a user manual, so we weren't sure which color did what. And no one in their right mind would just go flipping switches around here.

"Okay. We're gonna try the red one first." Clearly, Kevin was not in his right mind. "Hold on to your butts."

"Why would you start with red? Are you nuts?" DeeDee protested, but Kevin must have hit the switch anyway.

The fluorescent fixtures flickered. A low hum rattled the shelves. Metal shades that looked like storm shutters slid down over the doors and windows.

Aaaaaaah! Now we're trapped inside here forever! WE'RE ALL GONNA DIE!

Or not. Suddenly, the shutters and red lights stopped, then changed course, sliding back up out of view. Kevin must have switched them off. "Where were those shutters last week? We coulda used 'em to keep your tragically hip boyfriend out of an octopus mouth."

"Will you lay off already? *Ex* boyfriend, and technically he was *never* my boyfriend. You know that," DeeDee said.

And my heart soared. Woot! Woot! Take that, Tristan! A curse on you and your stupid hip name! I took a celebratory sip of slushy. Blech. This flavor was gross, but I was committed. I wasn't sure angel eight ball would let me trade it for something better.

"Anyway, I'm pretty sure it's the green one," she said. "That's the one I flipped last night."

"Yeah. And how many jackasses wandered in here? Four! I had to hold my tiger stance for forty-five minutes while those jerks took their sweet time shopping. And for nothing! They weren't even desperate. My legs are still sore."

They argued for a good ten minutes about which button to try next. I stood by the beer cave door holding on white knuckled to my crappy bronze hammer, praying the next button they hit didn't suck me into an alternate dimension run by giant spiders. Don't laugh. That shit was totally possible.

I prepared, just in case. I examined the hammer, looking for an on button. It had to do more than hammer, right? But there was nothing on it. No magic buttons, no carving. Nothing. It was just a normal, albeit long and oddly sharp, hammer. Great. This would come in handy if I were attacked by a giant nail. Super lame.

Suddenly, the hammer shook right out of my hand. The head lit up ice blue. Great. I'd pissed off a hammer. Just my luck. It spun around so fast, I had to double dutch jump out of its way. I was half expecting it to rise up and clobber me for calling it lame. But the hammer slowly stopped spinning, and when it stopped, the claw pointed at the beer cave.

"Is the hammer spinning, Lloyd?" DeeDee's back was to me. Man. She had some serious spidey senses.

"Yes?"

"What color is it?"

Dude. How did she know it had a color? "Uh, blue?"

"Okay. Let me know if it turns red."

"What?" Red? This thing was color coded?

The hammer vibrated, then the beer cave door creaked open. A red thing—fat as a Coke can, but long—poked through the top edge of the door, then unrolled up the wall. Huh. It looked like a leaf on a fat red vine. There was an oval-shaped bump on the end that looked like a sock puppet. A second one slid out and snaked up the wall, leaves unfurling. Then another. And another one. It looked like a vine, climbing the drywall like hell's rose bush.

The door kicked open, and the rest of it slid out. Oh God. "Help! Help!"

My voice was barely a squeak. "Triffid! Triffid!"

That was no joke. I was pretty sure I was staring down a sentient plant. I mean, it looked like a plant. Ten feet tall, bright red, with dozens of stems shooting up around a central stalk. Every stem had a sock puppet knob on the end. The center stalk was thick, orange and had a gigantic red and green striped oval on top. It looked like a mutant watermelon had been stuck on there sideways.

Here's the rub. It looked like a plant, but it moved like an animal. It used white stubby roots to pull itself across the floor, out of the gate. The vine-like stems wiggled and snaked, and every single one of those sock puppets moved up and down like it was looking around.

I lunged for the hammer. Okay, yeah, I had to do a fat sloppy man roll that I sincerely hope was not caught on any sort of film, but I did manage to grab it. I spilled a bit of slushy, but held tight. What? Lloyd Wallace did not waste slushy. The end.

Hammer and slushy in hands, I steeled myself and faced the monster. I didn't need to read the employee manual to know the most important rule: Only creatures that can pass for human are allowed out. "Stop right there!"

The big oval melon in the center must have ears, because the big stalk twisted around and down, until the widest part was an inch from my face. The center split open, revealing shark-teeth rows of ivory spikes. Oh God. It was a mouth. A green leaf tongue that looked like a wide palm leaf rolled out over the spikes and licked me. Oh. Dear. Baby. Jesus. Help.

The sock puppets opened. Yep. They were mouths. Little versions of the big one, lined with rows of spiky teeth. They stuck their tongues out and shook, *chhh chhh chhh chhh chhh*, rattling at me like maracas.

Vines wrapped tight around my ankles, and the next thing I knew, I was upside down. The big melon mouth slid underneath me and opened wide. I dropped my slushy straight in. I had to. I needed both hands to grip my hammer and prepare to strike. Well, if strike meant stick the hammer in his spiky mouth like Luke Skywalker stuck the bone in the rancor's mouth in Return of the Jedi. Then, yes. I didn't have time to come up with a better plan. I didn't do my best thinking upside down.

"Stop." I squeaked. I'd like to say I was confident, that bravery percolated through me, fortified by the power of Jesus, but nope.

The big mouth ignored my command. He was too busy chewing my slushy cup. I could see it, crunching and splurping green goo all over the inside of his horrifying mouth. The plant shook with excitement. Yep. It was hungry. I was about to be lunch. Death by Venus flytrap—mantrap? —from hell. This is it, Lloyd. You're plant food. A midnight snack, a Lloyd Cheez-It in a bad T-shirt.

The mantrap opened wide, lifted me up over his mouth and shook me.

"Larry!" The big head turned toward DeeDee.

Save meeeeeeeee! Wait. Did she just call him Larry?

"Do you like that? I can get you another one. See?"

Uh, it didn't sound like she was rescuing me. It sounded like she was serving me for lunch. The big mouth turned and watched DeeDee walk to the slushy bar, grab a Colossal Super Slurp cup off the stack and hit the lever on the very last machine. An emerald green liquid with black specks in it blurped into the cup. Hey. That's the same flavor I just had.

The nozzle clogged before the cup was full, so DeeDee jammed a straw into the machine, trying to clear it. "The legs always clog up the nozzle."

"Did you say legs?"

"Of course," she said. "Spanish fly is made of beetles."

Vlurp. Yep. My stomach flipped upside down, which was right side up, because I was still upside down. Either way, bile tickled my tonsils. Bugs in my slushy. Was nothing sacred?

When the cup was full, she put at least a dozen straws in it and handed it to Larry. Okay, he didn't have hands, but two of the smaller stems wrapped around the cup and that did the job. Soon enough, each straw had a hell plant mouth around it, sucking hard and rattling with what appeared to be joy.

Crunk. Ow. The plant dropped me on my head, smack on the linoleum. Jerk! I gripped my hammer and prepared to fight. But DeeDee stepped between me and the monster shrub. Then she hugged its central stalk. Hugged it!

"Aw. I'm so glad you like it. It's formulated to make birthing season easier."

Birthing season? You heard that, right?

The hell bush squeezed DeeDee. Too tight. *Stand back, DeeDee! I'll save you!* I raised my hammer. But before I could move, DeeDee kissed the plant on the cheek next to his mean, teeth-lined mouth. All the stalks stopped chitting and wrapped around DeeDee.

Unhand her! Oh. Wait. They're hugging. And it looks consensual. My bad.

She went stem to stem kissing every little cheek next to every little spiky monstrous mouth. "Hey little Larry. You guys are growing up so fast!" She kissed the next one. And the next, calling each one of them Larry. Each Larry made a clicking noise and turned a brighter shade of red after she kissed it.

The big mouth said something to her. I think? It sounded like a bunch of clicks and snaps to me. "That's Lloyd. It's my fault. He's new. I lost track of time. I didn't tell him you were coming. He didn't mean to scare you," DeeDee said.

"Scare *him*? Seriously?"

"Larry didn't want to eat *you*, silly. He wanted your drink."

Huh. Maybe she was right. That plant emptied that slushy in under a minute. I was intimately familiar with the sound of scoop straws sucking and scraping at nothing on the bottom of a slushy cup. The red plant squeaked, presumably from happiness, then the beast pulled itself by its tiny nubby roots across the room to get a refill. DeeDee filled five or six more Colossal Super Slurp cups with bug juice and attached them like baby bottles to various mouths.

"What the fuck is going on?"

"That's Big Larry and all the little Larries. He reproduces with runners, like a spider plant, so all the babies are clones. Technically they're all Larry," she said. "He lives in the wetlands in circle three. He's an endangered species. We're part of a special breeding program. He's carnivorous. Pretty cool, right?"

Carnivorous? There were at least ten ways this could go sideways.

"He comes up when it's time for the babies to leave home. It's safer that way."

"Safer for who?"

"The babies need a carbon dioxide boost before they can split off on their own. Hell's atmosphere has too much sulfur. Years and years of climate alteration. Mining. Running all those furnaces. It's so sad." She sighed. "It's nice to do something good for the environment, to make a difference, isn't it? Look at all those Baby Larries. I've helped birth two generations of him. This batch will be my great grandplants. Aw. They grow up so fast."

Uh, I was looking at them, and it wasn't making me feel nearly as warm and fuzzy. Did the world really need more Larries? This shit could go full Resident Evil Plant 42 any second now. "How long is he staying?"

"It usually takes about a week. Sometimes two. Hmmm." She looked around. "I wonder where the construction crew put the pots? We need to cover his roots. He's probably been out of the ground too long already."

Apparently my job description included hell's gardener, because thirty minutes later, I had successfully transplanted Big Larry into a pot as big as a whiskey barrel. We sat him right next to the Spanish Fly slushy machine. The little Larries hugged me after I spread the last of the potting mix—the bag said "Cryptid's Choice: Honey Island Swamp Rougaroux Peat"—over his wiggling roots. Toes? Ugh, my brain. Whatever. They were short and white like plant stems, but they had joints and wiggled like toes. Yes. It was creepy.

DeeDee supervised, flipping through an old leather-bound book entitled *Dante's Guide to Flora of the Lower Circles*. "It says here we need to keep the soil moist at all times. No fertilizer. Larry will get all the nutrients he needs from slushies and rotten meat. We usually feed him fifty pounds of spoiled hamburger every day. Hopefully Chef's got some in back. Larry gets really testy when he's hungry. Isn't that right?"

DeeDee patted him on his biggest head. He leaned in like a house cat when she scratched him where his ears should be.

"Can you stop messing with your pet plant and help me figure out the stupid Go Away charm? It's after midnight and your pal there is pretty conspicuous." Kevin snipped.

"Geesh, Kevin. Relax. I'm coming." DeeDee huffed. "Here. Read this. Let me know if you have questions."

She handed me the book. It was open to a page with a red plant that looked just like Larry. A jumble of letters on the bottom said C2H5OH. See? This is why I don't read these books. What the hell did that mean?

On the opposite page was a drawing of a pretty green meadow, with tall waving grass with red flowers on each stem. Aw, how pretty! That's what I'm talking about. Why can't we have nice plants like this up here?

I looked closer. *Gulp. Scratch that.* Those weren't flowers. Each blade of grass had a mouth at the end, red and angry, open and lined with sharp pointy teeth. The title said "Hungry grass." *Nope.* I flipped the book shut. *Can't deal.* I picked up the watering can and started in on Larry's pot.

"Found it!" DeeDee announced. She stood behind the counter with her arms up triumphantly. "It wasn't on the console. Look. There's a separate button right here."

"What? Where?" Kevin asked.

"Next to the stereo. Under this." She held up an album with a fist and a rainbow on the cover. "Was 'Rainbow Rising' really worth putting innocent lives on the line?"

"You shut your dirty mouth. Of course it is. That's the greatest heavy metal album of all time. A few stray customers is a small price to pay for that bit of ear gold. You guys clearly don't appreciate me." Kevin crossed four of his arms. "I need a break. Hey, dumbass."

It took me a minute to figure out he was talking to me.

"The line's died down at Monster Burger. I'm heading over. Do you want me to pick you up a combo? My treat! I owe you one, remember?"

"But they're free tonight." FYI, Kevin never did Venmo me the seven bucks he owed me.

"Look. I told you I don't have pockets. How am I supposed to carry a credit card?" Kevin said. He'd zoned in on my brain. Again. "It's the thought that counts."

"If you hadn't noticed, Kevin is so cheap, free is his favorite four-letter word," DeeDee said.

"Oh, ha ha," Kevin snipped. "You know I'm saving up for my own place. You know how bad my roommates are!"

"Sure I'll take a combo." Why look a gift roach in the mouth? "But, how are you gonna carry it back?"

"I've got a portal between here and there," Kevin said.

"How long have you had that?" You mean all this time all I had to do to get a Monster Burger combo was reach through a hole?

Angel eight ball rolled out from behind Larry's pot. "We didn't tell you because you'd be as big as a house by now. No shortcuts for you, chubby."

I am so done with you. I smacked him away.

"Faust set it up years ago," Kevin said. "Sometimes, I go over there after they close and lick crumbs off the deep fryer. Makes me feel better."

"That's kinda gross," DeeDee said.

"You need to relax. I'm a roach, remember? So, that's two number one combos for the boys and a big fat nothing for Miss Eats Carrot Sticks and Judges the Rest of Us here. Hold the fort. I'll be right back."

He scuttled across the counter and stood by the cheap cigarette packs, staring at them, as if waiting for them to dance. Nothing happened. "Hmmm. What's taking so long? Why isn't it opening?"

He snapped his leg tips. Nothing happened. "God dog it! My portal's broken." He kicked the lighter display onto the floor in a fit of rage. "Wait til I get my hands on Steve! Well, kid. You're up. You're coming with me."

"Okay." Anything to get me out of hell's greenhouse.

"Uh, he's not going anywhere," DeeDee said.

"I'm not?"

"The gate has a routing error, and it's opening and closing randomly. Plus, Larry is pregnant," she said. "We all need to be here if things go south. I shouldn't even let you leave."

"How am I supposed to carry all that food back alone?" Kevin huffed. "How am I supposed to order? Earl can't hear me."

"That's why we have Chef. He can make you something."

"Chef's good, but there's no substitute for the deep fried fast food delight that is Monster Burger. Right, kid?"

They both looked at me. I agreed with Kevin. Plus, now that I knew Chef was dead, I didn't really want to put anything he touched in my mouth. But I didn't dare say that. DeeDee's dagger eyes had lasered in on me. I wasn't stupid. My lips were zipped.

"Way to grow a spine, kid." Kevin huffed. He jumped off the counter, tucked and rolled across the floor mat, then slid between the metal threshold and the rubber weather seal on the bottom of the front door. He flipped us off as he scuttled off across the parking lot toward the glowing yellow burger across the street.

CHAPTER 10

Fifteen minutes later, the store filled up with headless men. No joke. These guys had no necks and no heads. It's like the bit where those were supposed to be was flat and smooth. But oh, they had faces all right. On their chests, which I knew because I nearly fainted when the first headless guy rolled out of the beer cave and split open his shirt to ask for directions. His eyes were where his nipples should be and he had a mouth in place of his belly button. With lips and teeth. Surrounded by hair. Because it was still a belly. Nope. Can't unsee that.

Thankfully, DeeDee stepped in when it became clear I was unable to listen to or process anything the dudes were saying. Because I had so many questions about the mechanics of it all. Plus, when someone's eyes are on their chest, it's hard to know where to look. The whole "eyes up here" thing just didn't apply.

I did absorb enough to know they were on their way home from a convention and had been rerouted here accidentally, due to an internal portal error. A convention. Of headless dudes. It must have been quite an event. They all wore polyester suits with button-down shirts opened to their waists, and red fez hats strapped to where their actual heads should be. Every bit of their exposed skin was dotted with lipstick kiss marks.

"You have my sincerest apologies, gentlemen. The portal at the hotel was supposed to take you to Isle Brisone," DeeDee announced. "We're having a gate routing problem, but there's no indication that it's system wide, so please help yourselves to a snack, complimentary of course, then step back through the portal. It should take you home. Thank you!"

A handful of headless conventioneers hit the chip aisle, others surrounded DeeDee, peppering her with questions. I kept my head down. Because you cannot *not* stare at a guy whose eyes are where his nipples should be. You just can't, so in the interest of being polite, I kept busy with other tasks, like refilling all of Larry's Colossal Super Slurp cups and sweeping off the welcome mat.

I was sweeping by the front door when I noticed a white orb hovering a foot above the ground at the far end of the parking lot. Floating toward the store. Oh Jesus. What now? It'd already been a doozy of a night. "DeeDee," I whispered. "Something's coming."

She was too busy ushering headless conventioneers through the portal, one by one, like she was hell's gate agent.

"DeeDee!" I whisper screamed, desperate to get her attention.

She was by my side in a split second. "What is it? I'm kind of busy here."

I pointed at the orb, floating ever closer. She squinted out into the darkness. "Is that...?"

She pushed open the door and ran out into the lot.

Shit! Shit! Shit! She left me. She left me! With the headless dudes! Aaaaaaaah!

I turned around and saw one of them eating Twizzlers, sucking red licorice into where his belly button should be. It had teeth. Belly button mouth teeth. Nope. Didn't want to see that. I immediately wished I could take out my eyes and scrub them. But there was no time. Something was coming, and I needed a weapon.

I grabbed that wonky weird hammer and whirled back around, ready to face the horror creeping across the lot. DeeDee stepped in, her arms around a giant pile of Monster Burger carry out bags that had been bungeed together and strapped to a dirty pink roller blade. Kevin stood on top, chest puffed up and proud like a victorious general.

What the hell?

"Well, Kev. I'll give you credit for ingenuity," DeeDee said. "But where did you get the skate? It's filthy."

"Out of the dumpster," he said. "I had to get creative after you two jerks refused to help me. Hold up. What are these guys doing here? They're never supposed to leave Africa. Was it the damn gate? Give me the phone. I'm calling Steve again."

"No, you're not." DeeDee sighed. "It's taken care of. They're on their way home now."

"They better be," Kevin said. "Jesus. Look at them. Chewing with their damn bellies. Disgusting!"

The last of the headless conventioneers popped an Utz cheese ball into his belly button mouth, then shot Kevin two nipples worth of stink eye before he stepped into the gate.

"What are you looking at, freak?"

Well, that was rich coming from a talking roach.

"What did you say, kid?" Kevin glared at me.

"Uh, who is all that food for?" When in doubt, change the subject, right? Kevin had brought back one, two, three...fifteen combo meals.

"For me. Duh. They're free!"

"Are you saying they gave you fifteen meals for free?" DeeDee laid the bags by the register and wet-wiped dumpster roller blade goop off her arms. "Didn't they have a limit, like one per customer or something?"

"Maybe. I don't know. I filched them off the counter," Kevin said. "Earl was too busy cooking to notice, and his new coworkers? They had a ton of bags lined up, filling them like a factory assembly line. I grabbed a few off the end. They won't miss them. Besides, the new guys were too dead on their feet to stop me. Heh? Get it? Dead on their feet?"

We looked at Kevin. Kevin looked at us.

"Geesh. Tough crowd. Not even a chuckle? Really? They were zombies, stupids. All zombies! And here's the best part: Earl has no idea. I'd kill to see the look on his face when he figures out his coworkers are dead."

CHAPTER 11

The bad news? Monster Burger had a zombie crew. The good news? One of the fifteen combo meals Kevin pulled across the parking lot strapped to a greasy dumpster roller blade was actually for me. The rest were for him. Seriously. Fourteen combo meals. Just for Kevin. That had to be a hundred years' worth of food for a roach. Apparently, Kevin planned to enjoy the sweet sweet taste of Monster Burger in perpetuity. For free. He really was an epic cheapskate.

"You say that like it's a bad thing," Kevin said, zoned in on my brain. Again.

DeeDee went in back to stash Kevin's hoard in the employee lounge and to prep some rotten meat for Larry. Kevin unrolled two burger wrappers and spread out a burger and an order of fries on each. When I walked up to the counter, he bit open a ketchup packet. It squirted in two thin arcs up into the air. He then picked up a fry, drug it through the ketchup lagoon, opened his mouth and shoved the end of it, whole, into his mouth. He swallowed it all without chewing. Like an anaconda. Or a sword swallower.

Jesus. How did he do that? That fry was as long as he was! Blech. I couldn't watch. He ate like an absolute pig.

"You're no Hemsworth either, kid," Kevin said.

Shit. Zoned in again. I glanced at my paunch. Well, he wasn't wrong, and I was too hungry to care. Pure joy welled up inside of me. I never thought I'd get to eat Monster Burger ever again. I took a giant bite out of my burger, preparing for the endorphin flood of pure salty meat happiness to pulse through me.

Wait for it. Okay, any minute now. And nope.

Weird. Monster Burger usually gave me a fast food high. "Does this taste different to you?"

"Mmumm mummbup." Yes. He was talking with his mouth full. He swallowed, thumping his chest a couple of times so he didn't choke. "Different and better. See?"

He pointed to the empty carry out bag. "Monster Burger: The new healthy fast food treat you can *never* get enough of!"

Then it listed all the things that it didn't have in it. No sugar. No sodium? No wonder Kevin liked it. He hated salt.

Fuck me. Was nothing in this world sacred? The new owners had changed Monster Burger's recipes and were magically marketing it as health food. No wonder they were giving it away for free! If there was one pure truth in the universe, it was this: Healthy food was not nearly as delicious as junk food. Period. The second you tried to make junk food healthy was the second you made it taste like crap. Or cardboard. Or both. What was the point of french fries if they weren't covered in salt? I'll tell you: There was no point.

I marched to the grocery aisle, filched a can of Morton's off the shelf, then liberally applied it to my burger and fries. I mean, I turned that umbrella girl upside down. I offered some to Kevin, but he held one leg up to stop me. "Nope. I like my fries like I like my women. Naked."

Uh. Weren't all roaches technically naked, even the lady ones? Like, all the time? Now that you mention it, Kevin was naked, wasn't he?

"Duh," he said. "And you can stop lookin'. Pervert."

I kept shaking on the salt, but no matter how much I put on it, I couldn't get my burger to taste right. Maybe it was mental. I mean, Kevin did say they were assembled, in part, by zombies. No zombie could make a burger as well as Earl. Plus, the more I thought about it, the idea of a dead person making my food wasn't exactly appealing. I lifted the bun a few times just to make sure there wasn't a lost finger or ear in there. I mean, would zombies feel it if one fell off?

That's when Bob the Doughnut Guy stepped in through the front door, silver-streaked mullet in top form. He was clad in elbow-high pink rubber gloves, holding a fresh pink box of doughnuts. Or should I say nightmares? Dolly's doughnuts were bad news.

He stood still for a hot second, soaking in the music. "Hey is this Zebra? Man, I haven't heard these guys in ages," he said. "Most underrated album of 1983, that's for sure. Man. The eighties. Those were some good times, right brother?"

"You know it." Kevin nodded like strip-mall preacher.

Bob the Doughnut Guy hummed as he walked behind the counter to the doughnut case. "You wanna give me a hand, new kid?"

No, sir. I do not. But Kevin jerked his head toward him like I should follow. Resistance was futile, so my body moved on auto pilot. Autopilot of doom. I moved in next to Bob the Doughnut Guy, and my heart nearly kicked out of my rib cage as I watched him open his demon box of cursed fried deliciousness.

He lifted full doughnut trays out and stacked them in the brand new display case, which looked exactly like the old case. He filled it with tray after tray of the same cursed flavors. Devil's food with chocolate frosting. Glazed with pink frosting and sprinkles. Straight, unadorned glazed. I'd say plain, but come on. There was nothing plain about Dolly's.

Then came the last tray. It had two strange new doughnuts on it. Bob the Doughnut Guy pointed to them and leaned in close to me.

"Pssst. Looky here. Dolly's very own pumpkin spice fritter. First time we've ever made 'em. Totally new recipe." He whispered and looked around conspiratorially. "Kevin doesn't want them here, but someone ordered them for you. When Dolly says deliver a doughnut, I deliver a doughnut, so the doughnut stays. Got it?"

He pointed to the pumpkin spice fritter. There were two of them. The way Bob the Doughnut Guy talked about them, I expected them to look majestic, to glow gold like the holy grail. But no. They were brown bumpy blobs, like an apple fritter, only with some sort of orange icing on the top. The icing looked suspiciously like a slice of prepackaged American cheese that had been slapped, unmelted, on top. Honestly, they looked kind of gross. And this is coming from a guy who, two weeks ago, would have eaten any doughnut, any time.

"Before I forget. Special order." Bob the Doughnut Guy pulled out a box holding a single glazed with pink frosting and rainbow sprinkles. He handed it to me. "Oops. My bad. Two for Doc today."

His arm disappeared, elbow deep, into the Dolly's box again. He handed me a second small box containing the same kind of doughnut. "The natives must be restless over at the Pawn Shop, huh?"

He winked. Winked! Gulp. I'd seen what this doughnut could do. The real question was why on earth did Doc need two of them? Wait. No. Don't answer. Forget I asked.

"Your buddy's back." Kevin's face pressed against the window, watching the puffed-up guy in the tracksuit yank on the back door of the Dolly's truck like it was his job. "He really wants a doughnut."

"What? Not again!" Bob the Doughnut Guy stomped over to the door.

I was still hungry, so I followed him as far as my combo meal and took another bite of my burger, determined to give it one more chance. It didn't taste any better.

Before he ran outside to confront the puffed-up jogger, he turned back to me and said, "Let me know what y'all think of the buns. Dolly's is baking those for Monster Burger now."

Pfoooooot. Yep. I spit that burger straight out of my mouth. Zombie fry cooks. Buns forged in the devil's oven. And no salt? A man could only bear so much.

Kevin wasn't deterred. He ate his combo down to crumbs. "I swear it tastes better because it's free. Urrrrp."

Yep. He burped.

As we watched the pink Dolly's van peel out of the parking lot, addicted jogger running full speed behind it, a green light flashed above Kevin and a gigantic red hand with long black nails emerged. I froze with fear. I thought it was going to grab Kevin, but it reached right past him, aiming for my food.

"Aw, hell no!" Kevin bit down on the hand just as it descended on my fries. "Get a job, you no good freeloader."

Yep. That red monstrous hand belonged to Kevin's roommate. And from the size of that fist and the deep red of his skin, I could honestly say I prayed Kevin would never invite me over.

"Don't worry, kid," he said. "I won't."

The hand flinched and pulled back inside the portal, but relief was short lived. Another portal opened by the heat vent on the ceiling above us, and two red hands poked out and started rubbing together, warming themselves.

"See? This is why I'm saving up for my own place. I'm the only one with a job. The jerks can't afford to turn the heat on, so now I gotta put up with this shit. Freeloaders. All of them!" He screamed at the hands. "I can survive down to zero, you bastard. And I'll do it. I ain't paying the heating bill! Get a jooooooob!"

"How many roommates do you have?"

Kevin put a leg up. "Nope. Not talking about it. Puts me in a bad mood."

Wow. If this wasn't his "bad" mood, I'd hate to see what was.

The red hand fiddled with the lever, opening the vent wider. Hot wind gushed down on us.

"That's it. Stop messing with my stuff. Get outta here." Kevin scuttled up the wall, across the ceiling and jumped onto the hands. "Faust ain't paying to warm your dumb ass up. You got blankets, use 'em. Get a job if you want heat!"

A second later, three dirty pixies fell out of that same heat vent. They knocked Kevin off the giant red hands, and he went splat, belly up, legs kicking, in his ketchup lagoon. "You gotta be kidding me. Help me up, kid."

I threw him a french fry life preserver. He hopped up, drenched in ketchup, and immediately went into full Karate chop mode. But the pixies didn't want Kevin. They flew right for the doughnut case. They pressed their dirty naked little bodies against the Plexiglas and pounded and scratched their little fists, determined to get in.

"Holy shit!" Kevin screamed, unfurled his tiny wings, and bzzzzzz roach-flew across the counter. He immediately got into a fistfight with a pixie. "Get over here, kid! Keep 'em away from the devil's food, no matter what. If they're twenty foot tall, we're toast. You can kiss your fat ass good byyyyyyyyyye. Hi ya!"

Oh. I hadn't even thought of that. Nope. I definitely didn't want the pixies to eat the doughnuts, so I waved my arms, trying to swat them away. Of course, I hit nothing. Again. Those pixies were wily. I did get poked in the eye a couple times, though.

That's when DeeDee stepped through the stockroom door, Larry's rancid lunch in hand. "Kev. I caught your roommate turning up the thermostat. He set it to 130 degrees. Can you tell him to cut it out?" She stopped when she saw us swatting and flailing around the doughnut case. "Uh, what are you guys doing?"

"Pixies!" I squeaked. "Doughnuts! Help!"

That pretty much summed it up.

DeeDee sat a heaping tray of something wholly unappetizing next to Larry. Seriously. It was pink and dull brown and green all mixed together. Blech. She walked over and flipped a lever on the doughnut case. "There. Now they can't get in."

"What?"

"The case locks. I thought you knew."

Even Kevin looked surprised.

Then, DeeDee lifted one hand, watched the pixies hawklike for a minute or two, and slapped her fist down. By the time it hit the counter, she had grabbed all three pixies. They cursed and spat, and one bit her with its dirty yellow fangs. "Ouch." She shook them so hard they squeaked, growling, "I told you, you can't stay here. There's a cemetery on the other side of Monster Burger with plenty of nesting spots. Go live there."

She stomped right through the front door and dropped the pixies on the sidewalk. They fluttered up and around her and away as she yelled something at them and pointed at Monster Burger.

Another small green portal opened above the remains of my burger and fries. A red hand emerged, grabbed the corner of the burger wrapper, pulled in my combo, and disappeared.

"Are you kidding me? Get a job!" Kevin screeched, but it was too late. That red monster hand was long gone. "Know what? I'm done. Hold the fort. I'm gonna give that jerk a piece of my mind. I'll be right back."

Kevin somersaulted through the air and landed gracefully on the counter. He stood up, smoothed himself out, and crinked his neck back and forth like he was getting ready for a fight. He was in the zone. Until he glanced at the doughnut case. "Are you shittin' me?" He pressed his face against the Plexiglas "No good...recking freckin...God damn pumpkin spice! Hand me the tongs, kid."

I did.

"Unlock the case. I'm going in."

I did, and he did. With some sort of rage-fueled super-roach strength, he tonged those two pumpkins spice fritters out of the case. "Give me a hand with these, kid."

"I'm not touching those!"

"Fine." He stacked those fritters on top of each other and pushed them all the way to the end of the counter, through the cheap cigarette carousels, onto the floor.

They, and Kevin, landed by DeeDee's boot when she stepped back in. "Uh, do I want to know what you're doing?"

"Hold the door." As Kevin pushed those pumpkin spice fritters across the linoleum, I heard grunting. And lots of potty words, sprinkled in with some normal words, including, "No...gerd. Dang. Soccer mom. Pumpkin. Spice. Killing. Civilization. Marketing. Sheep. Basic. No!"

DeeDee and I watched Kevin push those pumpkin spice fritters outside onto the sidewalk. Then he jumped up and down on top of them, cursing Bob the Doughnut Guy's good name. When he had finished, he slipped through the doorjamb, put one leg up and looked away, signaling he never wanted to speak of it again.

Alrighty then. Nothing to see here.

"Okay. I'm going to feed Larry," DeeDee said. She tilted her head toward Kevin. "Good luck with that."

DeeDee did feed Larry. And the unholy stench of rancid meat he called dinner filled the store. Kevin was having none of it. "Hey, sweetheart! Can you feed that overgrown melon a little faster? I can smell that rotten garbage all the way over here. Geesh." He held his nose. "I'm sensitive, remember? Thanks to my delicate condition."

I looked at him. He looked at me. "Because I'm a roach. Duh."

Oh. Silly me.

"It takes as long as it takes, Kevin. You know that." DeeDee pulled on a pair of elbow length rubber gloves and started spoon feeding rotten meat to each of the baby Larries. "Hey. While the store's empty, can we talk? Something's bothering me."

"That time of the month?" Kevin said. "Heh heh."

My jaw dropped. Oh, man. Even I, who knew nothing about women, knew enough not to say *that.*

"Very funny." She didn't mean it. "Monster Burger has a zombie crew. Doesn't that seem odd? You have to be pretty high level to get a zombie permit. They don't hand those out to just anyone."

Kevin shrugged. "There's only one zombie plant in this region and Steve runs a tight ship. His shit's always in order. Well, except for mucking up my store. Other than that, he's always by the book, T's crossed 'n' shit."

"Yes. But who owns Monster Burger? Mr. Jimmy couldn't get zombies, and he tried for years."

Oh, snap. Mr. Jimmy *was* in on it.

Speaking of snap, Big Larry leaned over and crunched down on that rotten meat. He ate all of it right out of DeeDee's hands, tray and all. "Oof. Careful there, Larry. I asked Doc and Henrietta. They didn't buy it, and they don't know who did. If it were Faust, wouldn't he have told us? He's the shadow boss in this sector. He owns the only zombie permit."

"Look, Faust probably bought Monster Burger the second the ink dried on Mr. Jimmy's death certificate," Kevin said. "You need to unbunch your panties. Faust protects his interests and his gates. If he didn't buy it, he knows who did. It's all good. You'll see. Now, why don't you grab me one of my back-up combo meals? I'm still hungry."

CHAPTER 12

Two days off work. Thank God. I stepped in the front door and dropped my keys in the bowl. I sighed, relieved. Headless dudes? Hell plants? It had been a heck of a shift.

It was a little before seven in the morning, and the downstairs smelled like coffee. Mom stood in the kitchen in her fuzzy bathrobe with her back to me. "Morning, Mom."

"Uuuuuuuuuuuuuuuh." She didn't turn around. She just swayed back and forth, very slowly.

The hairs on the back of my neck stood up. "Mom?"

"Uuuuuuuh."

Weird. I know she heard me come in. My Mom had ears like a bat. Once, she pinpointed the exact moment Big Dan and I opened a bag of cheese puffs in the basement with a single crunch, mouth closed, even though she was in her bedroom on the second floor. (For the record I wasn't allowed to eat in the basement anymore, not since the ants/exterminator incident, but let's never speak of that ever again.)

I walked up behind her, slowly. She didn't notice. She was hunched so far over her forehead was nearly on top of the coffee machine. She moaned. "Uuuuuuuuuuuuh."

Something was wrong. Seriously wrong. What if—? Oh, God. She sounded just like the cleaning crew. The zombie cleaning crew. What if one got out? What if it got her? What if she'd turned? "Mom?"

My voice shook. I blinked back a tear and tapped her shoulder. Her head tilted back, oh so slowly, then she groaned and shuffled her slipper-clad feet around to face me. Her eyes were raccoon slits, puffy and red and streaked with the remains of poorly washed off mascara. Her skin was pale. "Uuuuh."

Nooooooo! They got my Mom! It's not fair. I did everything you asked, God! Why are you punishing me!

"Uuuuuuuuuuuuuuuoooooooohi honey," Mom said.

Phew. False alarm. Not a zombie. Just plain old Mom, comatose by the coffeepot, desperately waiting for it to finish brewing. Did I mention she wasn't a morning person?

She yawned and her breath smelled like a camel had taken a dump in her mouth. "Oof. Sorry, honey." She waved her hand in front of her face, in a vain attempt to waft the camel away. "Book club decided to meet at a wine bar last night. I'm never drinking on a week night ever again."

She yawned again. "Howa wah wooook?"

"Oh. It was fine." No one died, and the world didn't end. I count that as a win.

She managed to open her eyes partway, but only by raising her eyebrows up to her hairline. She saw me and seemed confused. "Uuuuuh...How did you get all this dirt on you?" She put a fingernail on my shirt and started scratching chunks of Larry's potting mix off my chest.

I shrugged and said, "I'm going to bed."

"Okay, honey. I put your mail and your clean laundry in your room."

"Thanks." I turned to go.

"Uuuuuh, while I'm thinking of it. Can you clean your closet? It sounds crazy, but I swear I heard something rooting around in the bottom. It sounded like grunting! Little Scooter next door lost his hamster. Maybe it's hiding at our house?"

I froze. Grunting? That was no hamster. I knew who—or rather what—that was.

The coffee maker *beep beep beeped.* "Oh, thank God!" Mom descended on the pot like a caffeine-seeking missile, so desperate and elated she no longer cared about the mystery creature in my closet.

Phew.

I tried to play it cool, but as soon as I rounded the stairs and Mom couldn't see me, I ran to my room, taking the stairs two by two. Sure enough, the second I stepped in I heard snorts that reminded me of the sound cartoon pigs make when they root around in muck.

"Appropriate, given the state of your closet." Angel eight ball lay in a short round basket of clean folded laundry. Well, it *was* clean. Gertrude was asleep in the middle, rolled up around angel eight ball, shedding, and snore-drooling all over my "D.A.R.E. To resist drugs. Those are mine." T-shirt.

Ahem. Yeah. I should probably get rid of that shirt, now that I think about it. It's not helping the Mom situation.

"Cleanliness is next to godliness," angel eight ball said. "You might want to get on that."

Groan. The nagging never stops, does it?

"I could nag you from now until the day you die. Literally. I have an eternity. Also literally. Now go see why your employee manual is making weird noises."

"Hell no. I'm not touching that demon book."

"You really don't want your Mom to find it first."

Shoot. He had me there. No. No, I did not. If paying my bills made her think I dealt drugs, that book would induce full on satanic panic. Nope. Nope. And more nope.

Gruuuubbble fffftt. Splurrrrrpppppp.

Jesus. What was it doing in there?

I grabbed an old carnival toy off my dresser, one of those foot-long sticks with a bendable white hand on the end, bent into a middle finger. Because I was that kid. Hey. I won it when I was eleven. Cut me some slack. I slunk to the closet, steeling my nerves.

Gruuuubbble fffftt. Splurrrrrpppppp.

Seriously. What kind of book grunted like an animal? The kind no reasonable person would read, I'll tell you that. I carefully slid the closet door open. Clothes were piled up inside. Mostly stuff that had fallen off the hangers that I'd never bothered to put back. Plus the stray socks I threw in every time Mom told me to clean my room. Come on. Don't act surprised. We all know a clear floor and a closed door = good enough to fool Mom.

My pile of dirty socks and clothes moved up and down and side to side. The snuffling came from underneath. I poked the wiggling pile with my middle finger—the toy one—and the wiggling lump moved to the right.

Ruuuurh?

I poked it again, and it wiggled to the left.

Roh ruuuurh?

Jesus. The damned thing sounded like Scooby Doo under there.

It stopped moving. I mustered the nerve to lift up a corner of the pile and look underneath. My employee manual was near the bottom, in a hobo cave it had made out of my old winter coat and some cardboard game boxes. It had the corner of a long-abandoned Candy Land board in its mouth. It had nearly chewed the Licorice Lagoon down to shreds. A stray beam of sunlight hit the book, and it froze, confused, like it suddenly realized the closet door was open. I swear it looked up at me. I mean, I'm guessing. Books don't technically have eyeballs, but it sure felt like it was looking at me.

Grrrrrrrrrrrrrrrrrrrrrrrrr.

Yep. It growled. "Uh, are you okay in there?"

Grrrrrrrr. The pages opened, and it bit the rubber hand off the end of my stick.

"Nope." I closed the door and walked away.

"Holy moly, it's gone feral," Angel eight ball said. "I have never seen a book do that before, and I've been around since day two. THE day two. Tell you what. I'll give you a pass on cleaning the closet if you put the laundry away before this three-legged disaster pees all over it."

Angel eight ball rolled out of the basket and plunked onto the floor.

"Fine." I shooed Gertrude out of the basket. It didn't go well. She got her leg stump stuck in the basket mesh and was so fat her back legs couldn't get enough leverage to push her rotund body up and out. After a few minutes, I mercy lifted her onto the floor, lest she pee all over everything from the strain. She really did have a weak bladder.

I plopped her on the floor, and she waddled away. Turns out she'd been sleeping on my mail, which was an oversized postcard from my community college that said, "When are you coming back? We miss you!" Mom had stuck a Post-it note to the front with a question mark on it. Ugh. Under that was a book with a full-on handwritten note taped to the cover. It said, "You can always talk to us. No matter what. Make good choices, honey. We love you very much. Mom."

What the...? I lifted the note. The book title was *It's Brave to Say No. Drug Use and You.*

"Called it," angel eight ball said. "She thinks you're doing drugs."

"Shut up!" I snipped. "She does not!"

But she totally did.

His triangle floated across the top edge of the plastic window, like he was rolling his eyes at me. "Silly me. You're right. I'm sure she buys that book for everyone."

CHAPTER 13

I'd like to tell you that my two days off were relaxing, rejuvenating even, but no.

Mom kept poking her head into my room to say hello and to see if I was "okay" or "needed anything," which I suspected were code words for "are you on drugs? Are you high right now? How did it come to this? Where did I go wrong? I'm a terrible mother! Hurp hurp ha hurp."

I mean, I'm guessing. But when you live with the same chick as long as I have, you pick up on a few things. Every time I went downstairs, I half expected to find a handful of loved ones sitting in a semicircle in the living room, flanking my sobbing mother, ready to stage an intervention. She'd been on me for two days like white on rice.

Speaking of rice, I was absolutely starving. Angel eight ball followed me around for two whole days lecturing me about diet and exercise. When the judgmental comments didn't alter my habits, he upped his game. He knocked a root beer out of my hand. He hopped out of the meatloaf dish and broke my plate when I went back for seconds. He slipped me a bowl of straight up plain lettuce, no dressing, by scooting it across the kitchen island when my Mom wasn't looking.

Seriously. Can't. Deal. I even caught him in the pantry hiding the Doritos behind the cat food bin. He said, "Eat carrots, fatty" before he rolled away.

My stomach rumbled. I was so hungry, I could eat my hand.

And don't get me started on my crazy-go-nuts employee manual. I caught it dragging the month-old remains of a half-eaten ham sandwich out from under my dresser in the middle of the night. I said don't judge. I told you I'm working on the cleanliness and godliness thing. He and Gertrude even got into it. I had to put her outside after she hissed and swatted at it.

Work wasn't shaping up to be any better. When I walked up to the front door of Demon Mart at ten on the dot, thanks to my "Wake up or God will smite you" alarm clock—which consisted of the entire house shaking, Gertrude nearly being struck by lightning, and Angel Eight-Ball falling directly onto my genitals from what felt like one hundred yards up —there were at least fifteen pixies gnawing on that discarded pumpkin spice fritter.

Dude.

They did not even care that it'd been lying outside on a dirty sidewalk for two days, visited by flies and stepped on by human shoes. (It had a boot print on it. I swear.) No sirree. They fought each other for crumbs, shoving dirty scraps into their mouths, grunting and groaning like it was delicious.

The sad part? I was so hungry, I wanted to shoo them away so I could eat it.

Bump. Ow. A guy walked right into me like I wasn't there. My shoulder snapped like a slingshot. "Hey. Watch it!"

"Uuuuuuuh?" He stopped walking. He had his back to me. He stood there for a minute, hunched over and swaying.

Well, that's odd. Maybe he tied one on a little too hard at the Temptations Tavern.

"You okay, buddy?"

His head turned, and he sniffed the air, up and around, his nose moving like a rabbit's. Uh oh. Maybe he's not drunk. Maybe he's the walking dead. Hard to tell. Could go either way.

"Are you okay?" I backed up slowly while I waited for his answer, putting one hand on the door. Because yes, I was totally gonna turn tail and run if this guy was a zombie.

He shuffled around to face me. Drool trickled from the corners of his mouth. He seemed to be looking past me, not at me. He lurched forward and said, "huuuuuuungreeeeeee."

Phew. Drunk it is! Because zombies can't talk, right? Right? (This is the part where I really need you to agree with me so I can feel better.)

He reached out to me and said, "buuuuuurger."

"Across the street, buddy." I pointed at Monster Burger.

His gaze followed my finger. Then he shuffled the rest of the way around, and off he went across the parking lot, drawn to the giant green Frankenstein like a moth to a flame.

Wow. Dude needed to cut back on the booze. I did feel a little bad for him, though. He really needed to eat down that buzz, but he was gonna be waiting a while. Monster Burger had quite a line. Around the block. Again.

I went inside. Kevin had one of his back up Monster Burger combos laid out on the counter, eighty percent eaten. And oh my God, I knew Monster Burger didn't taste as good as it used to, but the sight of it made my mouth water. "Guys." I held my stomach, hoping to curtail the rumble. "The pixies are back and they are all over those pumpkin spice doughnuts."

"Muhmmm vummmm mummmm." Kevin's cheeks were so stuffed full of food he couldn't close his mouth, but it was pretty clear it was not a proclamation of joy. His face flushed a shade darker. He shook his tiny roach fists. Then, he disappeared behind the counter and emerged with a fresh new draw-string garbage bag. He stomped to the edge of the counter, swallowed hard and said, "Kid. Call Henrietta and ask her why the Pixie Rid is taking so long. Tell her we need a whole case. Now watch and learn. Uncle Kev's about to take out the trash."

He said it like an action movie one liner. He jumped off the counter, tucked and rolled across the welcome mat, and slipped through the door crack. And got stuck. His back half wiggled. "Can you give me a hand, kid? Oof. The door must be crooked or something."

I opened the door for him and noticed that he was bigger around the middle than he used to be. He waddled outside, pulling the garbage bag behind him. A second later, he was kick-boxing pixies and pulling the remains of that pumpkin spice fritter into the trash bag.

"I really hope those are regular doughnuts. We sure don't need mutant pixies around here." DeeDee, clad in elbow-length rubber gloves, stood emptying a pink watering can over the Larries' pot.

Holy shit. Big Larry was Bigger Larry, so tall his giant melon head had to hunch to keep from bumping out the ceiling tiles. The baby Larries' sock puppet heads had doubled in size, and each was sucking on a Colossal Super Slurp cup filled with Spanish Fly. Not sucking, so much as rattling. The cups were empty.

"Can you give the boys a refill? I can't keep up. These babies are the hungriest we've ever had."

Sigh. I collected an armload of empty cups and shuffled to the slushy machine. Another day, another dollar, right?

I had just about filled the last cup when the front door chimed. I assumed it was Kevin, but the look on DeeDee's face said otherwise. She nearly dropped her jaw and her watering can. Even the Larries all froze in place, not so much as a leaf or root moving.

Great. There was a monster behind me, wasn't there? I turned around, slowly, and when I saw what was there, I wished I hadn't. I should've stayed home where it was safe. It was a monster all right. The worst kind.

Caroline Ford Vanderbilt stood in the doorway. Well, stood isn't quite the right word. She balanced on the sleekest, most advanced set of shiny black crutches I had ever seen. Of course. If designer crutches existed anywhere in the world, Caroline Ford Vanderbilt would own them.

An impossibly long man held the door open for her. He had to be nearly seven feet tall. He wore a black double breasted suit, a chauffeur's hat, and a frown. The brim of his hat cast his eyes into complete shadow. He stood silently by the door as Caroline Ford Vanderbilt click click clicked in on her top-dollar crutches.

Caroline Ford Vanderbilt. Ugh. Where do I even start?

She's the snooty socialite who's so upper crust she uses two full last names. Her family was a founding member of the Country Club, and she never let you forget it. She was head of the Charity Ladies' Auxiliary, not from any philanthropic urge, but because she enjoyed bossing people around. She also gave birth to my high school arch nemesis, snooty Yale law student and head cheerleader Madison Ford Vanderbilt. (Three last names. See what I mean?) Oh and did I mention Caroline Ford Vanderbilt was once possessed by a failed Internet cult leader in aisle five? Yeah. It didn't end well. That's why she needed those designer crutches. At one point, her foot was on backward.

Caroline wore a long fur coat—real fur—and stood up stick straight. She usually did. Better posture put her surgically perfected nose at a higher angle. Better for looking down it. At you. Although, she had a little medical assistance with her posture tonight. A fat black cast ran up one leg, from her toes all the way up her pencil skirt, and although I couldn't see it, I'm pretty sure it went up over her hips. I mean, that cult leader had busted her thigh into bits and worn it backward. You didn't get up and walk away from an injury like that.

"Is that you, Lloyd? Why, I didn't know you still worked here!" Caroline's voice was sweet and sticky as syrup, as she glanced around the store with a tight mouth, obviously disgusted. "It's so great you still have this little job. More businesses should employ those with special needs. It's such a noble cause."

Oh, did I forget to tell you? Caroline Ford Vanderbilt believed that I was in some way disabled. I didn't know why. Maybe in her world, that was the only conceivable reason a man my age would live at home and work in a convenience store.

"I see you have an aide now." She turned to DeeDee and grinned, baring perfectly white straight teeth, capped to disguise the shark teeth that lay underneath. "It takes a special person to do what you do. I couldn't do it, personally. The salary. My word! Peanuts! But I suppose this is more of a calling than a career. I'm Caroline Ford Vanderbilt, and you are?"

DeeDee said nothing. Caroline had met DeeDee before, but she wasn't high enough status to remember.

"Lloyd is a capable adult and can take care of himself," DeeDee said, ice cold.

"Oh, yes. Yes, you certainly are. Bless your heart." She leaned in and pinched my cheek. Her fingers clamped hard, like manicured vice grips. "There's nothing more heartwarming than people who overcome difficult circumstances."

My entire face burned. Dear Jesus, why? In front of DeeDee? I wished I could melt into the floor and disappear.

"What brings you in tonight?" DeeDee inserted herself between me and Caroline, like a human shield.

No, DeeDee, no! Stay out of the line of fire!

"I meant to stop by days ago, but I have been such a busy little bee. Cocktail hours, tee times. I'm president of the welcome committee at the Country Club, you know. It was a stretch, but I just had to pop by to meet my new neighbors."

Mic drop. What?

She opened her big brown Louis Vuitton bag and pulled out a stack of glossy business cards, which she handed to me. "These are for you. A token of goodwill. And yes, I have some for you as well, sir."

She held out more cards, but they weren't for me. I turned around. Doc, clad in a blue work jumpsuit and brandishing an oily wrench, had stepped out of the beer cave. He took one look at Caroline, said nothing and walked right back into the beer cave.

"Well, I never. Some cultures just do not value manners and civility. Now, where was I? Oh yes. As I always tell my friends, you must be kind to the locals when you're revitalizing a downtrodden area. The poor have endured so much already." Caroline shook her head and tried to look like she had empathy, which must be extra hard when your face is frozen by that much Botox. "You know, I really admire the poor. So thrifty. Pinching pennies. Minimum wage. Can you imagine? It's such a romantic, old-fashioned ideal."

While Caroline waxed philosophical, I glanced at the cards. They were coupons for free Monster Burger meals. There had to be forty of them here. Oh God. Did that mean? "Monster Burger?"

That was all that came out. Seriously. No wonder she thought I had problems.

"Why yes. You dear sweet boy. My business partner and I are reviving that sad old restaurant across the street. It was such a unique opportunity, we just couldn't pass it up. It's the first step in turning this neighborhood around. It's certainly overdue for reinvestment. We have a vision that will revitalize this corner and bring prosperity to all. After we sweep out the trash, of course."

It was subtle, but I could swear her eyes darted between me and DeeDee as she said it. Yep. We were the trash.

"Our commercial corridors reflect who we are as a community. They should meet the same rigorous standards we set for our residential neighborhoods, don't you think? The restaurant is just the start. You won't even recognize this neighborhood in a year!"

Jesus. She sounded like a real estate brochure.

Click. Click. Click. She clopped over to Big Larry, who hadn't moved a leaf or a root since Caroline walked in. "Goodness, what an *interesting* plant." Her nose squinched up like she'd smelled something bad, and to be fair, she probably did. Big Larry's diet didn't lend itself to floral notes. "Is it real? So exotic."

She rubbed one of his leaves like she was trying to figure out if he was alive or plastic. I knew that rub. My Mom did that at TJ Maxx. A lot. Like every single time, even though the plants there were always plastic.

That's when Kevin pushed open the front door, dragging the trash bag behind him. Except this time it had something in it, and that something was moving. Well, shit. He put the pixies in there, along with the doughnut, didn't he?

"Damn straight. Disgusting jerks." He jabbed a leg up at the chauffeur. "What's up with Lurch?"

I pointed at Caroline.

"Good luck with that." Kevin shook his head, then cracked open the stock room door and dragged that wiggling trash bag in back.

Caroline turned around and looked at DeeDee, head to toe, like she was seeing her for the first time. "My. That's a bold outfit. I just love how you don't care how you come across."

A dozen of Larry's arms—stems?—rose up behind Caroline, and the tiny mouths on the ends opened up, baring spiky yellow teeth. The Larries lunged at her like she was lunch. Easy mistake. They liked to eat rotten meat, and Caroline was rotten to her core.

"Bad Larry!" DeeDee swatted Larry's vines as they moved to grab Caroline. "Bad!"

"Anyhoo," Caroline cooed, unaware that she was almost lunch for Satan's ficus. "Please do come see us at the restaurant. Food is free for all the neighbors. Company policy! It's the least we can do." She closed her eyes, tilting her head like a statue of the Virgin Mary, as she attempted to look pious, as if free burgers would save the world. "Well, I really must be going. This area can become quite unseemly at night. Stay strong. We'll change that."

The looming silent chauffeur held open the front door, and Caroline

Ford Vanderbilt click click clicked right on out into the parking lot. We watched him insert Caroline into the backseat of a Hummer stretch limo.

"Let me see that," DeeDee snatched a coupon out of my hand and flipped it over and over. "There has to be a catch."

"What makes you think that?"

"The broken leg? The possession? She sued Faust and the store."

I shouldn't be surprised. Caroline liked to sue. She convinced the school board to fire my middle school gym teacher because a kid accidentally kicked a soccer ball into the side of her SUV while she was in the carpool line.

"She lost, even though she subpoenaed the security tapes."

Gulp. Cue Reddit thread with video proof of ghosts/monsters, starring me in three...two...one. "Oh, God."

"Don't worry. There are a zillion magic spells on this place. The lawyers and the judge saw Caroline deliberately squirting dish soap on the floor, falling, then paramedics taking her out. It looked like she did the slip and fall on purpose. Case dismissed. Frivolous lawsuit. Still, Faust paid all of her medical bills. I mean, he's not a monster. Well, he is, but you know what I mean."

"That still seems dishonest."

"Yeah. It is. And if it were anyone but Caroline, I'd feel bad," DeeDee said. "But this is the way it has to be. There can't be any evidence. We've got the answers to the mysteries of heaven and hell, life and death, what lies beyond. We can't let that out. It'd be a nightmare. If Jesus' face on a screen door can draw a crowd of a thousand people, can you imagine the mob of crazies that would descend on us?"

"Good point."

"Anyway, when her case was dismissed, Caroline lost it. I mean, she unraveled. Faust offered her a million-dollar settlement, but she refused to take it. She said it wasn't enough. She said she'd find a way to ruin him."

A million dollars? She must be nuts. That was a lot of Prada.

"She's up to something. She didn't buy the business right across the street from us for the good of the neighborhood. Hmmm. What's this?" DeeDee pointed at some impossibly tiny marks on the bottom of the coupon, so small they looked like scratches. She put the card nearly up to her nose. "HHNF, Inc. dba Monster Burger. Not responsible for any injury that may occur from use of this product. Interesting."

"What does that even mean?" Did you catch that? Reminds me of every online terms and conditions form I'd ever ignored before I clicked "agree."

"Well, dba means 'doing business as,' which means HHNF is some sort of parent company, which must be owned by Caroline and her mystery business partner." She slipped the coupon into her pocket. "This one's mine. For research. Because if Faust didn't buy Monster Burger, we really need to find out who did. Caroline is definitely in over her head if she's got a zombie permit."

"Are those coupons for free food?" Kevin had somehow managed to scuttle back to the counter. He was lying on his burger wrapper, surrounded by crumbs. His midsection was bulging and taught. He looked like he'd swallowed a tire, whole. Okay, a Barbie tire, but still.

Pffffffffffffffffffffrrrrppppptttt.

And...that was a roach fart.

"Oof. Excuse me. Something must a hit a bump on the way down, heh heh. Why don't you run across the street and get me a Number Three, kid? No onions. I'm starving."

"What are you talking about?" DeeDee asked. "You've got a dozen combos in the fridge."

"I *had* combos. I ate them all. Now I got none. Zero," Kevin said. "And I'm starving."

"Are you telling me you ate all fourteen combo meals already?"

"Sweetheart, I finished those off yesterday, and I'm too tired to keep walking all the way over there on these tiny legs to get more. I been there four times today already. A man's gotta eat."

We looked at Kevin in disbelief.

"What? They taste good, and I'm hella hungry. Maybe I'm hitting a growth spurt or something. Who knows? So come on, kid. Do me a solid. Walk one of those coupons across the street and bring me back a free meal. I'm a roach. It's not like I have a lot of sources of joy in my life."

CHAPTER 14

For the record, I did not get Kevin another combo meal. Even if I wanted to, DeeDee wouldn't have let me. She made Kevin go get it himself. Let's just say this turned his complaint dial up to eleven. Before he left, he did not let us forget the portal was broken, he had to walk, DeeDee had thrown the roller blade away, and Monster Burger had yet another line out the door.

He only dragged one bag back this time, and judging by the squinty side eye he gave us as he pulled it inside onto the welcome mat, so out of breath he was wheezing, he would not be doing either of us any favors anytime soon.

"Hey, dumbass. Give me a lift, will ya? I'm spent." He bent over and put four hands on two knees—four feet on two legs? Jesus, I'm confused—while he caught his breath.

I sat him and the bag by the register. When he had fully recovered, he scuttled over to the stereo, hit play, then scuttled right back across the counter straight into his Monster Burger bag. It ruffled as Kevin moved around inside. I could just make out yummy noises over the pounding of drums and the slide of an electric guitar.

"Mmmmm mmmmmm. Oh yeah. Delicious. Come to daddy. Mmmmm."

The voice of a man singing something about wizards and selling souls boomed through every speaker in the store.

"Is this Dio again?" It had to be. That dude loved to sing about wizards.

"You know it." Kevin poked his head out. "Stargazer. You're welcome."

He ducked back in. The bag rippled, and the edge of a burger inched out. "This one's for you, kid. I owe you one, remember?"

Aw. My heart softened a little toward Kevin. He was actually paying me back!

"Of course I am. I'm no deadbeat." He pushed a small baggie of fries out, too. "I pay my debts. I'm not a freeloader like my freakin' roommates."

It couldn't have come at a better time. I was so hungry, I didn't care that the recipe had changed. My stomach growled as I laid out the food and hit it with some salt. I was just about to take a bite when angel eight ball rolled right on out from behind the cheap cigarette racks and onto my french fries, window side up. "Drop the burger." The triangle turned. "I said I'd give you a free pass on Monster Burger for saving the world. ONE free pass, and I did. But you can't transform that sad dad bod into a physique worthy of a world-saving hero eating this crap."

"What? I didn't agree to that!" If God wanted me to get a hot bod, He was gonna be waiting a long time. I hadn't had a visible ab muscle since puberty.

"You *did* agree to that."

"No, I didn't!"

"Look. Deny it all you want, but you signed a blank check. You made vague, open-ended promises to God. You weren't specific, so your contract is wide open. Ergo, if He wants you to get fit, you get fit."

Nope. Screw you. I took a gigantic bite out of the burger and chewed, hard, making as many *mmmms* and *yums* and *it's so delicious* as possible, even though the new and improved Monster Burger wasn't really that good. It tasted like Caroline Ford Vanderbilt had infused every bite with bitterness and judgment.

"Blech. How can you eat that?" angel said.

I looked him right in the triangle and shoved a fistful of fries directly in my mouth. "It's delishush."

"Really? Is it delicious? You like the taste of maggots?"

"Wha?"

Angel eight ball's triangle flashed an arrow. Pointing down. At my food. Which was covered in maggots. Big ones. Undulating and blubbing around all over. Darting in and out of my bun. *Pffffffffft*. No, that wasn't a roach fart. That was me broadcast spitting a mouthful of chewed up potatoes all over the counter.

"What the hell?" Kevin took shelter under the edge of his takeout bag as the food bits fell. "You're cleaning that up."

"Aaaaaah!" Yes. I screamed, okay? Because I'd eaten maggots. I scraped my tongue with my hands, my napkin, anything to get the maggots out. I never should have eaten food made by zombies.

"Okay, well that was easier than I thought it would be," angel eight ball said. "Why don't you grab a salad out of the employee lounge. I saw one in the fridge when I was rolling through there. Oh, and Chef got loose. You might want to take care of that while you're back there."

I gathered up my food to throw it away. "Where did all the maggots go?" I looked up, down, all around. I had the creeped-out chills. Disgusting things. Where could they be hiding?

"Relax," angel eight ball said. "There aren't any maggots. I faked it. I stole that move from Lost Boys. Funny, right?"

"You what?" So. Mad. Right. Now.

"I thought it was funny," Kevin said.

"Thanks. Oh, wait." His triangle turned. "Outlook not so good."

"Whatevs," Kevin snipped. "We all know you're in there."

Apparently, that's when my maggot shock wore off, and it dawned on me that I didn't have to put up with this. I picked angel eight ball up and threw him across the store. He hit the glass door of the reach-in cooler then thunked to the floor. He lolled around on the linoleum for a minute, then stopped, stone still.

I marched straight to the candy aisle. I was gonna eat a whole pack of something. Take that, angel. Just try to stop me. I found a big bag of Raisinets and ripped it open right there. I shoved a fistful into my mouth. "Take tha, azzhull."

Man. I really had to work on smack talking with my mouth full. Mmm. Totes worth it, though. Raisinets were like fireworks of fruity chocolate awesomeness in my mouth.

DeeDee poked her head into the aisle. "Hey. I'm going in back. I think I hear Chef rattling around. Do you need anything? Wait. What are you doing?"

"Nuffing." I turned and fled, cheeks flushing hot. Great. Nothing said, "I'm the man of your dreams" like a fat dude's cheeks stuffed with candy.

"Smooth. Real smooth," Kevin shook his head when I walked back up to the counter. "We're gonna have to work on your moves."

Yeah. I know. "Want waaan?"

I plopped the bag on the counter and it split, sending assorted bits of chocolate-dipped raisin heaven rolling all over. Man. I couldn't catch a break. I popped one in my mouth and bent over to pick up a couple that landed on the floor. Blech. This one must have gone bad. It tastes like dirt.

Angel eight ball hit my foot. "That's not a Raisinet. That's pixie poop."

"Yeah right."

"No. That's pixie poop. For real."

Pffoooot. I spit it out.

"Don't just stand there, kid. Help me!" Kevin yelled.

"What?" I stood up and my nose landed in pixie butt crack.

Seriously. My nose slid right in between a pair of cheeks like it was a bookmark.

I swatted that pixie away at the same time it dug its feet into my cheeks to push off. She twisted her ginger head around and looked at me like I was some kind of super pervert. Dude! Neither one of us was happy about this! The pixie flew off just as Kevin roundhouse kicked the old grandpa pixie with the giant mole right in the groin.

Aw, man. That had to hurt.

"Uh, Kevin." Pixies, too many to count, hovered in the air. They had us surrounded. He hadn't noticed. "Maybe you should dial it down?"

That would be a no. He waved a french fry back and forth like it was a light saber as he stomped and yelled, "How did you pricks get out of the dumpster? I closed the lid and sealed the bag!"

In response, a couple of pixies fluttered up off the floor, holding the shredded remains of Kevin's draw string trash bag. It just made him more angry. "How did you get back inside?"

Grandpa pixie pointed to the heat vent in the ceiling. Of course, his other hand cupped his aching balls. A pair of red hands poked out of a portal above us. Kevin's red-armed demon roommate warmed himself while adjusting the heating vent.

"Deadbeat!" Kevin shook his head. "You! Pixies! I told you once, and I'll say it again. You can't stay here. You go outside, we won't bug you. You come inside my store? It's war."

They chitted to each other like they were considering it. For a minute, it looked like we might have a truce. Grandpa directed the younger ones around. They dipped down and grabbed the corner of Kevin's Monster Burger sack and started to fly off toward the door.

"Oh, hell no! That was not part of the deal. That's mine." Kevin jumped up, trying to grab the corner as they flew up and away.

"Dude. Just let them have the burger!"

"No way, kid. MINE!" He screamed at the pixies, "Deal's off. Drop the burger and get outta here! Go on. Git."

The fat white-haired grandpa pixie—oh my God, I seriously could not stop staring at his hairy mole—raised two middle fingers and spat words at us. Fighting words. He had no intention of gitting anywhere, anytime soon, and no intention of leaving without Kevin's burger.

"So that's how it's gonna be, huh?" Kevin sighed heavily and shook his head. Then he slowly moved his legs in circles and breathed deep. It looked like some sort of roach Tai Chi. He whispered, "I want you to be nice until it's time to not be nice."

He said it over and over again.

"Are you talking to me? Do you want me to be nice, or do you want me to fight?"

The pixies buzzed around us, chittering to each other, equally confused.

"Shut up, kid. I'm Roadhousing. I gotta get in the zone."

"You're what?"

"Roadhousing. You know. Channeling the power of the Swayze."

I blank stared at him.

"Kids these days. You know nothing about the classics. Never mind. Moment's gone. You ruined it."

When I looked up, there were more pixies. Oh, so many pixies. Clean ones. Dirty ones. The naked old one. And every single one of them looked pissed. Naked and pissed. They'd started ripping stuff up and throwing it at us. Lottery tickets. Cheap cigarettes. A few of them grabbed key chain laser pointers off the display rack and zinged me in the eyes.

Kevin stretched his legs, then declared, "Bring it!"

He flew through the air, legs out, ready to karate chop right through a cluster of pixies, screaming like a tiny brown Jackie Chan.

"What are you doing?" Had he lost his mind? We were outnumbered. By a lot. Like, a lot a lot.   Kevin kicked a pixie right in the face, and the swarm descended on us.

A dirty pixie jumped onto my shirt. I screamed and batted him off. He thunked to the floor, but that didn't stop him. He rolled over, crawled right up my leg, and proceeded to pull leg hair out by the fistful while sinking his fangs into my shin bone.

"Aaaaaaaaaaaaaah!" Yep. I screamed. And flapped my arms and shook my leg. Because I was a totes cool cucumber ready for any crisis. Ahem.

Kevin had a pixie pinned on the counter and punched him repeatedly in the face. Then he scuttled up onto the intercom. He hit the button, and his voice boomed across the speakers. "Drop the bag, scumballs!"

The pixies flying off with Kevin's burger were nearly to the door. He was so fixated on dinner that he didn't see the phalanx of pixies that swooped in and grabbed him from behind. They each grabbed hold of one leg and pulled him up off the intercom and into the air.

I tried to swat them away and save Kevin, but they flew out of reach. The rest of them descended on me. Sadly, coming to Kevin's aid had landed me the new top spot on the pixies' shit list. There were so many on my face I couldn't breathe. They started to suck up into my nostrils every time I took a breath. I tried to scream for help, and they stuck their dirty little legs in my mouth, choking me. I could feel the weight of them all over my head, pulling my hair, and scratching my ears. This was not going well. We were totally losing.

"Oh, dear," I heard a tiny sweet voice. Then kissy noises that sounded like someone trying to con a cat into coming closer. "Looky what I've got. Here, boys. Here you go, fellas. Oh yes. Good stuff. Yummy, isn't it?"

One by one, the pixies lifted their fangs out of my face, let go of the hair they were pulling out of my scalp, and dislodged themselves from my nostrils.

When I opened my eyes, a small grandma stood on the other side of the counter, staring into her huge floral-print quilted handbag. It took me a minute to recognize her. It was Henrietta, the owner of the Jesus Saves Discount Religious Supply store. She quickly pulled the zipper shut on her bag and looked up at me sweetly.

"Good evening, dear," she said. "Pest problems?"

Her bag wiggled and writhed. Huh. Were the pixies in there? No. That's crazy. I looked all around, but didn't see them.

"Is your manager here, young man?"

I noticed she was disheveled. Her white orthotic tennis shoes were coated with black muck, like she'd been standing in a horse stall. She had a broken stick stuck in her white cotton ball hair, and the embroidered pumpkins on her sweater were streaked with mud.

"Jesus Christ." Kevin crawled onto the counter and brushed himself off. He turned to Henrietta and said, "Where's that case of Pixie Rid I ordered? If you hadn't noticed, the place is infested!"

"That's why I'm here, dear. It's out of stock. The supplier said someone bought up every single can in North America. One big bulk order, nearly two weeks ago."

"Then import it from somewhere else!" Kevin snipped. "This is an emergency. They almost quartered me!"

"I can't, dear. The factories can only make so much. It's barrel aged. What they have on hand isn't ready yet. It's not potent unless it ferments. I ordered an alternative for you. It hasn't arrived?"

"No it didn't arrive. Look around! We've been up to our eyeballs in pixies for a week now!"

Kevin ranted, and she shook her head, declaring "oh my" and "oh dear" as he spun his tale of pixie woe.

"It seems like everyone in the neighborhood has a pixie problem. At first, I said to myself 'Henrietta, it's just a bad season,' but when I went to the cemetery to put out a feeder for them, all of their burrows had been dug up. That's why they're nesting in the shops."

"Yeah, so? It coulda been a skunk or a raccoon or something. They dig 'em up all the time," Kevin said. "They can rebuild."

"I don't think so, dear. They can't rebuild. The soil has been completely removed, scraped away. Like someone took a bulldozer to it. An animal couldn't do that. I'm afraid someone sabotaged the burrows."

"What? Who would be dumb enough to do that? Shit. No dirt? Really? They'll never leave." Kevin held his head like it hurt.

"There there, dear. But please be kind to them while we sort it out. Pixies do tend to hold a grudge," she said.

Did she say grudge? Uh oh.

"I have a bad feeling. I sense a darkness over the neighborhood." Henrietta shivered, then sunk one wrinkled hand into her pocket and produced a glass bottle. She slipped it to me—Kevin was too busy stomping and spouting pixie-related expletives—and said, "Just in case, dear."

The bottle was filled with what looked like lime green milk. The label said "Quita Maldicion Curse Breaker Floor Wash."

Doc stepped out of the beer cave. "Is the mean woman gone?"

"Yeah. It's safe," I said.

Famous last words.

"Hey. Loverboy. You're taking your sweet old time back there," Kevin snipped. "You fix my gate yet?"

"Bug man, I have examined the components. There is no error. The gate is functioning properly."

"What? Properly my butt!"

The last word wasn't even out of Kevin's mouth when a wave of thick white puffy ooze blubbed up and out of the beer cave door. And it kept coming. It didn't stop until we were all knee deep in hell's marshmallow fluff.

CHAPTER 15

If you're waiting for me to tell you Henrietta snapped into psychic mode and gave me a magic poem containing the clues we needed to solve all of our problems, you can keep waiting. I sure did. With pen and paper, so I could take notes. But she didn't go into a trance. She didn't tell me Dwayne Johnson and Ronnie James Dio would save the world. Nope. Not this time.

She bought a tube of Rolaids, Doc pulled her free of the mysterious marshmallow muck, then she carried her giant quilted bag full of pixies across the street, back to the Jesus Saves Discount Religious Supply store like it was no big thing. We haven't seen her since. It's been seven days.

Dude. You don't just slip someone a bottle of curse breaker if everything is hunky dory, then go about your daily life like nothing's up.

Because something was definitely up. There was that weird white fluff, which was harmless but messy, and the result of yet another gate routing error. Then we had a hard time getting the zombies back in the cooler after they ate it all up. Those collars? Apparently, they were remote controlled. But no one could find the remote. It had gone missing.

Last night, a portal opened by the boner pill display and some giant shrimp looking thing popped out and ate half the rack, pills included. His legs and antennae got so hard, we had to wait until they got soft again to poke him back through the portal. With broomsticks, because come on. No one in their right mind would use bare hands to touch a giant hell shrimp with a full body boner.

Even without all that, the store's rhythm was completely off. Customers used to wander in to load up on beer and chips like this was any normal corner store. At least until midnight, when the Go Away charm flipped on. But now? We didn't have any customers to shoo away. None at all. Even Junebug, fresh off the day shift, said as much. Dead as a doornail. All day.

No one had customers, not even Sinbad's. I'd been pulling demon strippers out of the beer cave every night. Butts and legs, and other random lady bits getting stuck in the wall was a regular thing now, because the wonky gate kept closing on them. All that trouble so they could go to work at an empty club.

The only business that was hopping on this block was Monster Burger. A line of people three wide spilled out the front door and looped halfway around the block. You couldn't even see the patch of grass where poor Mr. Jimmy had died for all the people standing on it. Poor guy. Monster Burger never had a crowd like this when he was alive. And now Caroline Ford Vanderbilt was making all the money. Remind me again how life is fair?

Geesh. Shows you how gourmet I was. I thought the new recipes tasted like crap.

"What are you talking about? It's better than ever. Speaking of, I hope that line moves fast. I'm starving." Kevin paced back and forth across the window ledge, staring at Monster Burger. Although, maybe pacing wasn't the right word. More like slugging. He wasn't as sleek and fast as he used to be. I had watched him eat at least two Monster Burger combos per shift this week, and I had a feeling he ate even more off hours. The calories were starting to show. Kevin had become a wide load, if you get my drift. He was as big around as he was long, and thicker. Much, much thicker, with full blown muffin tops rolling over each of his body segments. The poor guy was one french fry away from his own show on TLC.

"You're no slim pickings yourself." He glared at me. "Make yourself useful and finish stocking the frozen dinners."

Sigh. Fine. I shuffled off to the very end of the cooler, where we housed our selection of premade plastic wrapped sandwiches and single serve frozen dinners.

When I rounded the end cap, I jumped. Oh shit! We had a customer! I didn't know how this guy managed to sneak past us. A dude, big and juicy at six feet four and four hundred pounds, leaned against an open cooler door, staring at the six packs like they were the most fascinating thing on the planet.

I looked at DeeDee. DeeDee looked at me. I pointed at the customer, all "WTF?"

She shrugged and pointed at the clock, indicating that it was not yet midnight ergo this was weird but probably fine, then stuck her nose right back into *Dante's Guide to Flora of the Lower Circles*. Did I mention Larry wasn't looking so hot? He'd turned a bit brown and had started to wilt.

That's when I spotted two naked pixies fluttering down the candy aisle, making out, looking for a safe place to bang. Ugh. I didn't know which was worse. Knowing the pixies were back or knowing the little jerks were having way more sex than I ever would.

Look. I would like to say that I did the right thing here. That I grabbed a net and went after the pixies. I'd like to say I did a flip in the air and had them in that net in one swoop like DeeDee, but come on. Let's be honest. I could jump and grunt and wave a net around all night, and I'd never catch a pixie. They'd just flutter a little higher. So I turned back around and stacked those cardboard trays of frozen macaroni and cheese into the slot like the pixies weren't even there.

That's when Morty stepped out of the beer cave buck naked, and I mean full-on birthday suit, junk hanging out for all to see. Nekkid naked.

"Morty!" DeeDee snapped. "Where are your clothes? We have a customer. Cover up!"

"Sure thing, sweet tits, but first, do you like what you see?" His eyebrows wiggled as he pointed both index fingers straight at his...ahem. When it became clear that DeeDee had not changed her mind upon seeing the goods, he huffed and grabbed a bag of tortilla chips off an end cap and held it over his junk.

"Why are you naked?" DeeDee whispered.

"I can't decide what to wear, and I have to nail it tonight. Literally nail it. Somebody. Anybody. I'm starving. I haven't had sex in a week! The bar's been empty. I really gotta wow the ladies. I need a sure thing. I gotta get a read on the crowd. Just gimme a minute to check it out."

He moseyed—bare naked, apart from a bag of chips, right on past Big Juicy to the far wall adjoining the Temptations Tavern. He bent over, stuck his nose to the drywall, and drew in a long sniff. Full moon on display. Big Juicy, our lone customer, didn't notice. Lucky him.

"Hmm. A book club. Okay. I think I got it," Morty declared. He waltzed, buck naked, past our oblivious human customer, right back into the beer cave.

Boy. Those craft brews must be fascinating because Big Juicy didn't give Morty a second look.

Morty returned a minute later. In clothes. "What do ya think? Panty dropper?"

My jaw dropped. Did that count?

Morty looked like he'd just stepped off the cover of a romance novel. And not like a firefighter or cop. More like a pirate. His hair was flowy and blond. Don't ask me how he did that trick. He wore leather pants with a big belt buckle and a white shirt with no collar and a ruffled lapel. I'm pretty sure the last guy who pulled off that look was Prince.

DeeDee shook her head. "Try again."

"You're kidding. Horny book club housewives love bad boys!"

"Yeah. But it's not 1750. Try something a little more current."

"Women. You all are impossible to please." Morty huffed, turned on his heel, and stepped right back into the beer cave.

That's when I caught site of the pixie dude poking his head out from behind a bag of Bugles. He looked right at me and knocked all the bags off the little metal hanger. Like he wanted to remind me that he'd already defeated me in battle with that pointy, spicy snack. Bugles binked and bopped all over the floor. The pixie flew up and away.

Dammit. I followed him, trying to grab him. He locked eyes with me and knocked the trail mix and Combos bags off their hangers one at a time, leaving a trail of broken bits in his wake. Henrietta was right. These jerks held a grudge. He hovered in the air right behind Big Juicy, who still couldn't decide which beer he wanted.

I moved in on the pixie. He shouted at me in his teeny voice. Morty stepped out of the beer cave. The pixie looked at him, and my hand snapped out to snatch him. *Ha! I got you!*

Or not. The ginger pixie zipped up and away. All I'd managed to do was hit Big Juicy smack between the shoulder blades. Oh shit. He was gonna squash me like a grape.

"I'm so sorry, sir." My voice shook, prepping to sweet talk my way out of an ass kicking. But he still didn't move. He didn't even flinch. He just stood there, head in the cooler, staring down the beer.

"Whatda ya think?" Morty wore a very expensive looking suit, tailored tight, and a tie.

"Much better," DeeDee said. "Very fifty shades of Morty. Go get 'em stud."

"You know it." Morty said.

DeeDee straightened Morty's tie.

Big Juicy moaned. "Muuuuuuuuuuuuuuuuuunnnnnnnn. Buuuuuuuuuuuuuuuu."

We all turned to look.

"Is he okay?" DeeDee asked.

"Buuuuuuuuuuuuuuug."

Did he just say bug? I looked around. I didn't see Kevin.

"Buuuuuuuuuuuuuuuurrrrg."

Burger? There was a Monster Burger bag on the floor by his tan work boot. It looked like he'd dropped it there. It was rustling. *Shit. Demons.* No, wait. Kevin stepped out, pulling the jagged remains of a crooked, burned french fry behind him.

"Man. The fat bastard ate every last crumb. This is all that's left!" He shook his head, then opened his mouth and shoved that fry right in. He swallowed it whole, looked at Big Juicy and said, "God doggit. Is this guy possessed?"

"What?" If a human could be both on fire and freezing cold from terror, body dripping with sweat and mouth bone dry all at the same time, well, that was me right now. Possessed? *Dear Baby Jesus, why are you doing this to me?*

Angel eight ball rolled out of aisle five and looked right at me. "Leave Baby Jesus out of this." Then he rolled away.

"Woo boy. He's a big un, ain't he?" Morty sized up Big Juicy as he straightened his cuff links. "I'd help out but I gotta get the ladies while the wine is flowing. Good luck."

"Muuuuuuuuuuuuuuuuuunnnnnnnn. Buuuuuuuuuuuuuuu." Big juicy groaned, eyes still on the beer.

DeeDee whispered, "I'll grab the taser, you double check."

"Double what?"

"His eyes! Remember Caroline? Weird eyes, weird drool equals possessed. Now go."

She tucked and rolled toward the safe, silent as a ninja. I stared at Big Juicy's back. Gulp. The man was gigantic. A burly hulk of a man. He looked like he could pull an eighteen wheeler out of a ditch all by himself. There really needed to be a height and weight limit on demonic possessions.

I slid to the right, far enough to get a side view of Big Juicy's face.

"Buuuuuuuuuuuuuuu." He moaned.

Huh. He was drooling, but it was normal clear drool, but a lot of it. Enough to get his chin wet. His eyes looked normal, too. They weren't all white, all black, red, glowing or glazed over. They were normal eyes, just open really wide and staring at a microbrew six pack. Well, not at it, more like through it. Huh. He didn't seem possessed. "Sir? Can I help you with the beer?"

"Buuuuuuuuuuuuuuu."

"Sir? Are you all right?"

"Buuuuuuuuuuuuuuu."

I touched his massive meaty shoulder, and he slowly turned toward me. We locked eyes. His were still blank, like he only half understood that someone stood in front of him.

"Do you need help?" That was as specific as I could get, really. Seriously. I was trying to keep this cazh and normal. I couldn't just flat out ask, "Sir, are you possessed by a demon and do you need my unholy assistance?"

His wide, blank eyes looked right at me and said, "Muuuuuuuuuuunnnnnnnnsssstrrrrrrrr. Buuuuuuuuuuuurrrrrrrr."

"Oh, my God. He's so drunk!" Kevin stood next to Big Juicy's takeout bag with his legs on his hips. He called to DeeDee, who was slinking back up the row with a bottle of holy water in one hand and a taser in the other. "False alarm. The guy's not possessed. He's totally shit faced. Sorry, pal. This Bud's not for you. Kid, don't sell him any beer, okay? I ain't paying a fine."

"Muuuuuuuuuuuunnnnnnnnsssstrrrrrrrr. Buuuuuuuuuuuuuuuurrrrrrr?" Big Juicy's eyebrows wrinkled. He looked like a sad, desperate puppy.

"Huh. I don't think he wants beer. I think he wants Monster Burger? Here." I leaned down and grabbed his takeout bag off the floor. Oof. Kevin was right. Totally empty. Nothing but wrappers and memories in there.

I handed it to him. Big Juicy looked at it for a moment, then slowly opened the bag. Dude. He was drunk. He swayed and moved so so so slowly. When he saw the bag was empty, his eyebrows squinched together and his eyes went even bigger, like he couldn't believe what he was seeing. "Buuuuuuuuuuuuuuuurrrrrrr?"

"Sorry, man. It's all gone."

He stomped a boot. "Muuuuuuuuuuuunnnnnnnnsssstrrrrrrrr. Buuuuuuuuuuuurrrrrrr."

Okay, then. I gently turned him around and shuffled him to the front door. "Monster Burger is still open. You can go get another burger. See?"

I pointed at the neon Frankenstein. His eyes went wide when he saw the glow of that yellow burger bun.

"Muuuuuuuuuuuunnnnnsssstrrrrrrrr? Buuuuuuuuuuurrrrrrr?" He sounded hopeful.

"Yep. That's right. Monster Burger. Right over there."

I held the door open for him. He shuffled out, making his way slowly but steadily across the lot, his wide eyes fixed on that neon sign. He shuffled straight to the end of the line, which hadn't gotten any shorter. He stood at the back, staring up at that neon yellow burger in the sky. They all did. No one in line talked. No one looked at their phone. They all just stood there waiting patiently, silently, staring up at the sign.

Kevin leaned against the door frame, rubbing his portly carapace. "Kid, I better run across the street and nab me a burger before Big Juicy eats them all. I'm starving."

CHAPTER 16

After Big Juicy and Morty left the store, we turned our attention to the Larries. Something was seriously wrong. Their leaves had curled up, and all the stalks drooped. We tried to feed the babies Spanish fly, but they just turned up their noses. Well, they didn't have noses, but you get the idea.

I spritzed the little Larries with a plant mister while DeeDee combed through the book.

"I don't know what's wrong. It says he might need an occasional supplement during a high-stress pregnancy, but what kind of supplement? It doesn't say!" DeeDee snapped the book shut. "Dammit. These stupid books are so confusing. The instructions are never straightforward."

She handed me the book and grabbed Larry's tray of rotten ground beef off the hot foods island. And I mean rotten. Dude. It had a green film forming on it and smelled like boiled garbage. She tried to feed it to them, but the Larries turned away.

DeeDee stared at the tray. "He used to like it this way. I'm worried. He's never wilted or gotten this big so quickly. We can't screw this up. He has to survive birthing season. There aren't many Larries left in the wild."

Suddenly, as if to punctuate our failure, Larry's big head flopped over and crashed against the floor. His mouth opened, his tongue shot out, and his stalk convulsed. *Heeeeeerrrffff Heeeeerrrffff.*

Uh oh. He was making the same sound Gertrude made when she was about to hack up a hairball.

Heeeeeerrrffff heeeeerrrffff.

Dear lord, please don't be a hairball. Gertrude's were too disgusting for words, and she was a teeny little thing. Who knew what horror Larry would hack up.

Heeeeeerrrffff heeeeerrrffff.

I braced for it, but Larry went completely stiff and stone still.

Oh God. He's dead. We killed him. He's going extinct. It's our fault!

"Larry. No!" DeeDee gasped. Then I swear he looked right at her and moved. It was so subtle it was easy to miss, but he clicked his head toward the door two times.

A sweet voice came from behind us.

"Oh goodness, honey. Is that a Halloween decoration? Do you need help putting it away?"

Gulp. I knew that voice. I spun around. My Mom, Jennifer Lamb Wallace, stood on the welcome mat, looking at Larry.

This can't be happening.

I checked the clock. It was one in the morning. The Go Away charm was on. Which could only mean one thing: Mom was desperate. Really, really desperate. Because that's the only way a normal human could get past the Go Away charm.

I could see Mom's book club friends in the parking lot, waiting by Mrs. Miller's minivan, looking uncomfortable. The charm worked on the other ladies.

Shit. This was bad. This was very, very bad. I didn't know why Mom was here, but I had to get her outside, back in that minivan, before she got hurt. Or, you know, figured out there was a giant, pregnant carnivorous plant from hell in the store.

Right then, Angel eight ball rolled out from behind the hot dog station. "Remember the note she left in your laundry hamper? She's checking up on you. She thinks you're on drugs. Or dealing drugs. Probably both."

"Do you have something there? Behind your back?" Mom asked.

I held on white knuckled to DeeDee's book. There's no way I could let Mom see that. I mean, it wasn't growling in the bottom of my closet level bad, but still. Divert! Divert! "Is everything okay?" I asked, big fake smile on full display. "Is Dad okay? You're never out this late."

"Oh, yes, honey. Everything's fine." Her voice was sweet as syrup. "Just fine."

The worry wrinkle between her eyebrows furrowed into a deep eleven as she tried to peek around to see what I was holding. She swayed a little. Her cheeks were pink, and when she smiled at me her teeth were dark. Stained. With red wine. Uh oh. Mom was tipsy.

"The girls decided to mix it up and have book club at the bar again. We were next door, so I thought I'd pop in to visit you," she said. "So. This is where you work? I've only seen it from the outside, but it looks...nice?"

Mom glanced at Larry, playing dead. DeeDee stepped between Mom and the giant plant and introduced herself. "Hi. I'm DeeDee."

"Oh, my. He didn't tell me you were so pretty. I'm Lloyd's mom. It's so nice to meet you!" She wrapped DeeDee up in her arms. "Sorry, dear. I'm a hugger!"

I took my chance and ditched the book. I slipped it between some potato chip bags on an end cap. DeeDee looked at me over my Mom's shoulder and mouthed, "get her out of here."

Well, duh! I didn't want her to stay.

"Do you need snacks or drinks for the road, Mom? My treat." I pulled that fake smile up higher.

Mom let go of DeeDee and descended on me, locking me in a death squeeze. Like seriously. She was hugging me like she was never gonna see me ever again. "Aw. You're so sweet. You're my sweet, sweet boy. Are you okay, honey? Like, really okay?"

"Get your hands off my woman." Morty stepped in the front door and straightened his tie. "Don't waste your time with boys, Jennifer. You need a man, and this is what a real man looks like."

My Mom spun on her heel. She took one look at Morty and giggled. "Stop. You're such a flirt. This is my son, Lloyd. I told you about him."

"Son? You're pulling my leg," Morty cooed. "Your brother maybe."

Morty grabbed Mom's hand, went down on one knee in front of her, and kissed it. And I'm not talking a peck. He turned her hand over and sunk his tongue into her palm.

What. The. Fuck. Is. Going. On? Then it hit me. Oh God. My Mom was the book club babe he was trying to bed. Oh, hell no!

"Stop." My Mom blushed and giggled. "I told you, I'm a married woman."

Morty looked up at her and grinned. "You may have already ordered your entree, but it's time for dessert."

Noooooooooooooo!!!! Why God? WHY?

"You shoulda never let your hot mom within three blocks of that perv." Kevin dragged a Monster Burger bag in through the front door. "Told ya she was a MILF. Wait. What time is it?"

He glanced at the clock. "Man. You must be in deep shit, kid. What did you do, set the garage on fire?"

Morty put his arm around my Mom and whisked her dangerously close to the boner pill display.
"Are you hungry, beautiful? There's chocolate sauce in aisle three. I'd love to lick it off of you. Mmm mmm."

Room spinning. This is not happening. Make it stop.

So of course, things only got worse. Much worse. As soon as Mom's back was turned, Big Larry started hacking again. *Heeeeeerrrffff heeeeeerrrffff.* He reared up and bucked like a rodeo bull. *Heeeeeerrrffff heeeeerrrrffff.*

Not now, Big Larry. Please wait until Mom is gone. Please please please.

Nope. Big Larry let loose. A stream of neon pink vomit shot straight up out of his mouth, spraying down all around him like he was the fountain in the town square.

"Get her out of here!" DeeDee scream whispered and pointed at Mom. She ducked, trying to avoid Larry's projectile vomit. But there was no avoiding it. It was all over. All over the floor. All over the chip aisle, the wall, the slushy machines. Even all the little Larries dripped with slime. Pink slime. With thousands of black bug legs floating in it.

My heart jumped so high so hard, it nearly hit my tonsils. What were we supposed to do? How could we possibly hide this mess? What would I tell my Mom?

Angel eight ball rolled around the edge of the barf puddle. "Bear in mind that lying to your parents is a sin."

I kicked him. I didn't need a lecture. I needed actual help. The mop. I'll get the mop. Clean it up before she notices. Yeah. That'll work. Morty's smooth. He'll keep her occupied. Shit. Well, hopefully not too occupied.

I spun around, ready to make a run for the mop, when a yellow light began to flash by the Mountain Dew pyramid. The white door opened, and the zombie cleaning crew shuffled out. No. Not zombies. Not now! Is the room spinning or is it just me?

"Kevin!" DeeDee snipped. "Level one and two only!"

"Whatevs," he said. "I'm not cleaning that up. It's dinnertime. I don't want to lose my appetite."

A second later, those zombies were slurping up Larry barf like it was freaking ice cream.

Vlurp. Disgusting. My stomach turned so hard it felt like a double knot.

I looked back at Mom. Morty tried to wrap his arms around her, but she pushed him away. Phew, except she was smiling and giggling. A strong, sudden bolt of testosterone surged inside me. I was gonna punch that hell fiend right in the nose. Moms were hands off! I didn't walk into the beer cave and put the moves on *his* mom! Boundaries, people!

I closed in on Morty, fists ready. Wouldn't you know it, that was also the moment the dirty pixie couple decided to stop humping in the snack aisle and start flying around. Just my luck. You couldn't wait ten freaking minutes until my Mom left?

Nope. No, they couldn't. They flipped me four middle fingers as they looped through the air.

"Hey, Mom." I grabbed her and spun her around before she could see the tiny naked gingers. I also conveniently inserted myself between her and Morty. I couldn't let a succubus straight from hell seduce my Mom. Yeah. Read that sentence again and let it sink in. How did this become my life?

"Can I get you a Snapple? You like Snapple, right? Do you want a Snapple? We have Snapple. Come on. Let's go get a Snapple. You can drink Snapple in the car. On the way home. Yay Snapple!" Apparently, my brain had snapped for Snapple.

"Mmm. That does sound good, honey. That was my favorite drink in college," she said. "I need a little snack to go with it, though."

She looked around, then whispered, "I think I may have had a little too much to drink."

"I think you've had just enough." Morty took my Mom in his arms and leaned her back into a deep dip. She made a happy "oooo" noise as she went.

"Watch out, kid," Kevin said. "I'm not the only one channeling the Swayze."

Shit. I'm screwed. Dirty Dancing was my Mom's all-time favorite movie.

Morty undipped her and twirled her around. She stopped face to face with the doughnut case. Her eyes lit up. "Oh dear. Is that a pumpkin spice fritter? Oh yes, please."

"What? Are you kidding me? I told Bob no pumpkin spice!" Kevin pressed his face against the case. "Wait til I get my hands on that fat old bastard."

She started for the little wax paper envelope and the tongs.

"Welp. Here we go. No soccer mom can say no to pumpkin spice. That's why this shit is destroying civilization."

Geesh, Kevin. Hello! Bigger problem! My Mom was about to eat a cursed doughnut! I fwapped the little tongs out of her hand and closed the case.

"Lloyd!" she yipped. "What are you doing?"

"Technically, you can't stop her, kid. There's no rule against moms buying doughnuts." Kevin stood next to the case, rubbing his distended belly. "Errrrp. Excuse me. Mmph. That tasted like fries. Speaking of, I'm starving."

"What's gotten into you? You're acting awfully strange." Mom looked at me, waiting for me to explain.

"Uh, you don't want those, Mom. These are old. Stale. The fresh ones don't come for another hour."

"Oh." Her shoulders slumped as she considered this. "I bet they're still good. They look good."

She started to reach down to grab the serving tongs off the floor. "You might want to wash these, though."

"Mom. No!" I screamed and kicked the tongs all the way to the hot dog station.

"What's your problem? Why are you so jumpy?" She dug her fists into her hips.

"Uh. You don't want a doughnut. Trust me." Man, are you hot? Because I'm sweating bullets.

"And why not?"

"We've got a pest problem. See? Roaches!"

I pointed at Kevin, still leaning against the doughnut case. He froze. He looked at my Mom. My Mom looked at him. Mom recoiled. "Goodness gracious. I've never seen a roach that big! You really should call an exterminator."

"Way to throw me under the bus, kid." Kevin shook his head and waddled away.

"Maybe I'll try one of those drinks you like so much instead. A slurper? No, slushy. That's right. What's your favorite flavor? I'll try that one."

Mom turned around and went straight for the slushies. Which would have been fine, if there weren't twelve zombies licking hell plant barf off the floor and the walls. Never mind the naked pixies who just landed on the Salvation Strawberry nozzle.

Larry was gracious enough to play dead once Mom turned around. She stopped when she saw the men in coveralls. "Who are these fellas? I didn't see them come in."

"Uh, that's the cleaning crew," I said.

"What is that stuff they're cleaning up?" Her nose wrinkled up. Yeah. It smelled bad. Thanks, Larry.

"One of the machines is broken," DeeDee piped up. "It spilled all over everything. They hold a lot more liquid than you think."

"It smells terrible. What are they doing to the floor?"

"These three are plumbers. We have a broken sewer pipe," DeeDee pointed to the zombies on their hands and knees licking the linoleum. "They're trying to find the pipe before they cut through the floor."

"But it looks like they're licking—"

Oh shit. I grabbed Mom's shoulders and spun her around—again—to face me. "Uh, shouldn't you get going? It's late. Dad's probably worried, and Mrs. Miller's waiting. See?"

She looked out over my shoulder. "They're all fine, silly. But you're sure in a hurry to get me out of here. You're awfully jumpy. And sweaty.

You always sweat when you're nervous. Why are you so nervous?"

"I'm fine." I was so totally not, but that kind of lie didn't count, did it? "This neighborhood isn't the best at night. I'd feel better if you were safe at home."

And I don't want you to cheat on Dad with Morty. And there's a naked pixie flying through the air behind you. And it just landed on the shoulder of a zombie. A legit, real zombie. And the pixie just unbuckled his containment collar, then flipped me the bird. And...wait. Back up a second.

"Uuuuuuuuuuuuhhhhh." The newly free zombie lurched and sniffed, looking for lunch. Human lunch. Uh oh.

I yanked Mom forward and held her tight against me.

"What's gotten into you?" She wiggled.

"Nothing. I just want to hug you. I love you so much!"

I squeezed her tight like a ketchup pack, and inched her away from the zombie, to the front door. DeeDee had her hands on the errant zombie's collar as it bit and moaned. She had it under control. At least until two ginger pixies landed on her face, and she had to let go of the zombie to pull them off.

Gulp. We're screwed.

"I love you too, honey, but you're squeezing too tight."

She wriggled free, so I grabbed her hands and held tight, fumbling for something brilliant to say that would keep her distracted as the zombie stumbled toward us. "Uh. Uh. Uh."

"Honey, are you feeling all right? You look a little green. Are you coming down with something?"

She put her hand on my forehead. While she patted my head checking me for fever, Big Larry opened wide and clamped down on the errant zombie. Seriously. That zombie went tonsil deep. Big Larry reared up, and the only visible zombie bits were two legs, from the knee down, dangling out of his mouth.

Chomp. Chomp. Chomp.

Oh, my God. Big Larry ate the guy! Whole! DeeDee jumped up and grabbed the zombie's legs and tried to pull him out, but it wasn't going so well. She swung back and forth as Big Larry chewed.

Kevin crawled up on Mom's shoulder, grabbed a strand of her hair, and sniffed it. "Mmm. She even smells good. What is that, strawberry?"

What are you doing, Kevin! If you hadn't noticed, we're in the middle of an emergency.

"I got bad news for you, kid. I was just in your Mom's pocket and her browser was open to 'seven signs your son's on drugs.' She highlighted paranoia, so you might want to play it cool. You're sweating.

And your face is all twisted up. Relax."

Play it cool? RELAX? Considering the circumstances, I'm rocking this! Or not. I mean, Mom's worried wrinkle was nearly in Mariana Trench mode.

"You should go home, Mom. These guys have to clean up," I said. "And it smells terrible in here. I'm sure it'll only get worse."

Take that, angel. Still not lying!

Mom huffed. "You're probably right. Can you get me that Snapple? And some Twinkies. Ooh. Yes. Twinkies. Here. How much is that?" She went for her purse.

"My treat. I'll bring them out to the car. Does Mrs. Miller want anything?"

"No. They didn't want to come in for some reason."

Mom turned to Morty, who was craning his neck trying to look down her shirt. Yep. I was gonna kill him.

"It was so nice to meet you. Thanks for the lovely conversation." Mom gushed. "I hope you find the girl of your dreams. I better get home."

"Don't leave me, beautiful." Morty opened his mouth, locked eyes with my mother and moved in for a kiss. A french kiss. God help me. Nooooooooooo!

I stood there in horror as time slowed down to a snail's pace. As the gap closed between my Mom and Morty's filthy frenching mouth, I watched Big Larry swing DeeDee off the zombie's kicking legs. She skidded across the floor. Big Larry bucked back and crunched the rest of that zombie down whole in a single bite. No sign of him left.

Mom turned away from Morty, so his filthy mouth only managed to eat up her hair.

"Well, I'll see you at home," she said to me. "Oh. It looks like Monster Burger's still open. That sounds good. I'll take a rain check on the Snapple and Twinkies, okay, honey? I need something heavier. Something meaty."

Morty opened his mouth, surely about to make a comment about his meat. I glared at him.

She made for the door. She stopped for a moment and said, "Never mind. The drive-thru is closed. Darn. Maybe I can talk the girls into White Castle instead."

And with that, she walked across the lot, crawled into Mrs. Miller's minivan and drove away.

"You are an epic cock block," Morty sneered.

"That's my MOM!"

"So? She's married, not dead," he said. "And her vagina's had plenty of time to recover from pushing you through."

My jaw dropped. He did not even.

"I'm the one who's suffering here. Now I have to go back to the bar and start all over again." He slumped. "Oh well, you know what they say. If you can't get a ten, get five twos. Look out twos, here I come."

He straightened his crotch, kicked open the front door, and sneered at me as he walked back to the Temptations Tavern.

By then, the zombies had licked the place clean. DeeDee must have found the zombie remote, because she pressed a button and all the zombies shuffled back into their cooler of doom in the back hallway without so much as a grunt. Okay, not all of them.

The one that Big Larry ate? All that was left of Larry's late-night snack was a tan work boot lying on the linoleum. Oh, Jesus. It still had a foot in it. But it must have hit the spot. His stalks stood tall, no sign of droop or wilt. His healthy rosy red blush had returned.

"Well, now we know what kind of supplement Larry needed," DeeDee shook her head. "The book said C2H5OH. That's alcohol. There's some in the Spanish fly, but it must not have been enough. There's a lot of it in embalming fluid. That must be why he ate the zombie."

She rubbed her temples and groaned. "What am I going to tell Steve? We're short staffed now."

"Can't we just order a replacement?"

She looked at me like I had two heads. "Uh, no. There's a limited supply. People don't turn into zombies every day, you know."

CHAPTER 17

I pedaled my Huffy as fast as I could because if I slowed down, just for a minute, the sky turned into a fireworks display of thunder and lightning.

"And because you're late. Again. It must be *soooooo* hard to be on time for work at TEN P.M." Angel eight ball rolled his triangle at me. Did I mention he was riding in the cup holder attached to my handle bars? Lucky me. He was such a joy to be with.

Useless angel. I still didn't know why God wanted me to go back to Demon Mart. So I could watch Morty hit on my Mom? Get assaulted repeatedly by pixies? Or sit by as Kevin ate so much Monster Burger he ballooned up to the size of a kitten? Was that really worthy of a divine plan? "Can you cut me some slack? You don't have to scream at me."

"Your cat is still alive. That's plenty of slack."

I wanted to argue, but all that came out was, "Chhh chhh chhh chhh." No. I didn't go full Friday the thirteenth. That was the sound of my teeth chattering, because I'm riding my bike after dark. In November. In Ohio. And it's fricking freezing outside. Apparently, God wanted me to get frostbite.

"Relax. You've got plenty of insulation." The triangle hovered there, like he was looking at me.

"Did you just call me fat?" Again?

"I watched you eat an entire row of fudge stripe cookies last night. What do you think?"

"Every man is entitled to small joys."

"Lift your shirt. When I see abs, you can have some small joys. Holy cannoli! Watch out!"

"What?" I looked up. Ack! There was a dude right in front of me. In the middle of the street! I hit the brakes, swerved, and skidded across the asphalt. My tire hit the curb. I went right over the handlebars and face planted into the sidewalk.

Ow. That hurt.

I rolled over. I had nearly hit him, but the guy bopped along like it never happened. "What the hell, dude! Get on the sidewalk before you kill somebody!"

The guy stopped walking. Well, it was more like shuffling, and his head turned.

"Yeah you! Get out of the road!"

Angel eight ball rolled out from under a bush, streaked with dirt. "Yelling at strangers never ends well. Do you want to get beat up?"

"He shouldn't be stumbling—probably drunk—in the middle of the street at night!"

Yeah. I said it loud enough for the dude to hear me, but he didn't stop, didn't look at me, didn't react. He lurched away, down the middle of the street, moaning. "uuuurrrr gerrrr."

"Huh. Does that seem a little strange to you?" Angel eight ball asked.

"No. But that does." I pointed.

That guy wasn't the only person wandering in the street. Up ahead, in the two blocks between me and Demon Mart, dozens more people milled around. On the sidewalk. In the road, each one of them shuffling in the same direction, toward the glowing Monster Burger sign at the intersection.

"I don't like this one bit," angel eight ball said.

"Me either." An icy cold ran over me. They couldn't all be drunk.

"Hurry up and get to the store. You'll be safer inside."

"Yeah. I think you're right." Boy, I never thought I'd say that.

I heaved my bike up off the sidewalk, popped angel eight ball into the cup holder and pedaled as fast as I could. Which wasn't very, and not because I was out of shape. (For once.) The closer I got to Demon Mart, the more crowded the street became. The parking lot was wall-to-wall people, so packed I couldn't even walk my bike through. I had to ditch it on the sidewalk.

"Don't leave me out here alone!" Angel eight ball said as he rolled out of the cup holder.

"I wasn't gonna." Even I wasn't that cruel.

I picked him up and tiptoed through the crowd to the door, trying to avoid any undue attention. It didn't matter. I could have been screaming, naked, and on fire. Those people wouldn't have noticed. They came from all directions, shuffling toward one thing, and one thing only: that glowing neon burger. It's like they were in some sort of trance.

Crack. Thwack. Rurrrrr.

Lightning and thunder.

I'm sorry! I'm sorry! What did I do wrong? I jumped, but it wasn't crackling over me. A black storm cloud, blacker than the night sky, squatted over Monster Burger. The cloud flashed and crackled with eerie blue and yellow light.

"I think you're about to find out why God wants you here," angel said.

Something grabbed my shoulders. "Aaaah!"

Something spun me around. Oh, wait. Phew. It was DeeDee. "Get inside. Quick."

She didn't have to tell me twice. She grabbed my arm and dragged me through the front door. She shut it behind us and locked it, then peered through the glass. "We've got problems. Big problems."

Gee. You think?

She turned around and looked at me. Like really looked. Up, down and all around, like she was searching for something.

"Uh. Are you okay?"

She didn't answer. She put her hands on my cheeks and moved my head around. "How do you feel? Have you blacked out? Lost any time? Having any unusual cravings? Is a demonic force compelling you to do its dark bidding?"

"Um. No?" Did this seem weird to you?

Then she felt me up. Unfortunately, it wasn't sexy. It was a pat down. She opened my coat and ran her hands around all over my chest, then down over my love handles. Yeah. Maybe eight ball was onto something with the abs.

"Do you feel sick? Did anyone bite or scratch you?"

"No. Why?"

"Look." She took me by the hand and led me to the counter. The cigarette carousels had been pushed aside to make room for a big clear glass dome. It looked like my Grandma's fancy cake stand. It even had a big, fluffy brown pancake inside.

Tap. Tap. Tap.

Oh shit. That's no pancake. That was... "Kevin?"

Kevin was super fat and super wide. His head bumped the glass, over and over, like he was trying to walk but kept forgetting there was a piece of glass in front of him. His black eyes had lost their shine. He stared at nothing, as if he was in some sort of trance. "What's wrong with him?"

"He's one of them." She pointed out the window. "Does this remind you of anything?"

"Well, Big Dan dragged me to a hippy jam band show once. Everyone there was so high. Like soo soo high."

"Uh, I was thinking more like Sugar Hill."

"Is that, like, a resort or something?"

"Isle of the Snake People?"

"Oh, shit. Are these people really snakes?"

"No. Look outside." She huffed. "This is just like White Zombie."

"My dad has that CD."

"Oh my God." She rubbed her eyes. "The movie. Seriously? Bela Lugosi? It's a classic. They're all movies. Zombie movies. Do you live under a rock? All these people have been turned into zombies!"

Gulp. Zombies? I watched a few people shuffle past the front door. They walked like zombies. They moaned like zombies. But something didn't add up. They all looked, well, alive. Pink skin, clear eyes. I had seen real zombies up close. They had gray skin, milky white eyes, black teeth. They looked rotten. These guys on the street did not. "But they're alive."

"I hate to tell you this, but there's more than one kind of zombie. Dead ones and living ones. The living ones are turned into slaves using magic. Walking mindless slaves."

We both watched as more people stumbled across the lot, eyes wide and blank, lured to the glowing neon Monster Burger sign as if it were a beacon. Walking. Check. Mindless. Check. Slaves? Hmmm.

"How could I have been so stupid? It's so obvious." DeeDee paced. "It's just like the movies. People don't realize the zombie apocalypse has already started because they're too busy with their own problems. Someone turned people into zombies right next door, but we didn't notice because we were too busy with our own problems. The pixie infestation. The gate routing malfunction? Henrietta said someone bulldozed the pixie burrows. Doc and Steve say there's nothing physically wrong with the gate, yet we were knee deep in white goop and headless guys. Plus, the strippers stuck in the wall. We were sabotaged, Lloyd. Whoever turned these people into zombies deliberately kept us distracted so we wouldn't stop them."

"But Caroline couldn't..." That's all I could say, all right? Dude. This was a lot to take in. A. Lot. And I didn't have peak brain processing speed even on a good day.

"No. She couldn't, but her mystery partner could. Monster Burger has zombies on staff. You have to be supernatural to get a zombie permit. I did a little digging into her partner. That shell company, HHNF? It's owned by an anonymous, private trust. Whoever runs it is virtually untraceable. You only do that if you're trying to hide something. And now we know what they're hiding."

Lighting flashed above Monster Burger as DeeDee said it, like a big, ominous electrical exclamation point. Of course. Because my life had turned into a bad horror movie.

Angel eight ball rolled behind DeeDee. "At least your life isn't boring!"

"We should call for help."

"I did," she said. "No one's coming."

Uh oh. No help? Magic? Zombies? Woah boy. Room spinning.

"I couldn't conjure Faust. At all. Steve didn't answer, thanks to Kevin. But don't worry. Doc and Henrietta are safe in their shops, working on it. They'll call if they come up with any ideas," she said. "We don't know who did this or how or why. The good news is those people aren't after us, so we've got plenty of time to figure it all out. Here's the plan."

Cakunk cakunk heeerrrrf. Herrrrrrff. Herrrrrrrrrrrrp.

Big Larry heaved like he was choking, opened wide, and spat a giant ball of slime on the floor. He shook his big melon head, thumped his leaves against the walls, and suddenly turned completely purple. Like, bright, technicolor, My Little Pony level purple. And even though he didn't have a face or eyes or eyebrows, I could tell he was freaked out and in pain.

"You okay, buddy?"

Thump. Thump. Thump. His leaves pounded the walls.

"Oh no. Not now!" DeeDee, normally Ms. Cool Cucumber in a crisis, looked absolutely, completely and totally panicked. She grabbed my arm and squeezed, super tight. "Larry's in labor."

Great. Just great. There are magic hoodoo voodoo zombies roaming the streets, and we're supposed to switch into hell plant maternity ward mode? NOW? I have a bad feeling about this. A very bad feeling.

Crack! The lights flickered. That wasn't Larry. That was a bolt of lightning the size of Detroit striking Monster Burger. It lit up the neighborhood like it was noon, casting the whole block in an eerie green light.

"Lloyd. Help me. We don't have much time."

You could say that again. She meant with Larry, but come on. We were in deep, on multiple levels. But then it hit me like a brick. We weren't the only ones in trouble. I turned to face the glowing neon bun outside. "Earl."

CHAPTER 18

Earl picked up on the second ring. "Hey. It's Lloyd. From Dem—uh, Dairy Mart."

I tried really hard to sound casual. Really REALLY hard, because a large crowd had gathered around Monster Burger, a sea of bodies so thick you couldn't see the parking lot.

"Who?"

"Number seven combo, extra onions, extra salt, no mayo."

"Oh, hey. My main man! Whazzzup?"

"Earl. Listen carefully. You're in danger. Get out of the restaurant now. Come over here. Come to Dairy Mart. Right now."

"Are you kidding? Look at that crowd. I can't leave, we're about to get slammed! I've got six fry baskets down, a dozen guys working double time on the grill, and the boss lady's here. I can't leave."

"Earl. Please. It's an emergency. Come to Demon Mart right now. I'll explain everything when you get here. We'll protect you."

"I hear you B-boy, but that's wack," Earl said. "I gotta go. I'm 'bout to be slammin', and you know I'm 'bout to be jammin'. Hold up. What are you doing here? Back again, huh? You want some of this?"

"EARL!" I screamed. "Get out of there. Now!"

Clank ca-thunk.

"Earl? Earl?"

"Get off me. Gack!" His voice was far away. He must have dropped the phone. "Damn you, Ed McMahon. Stop stealing my lettuce. Get out of there. Stop! Stop it right now, you tiny bastard!"

"Jesus, Earl. Forget about Ed..." McMahon? Stealing his lettuce? Tiny bastard? Oh my God. All the random pieces clicked together in my brain. The white hair. The big nose. The wrinkles? The belly? That old naked pixie looked just like Ed McMahon! Well, if he were naked and the size of a GI Joe, but still.

Maybe Earl wasn't crazy. Maybe that Ed McMahon pixie actually did kill Mr. Jimmy. Something did buzz around him. A pixie could have knocked him off the ladder. "Earl. Ed McMahon DID kill Mr. Jimmy. Come over now and we can talk about it! Earl!"

"You tiny bastard! Ha. Take that. Wait. Where do you think you're going? Leave that guy alone!" Earl yelled. "Buddy, Ed's on your shoulder. Grab him. Ope. You missed. Come back here! I'll get you! Do you hear me? I'll get you! Wow. Did you see that? Hey. Buddy? Are you all right? You look a little green. Why are you growling? You mad?"

Lighting hit the restaurant, and the landline went dead. "EARL!"

I dialed again, hand shaking so hard I could barely keep a grip on the phone.

Beep beep beep. "The number you are trying to call is not in service."

Oh no. My stomach churned. I stared at the restaurant and tried to zone in on his brain waves. *Run, Earl. Run! Get out of there. Please get out of there!* I didn't know what else to do. It's not like I could run over and grab him. I'd never get through the crowd.

"Mmmm. Buuuuuuuuuuuuuuur," Kevin swayed back and forth, staring through the glass, a prisoner in a dome.

I felt a pang, an icy needle of fear, deep in my gut. What if we didn't figure it out? What if we couldn't save Earl. Or Kevin. Poor Kevin. I felt so bad for him, mindlessly bumping up against the glass. There was no sign of snark, no trace of the real Kevin. How did it come to this?

He'd left a full bag of Monster Burger on the counter. Probably his dinner. I fished out a french fry, cracked the dome and slid it in there. It was the least I could do. Small joys, right?

He immediately chomped down on my finger. Okay, he tried to. Thankfully roaches aren't known for their bite force. He stopped abruptly when he realized there was a fry in my hand. He crawled over and chomped down on that instead. I pulled my hand out and the dome clicked closed.

"Is Earl on his way?" DeeDee stood in front of Larry, wearing thick red rubber gloves and safety goggles.

"No. I don't think so."

She frowned, then motioned for me to join her. I did.

"Are you all right? You look a little pale."

"I'm fine." I couldn't even fake smile. Earl was trapped. And Kevin..."What if?"

"Stop right there. We do not go down the path of what if. We deal with one problem at a time, and we do the best we can with what we have, okay?" She put a rubber-gloved hand on my shoulder. "We will help Earl. We will help Kevin. But first, we have to help Larry. Fill this bucket with warm water. We're about to save an endangered species."

Okay, then. One thing at a time. I took a deep breath, and strangely I did feel a little better.

She handed me a bucket and some rubber gloves and sent me on my way. There was a utility sink in the stockroom, right outside the employee lounge. I plopped the bucket in and turned on the water. A pixie chick fluttered up off the spigot. Ugh. Seriously? Now?

She yelled at me in a teeny voice and shook her fists. She was soaking wet. She must have been under the tap when I turned it on.

"Shoo!" I swatted her away. "I'm busy. Go on. Get out of here!"

She tittered and gave me the stink eye as she flew away.

"Blah. Blah. I've heard it all before!" I yelled after her.

When the bucket was mostly full, I lifted it out of the sink. I'm a little ashamed to admit it took me a couple of tries. Oooooooof. Man. Why is water so heavy?

"Go on, do a few curls with that bucket while you're at it. Girls like muscles." Angel eight ball sat on a shrink-wrapped pallet of condoms.

"I have muscles."

"Correction. Girls like visible muscles. Never mind. Watch out!"

Something hit me hard right between the eyes. The bucket slipped out of my hand.

Ploosh.

The water spilled all over the floor. My feet when out from under me and smack. I landed flat on my back. *Eowch.*

Apparently, I'd been punched between the eyebrows by a couple of angry pixies wielding a Coke can. A cloud of them hovered above me, led by the chick from the sink. She spit shouted words at me.

"Uh. Okay?" I pretended to listen, but come on. Do you speak pixie? I sure as hell didn't.

"I'm a little rusty, but she says you giant fat apes destroyed their village. They have a right to shelter and food. Don't be stingy. Yada yada. Oh, and you'll pay for what you've done."

"Why do I have to pay? I didn't do anything wrong!" Dude. They pooped all over the store and poked me in the eyes with spicy Bugles. I couldn't let them stay!

They apparently thought otherwise. Because they dive bombed me, tearing at my hair and my shirt. I screamed and swatted and thwapped. "Jerks! How did they get back in here?"

Angel flashed an arrow pointing up.

There was a swirling green portal on the ceiling. A red demon hand poked out, warming himself by the heating vent. Kevin's dickhead roommate. Again. "Great. Just great."

A second later, the stupid naked jerks were all over my face. I swear I could feel a tiny butt hole on my nose. Again!

"Lloyd! Hurry up. It's started!" DeeDee called out.

Shoot. Gotta save Larry. I sat up, pixies clinging to my cheeks, and plucked them off one by one, losing a chunk of skin each time. *Ouch. Ouch. Ouch.*

I hopped up and grabbed the bucket. The floor wasn't that slippery because my "If I'm not back in five minutes, wait longer" T-shirt had soaked up most of the water. So had my underpants. Man. There was no worse feeling in the world than wet underpants.

The pixies didn't give up. They swooped at me, taking sucker punches as I made my way back to the sink. "Leave me alone!"

You know what? I didn't need to put up with this. My face throbbed. My underpants were wet as a swamp. Desperate, I grabbed a can of Kill 'Em Dead off the to-be-stocked pile, popped the cap, and started spraying the little bastards.

Pssssssssssssssssssssss.

"Put that down! Are you crazy? That isn't Pixie Rid. That's poison! Thou shalt not kill, remember?"

"Shut up." Stupid angel. "I'm not trying to kill them. I just want them off me."

And it worked. The pixies scattered. Sure, I felt bad. Even I was coughing and gagging in the noxious cloud of chemical poison, but pixies weren't bugs and I didn't spray it in their faces, so it wouldn't seriously hurt them, right? When they had all flown off, I refilled the bucket.

"We need to talk," said angel, who was somehow now balanced on the faucet.

"How do you move around so fast?"

"Listen. If you hadn't noticed already, pixies are vengeful jerks. For real. They aren't gonna let that poison thing go. You kicked this fight up another notch. Watch your back."

"Yeah yeah. Whatever."

Errp. Errp. Errp. Errp. Errp.

Oh no. The yellow light outside the cooler began to flash.

Cuhhhhhhhhhhhr. The seal on the door released, and the eleven remaining zombies ambled slowly into the store.

"Lloyd!" DeeDee screamed. "Get in here. Now!"

Well, here goes nothing. I grabbed the bucket and waddled as fast as I could with it. The tiny pixie chick rose before me—eyes puffy and red from the bug spray—to squeak out what I could only guess was a threat.

"I don't even know what you're saying." I snipped.

Angel eight ball rolled out from behind a stack of toilet paper. "Let me translate for you: You're screwed."

CHAPTER 19

"Duck!" DeeDee tackled me the second I walked out. The bucket clanked to the floor and sploshed, but thankfully didn't fall over. But we sure did. We landed on the floor, in a huge puddle of sticky red goop. Which looked like it was bubbling out of Big Larry's stems. Nope. Don't tell me what it is. Just don't. I don't want to know.

"Stay down." DeeDee squeezed me tight. She was so warm and soft my downstairs tingled for a second. Ahem. But that moment of pure carnal joy was fleeting. A fat red thing that looked like a gigantic rubber band crossed right over us and hit the wall, crunching a fist-sized hole in the drywall. The hole sizzled and smoked.

"What the hell is that?" I squeaked.

"Acid whips. In the wild, they keep predators away while Larry's giving birth."

Fwap. Another one hit the ceiling, and bits of acoustic tile sprinkled down on us.

"He has WHAT?" Holy shit. "Make him stop. We're not predators!"

"He can't control it. It's instinct. Just don't get hit."

DeeDee rolled off of me. She took cover behind a row of giant plant pots and bags of potting mix she'd stacked like sandbags around the pyramid of Mountain Dew 2-Liters. The zombies worked in teams on each of the little Larries. One zombie would hold a little Larry head, while the second plucked out his spiky ivory teeth, one by one. The Little Larries bucked and yelped.

"Dude. Stop! Don't hurt them."

"We have to defang the babies before we transplant them, or they won't make roots!" DeeDee yelled. "Didn't you read the book?"

"No. I didn't read the book. Duh!"

"When all the babies are separated from the main stalk, the acid whips stop. Lloyd. Watch out! Behind you!"

I curled up in full fetal position, expecting another acid whip to fwap, but that wasn't what DeeDee meant. An angry squadron of pixies swarmed around me, led by the faucet chick and a tiny, naked Ed McMahon. Great. Just great. Grandpa McMole was back. That murdering, lettuce-stealing prick.

Thankfully, Larry's acid whips didn't discriminate. There had to be a dozen of them wiggling around smacking stuff. It only took one to break up the pissed-off pixie formation. I rolled out of the way, but the angry Ed McMahon didn't see it coming. With a thwack and a fwap, a handful of the pixies fell, injured and smoking, into the oozing sticky muck on the floor. The rest scattered.

Unfortunately, after that whip waved around thunking pixies, it headed straight for me. I rolled out of the way just in time. And I kept right on rolling. If there was one benefit to being portly, it was that my body was essentially a big flubby tube. I could roll all day. I was made for it. Of course, the chip rack was in the way, so I only managed to roll nose deep into a bag of Mikesells. That was as far as I could go.

I should have run, but I didn't know where to go. DeeDee's sandbag fort wasn't big enough for two. Larry's whips had spread across the ceiling. They fwapped and wiggled and thrashed in every corner. Let's be clear here: Larry's labor wasn't fun for anybody. His main head had swelled to the size of a gigantic pumpkin. And I'm not talking a rinky dink porch pumpkin, either. I'm talking one of those thousand pound prize winners from the Circleville Pumpkin show. Larry's lips pursed, teeth grinding, and he panted like he was doing some sort of herbaceous Lamaze.

Although I could finally see why Demon Mart kept zombies around. Acid whips? Pixies? They kept right on working. They defanged the baby Larries, then used some sort of short sharp garden knife to slice them off of the main stalk. They worked, no matter what chaos raged around them, even though Larry had already eaten one of their friends.

But boy. Larry's stalk must have been made of pretty tough stuff, because it took two zombies to cut off one baby. Then another zombie to walk it over to the pot, acid whips thwacking, where DeeDee waited to transplant it. I watched her cover each Larry's roots with a scoop of peat, hit the floor to avoid an acid whip, then sit up and water him from the bucket I'd brought her. Man, she was smooth. Even with all that chaos around her, she took the time to scratch each baby under the chin and kiss the top of its head.

It's like she had a preternatural sense for those acid whips. She tucked and rolled out of the way before I even knew which direction they were gonna thwap. Then she'd roll right on back like it was nothing.

She was so busy, she didn't notice the naked Ed McMahon fluttering around Larry. Oh, but I sure did. That mole-ridden menace locked eyes with me. He held up his arm, then pumped it up and down twice like he was giving me the "Go" signal at a cheap drag race. Then he flipped me two middle fingers.

"What the? Jerk!"

He flew directly onto the shoulder of the closest zombie, grabbed hold of his electric collar and snapped it off. The collar clinked to the floor.

Holy. Shit.

My eyes shot from zombie to zombie, and that's when it hit me. That *was* a go signal. A pixie sat on each zombie's collar. Each one of those pixies looked right at me, unbuckled that collar, then chucked it to the floor. They fluttered up and away into an open heating vent, shooting me double birds the entire way.

Oh. Fuck.

I stared at the collars. Broken. On the floor. This can't be happening.

I shook all over. The zombies looked up and around slowly, confused, like babies waking up from a nap. They grunted and sniffed the air. They had stopped cutting baby Larries off stalks. They had stopped licking red Larry goop off the linoleum. That wasn't what they wanted to be eating. They'd rather be eating...*Gulp.* We're screwed.

DeeDee cooed at baby Larries, moving from pot to pot watering, rolling away from acid whips, unaware of the awakening unfolding around her. She didn't see. She didn't know. But the zombies sure noticed her. They eyeballed her like she was a glass of water, and they'd just shuffled through Death Valley.

Oh God. They were gonna get her. Just like my dream. I couldn't let them get her. I had to save her. I tried to move, but couldn't. My body felt like ten thousand pounds of solid lead.

"Dee—" My mouth was so dry the words got stuck. My tongue was glued to my teeth.

Uuuuuuuuuuuuuuuh. Uuuuuuuuuuuhhhh. Aaaaaaaaaaaaar.

Move, Lloyd. Come on. You can't let zombies eat the love of your life!

The vision of DeeDee as the drooling Lloyd-eating zombie in my dream kick started me into action. It was like having an out-of-body experience. I felt like I floated across the room, pulled by a supernatural tractor beam. *Must. Save. DeeDee.*

She was kissing a baby Larry.

Uuuuuuuuuuuuuuuh. Aaaaaaaaaaaaar. Uuuuuuuuuuuhhhh.

She didn't think twice about the moaning, probably because the zombies were always moaning. I tugged her sleeve, but she was too busy with the babies to notice. "You guys are safe now. We'll feed you. You'll grow up big and strong. Then daddy will take you back home, okay? I love you little guys so much!" She snuggled a couple of them like they were babies. Real babies.

Uuuuuuuuuuuuuuuuh. Aaaaaaaaaaaar. Uuuuuuuuuuhhhh.

The zombies moaned louder. They seemed agitated. We didn't have time to waste.

I grabbed her and shook her. In the moment, it was all I could think to do.

"What are you do—" she protested.

Until she saw what I saw. Containment collars scattered on the linoleum. Eleven hungry, restraint-free zombies zoned in us like senior citizens zone in on a free lunch buffet at a riverboat casino. They bared their rotten teeth and growled.

CHAPTER 20

DeeDee pushed me into the chip rack and ran.

She ran! She left MEEEEEE!

Sure, she saved me from an acid whip, and her escape looked like a hero montage cut straight out of a Kung Fu movie, all tucks and rolls and jumps, but still. As I lay there in a pile of chip bags, too terrified to move, she went to the counter and hit the control console. A red light flashed and metal storm shutters slid slowly down over the front of the store.

"What are you doing?" I squeaked. "We're trapped!"

"So are they," she said. "Standard zombie containment protocol. Didn't you read the employee manual?"

Um, no. No I didn't, thank you very much. It tried to bite me!

"Shouldn't we be on the other side of the metal shutters?" Did standard containment protocol include instructions on how we were supposed to get out of here alive?

"We can't leave the baby Larries alone, and we can't let a single zombie out of here. It'd literally start the zombie apocalypse," DeeDee said, calm and cazh as usual. "We have to risk our lives to save the world. I can't think of a nobler cause to die for than that."

Wait. What? Die? THAT WAS THE PLAN??

Vlurp. My stomach clenched so tight, bile lapped my tonsils. Great. Just great. If she wasn't planning to get out of here alive, we were both doomed. I screamed, "Letting zombies eat me is not in my job description!"

"Relax. We'll be fine. Probably," DeeDee yelled as she ran down the candy aisle. "Here's the plan. We need to stop the acid whips, so first we cut the last baby Larry off the stalk. Then we contain zombies."

Speaking of whips. One fwapped through the zombies and sent them flying like bowling pins. Then it came for me. I ducked.

Angel eight ball rolled into my foot. "If it's any consolation, if you get bit, only your body will be here, performing menial tasks for your corporate masters. For free. Until you rot. Wow. When you say that out loud, there are some real hard truths about end stage capitalism and the soul-sucking nature of work in there."

"What do you want?" I snipped.

"Relax. I'm cheering you up! Anyway, your soul will move on. I know for a fact that short fat guy is up here getting a sweet tan on Paradise Beach right now." His arrow pointed to the middle-aged zombie rolling around on the floor underneath the Perdition Peach slushy machine.

"Great. How comforting."

"It is. Sort of." Angel eight ball rolled away.

The zombies stood up and stumbled forward, sniffing the air, following the scent of the delicious hot Lloyd steak before them. I crawled away, but pretty soon I was up against the beer cave door. I was about to U-turn into the candy aisle to hide like an epic chicken shit when DeeDee hopped over me, yanked open the weapons safe, and started throwing stuff out. "Lloyd, cover me!"

The zombies moaned over the plunk plunk of falling gourds, tasers, and other weird stuff hitting the floor as DeeDee dug through the packed cabinet. A bumpy purple gourd rolled into a zombie's foot. He stepped on it, tripped, and landed flat on his back, buying us a few more precious seconds. An acid whip to the back knocked a few of them over again.

Then a single glazed doughnut with pink frosting and sprinkles fell out of the safe, onto the floor between me and the zombies.

A doughnut. Of course! It all clicked. I'd watched one of these crunch a giant hell spider down to nothing. The day is saved.

I scrambled across the floor and grabbed it. It was in a thick, clear plastic clamshell package. I pulled and pried, but the plastic didn't budge. Seriously? Zombies are closing in and I can't save the day because of a plastic clamshell? These stupid things are impossible to open!

A red hot rage burbled up in me. I hit that thing against the floor over and over again but the damn thing wouldn't crack. *Fwap!* I jumped out of the way as an acid whip crunched down, then snapped back. Oh. It split the plastic, and the doughnut rolled out. Thanks Larry!

It landed icing side down. Well. Zombies won't mind.

I scooped up as much icing and sprinkles as I could and rubbed them back on the dough. Which would probably seem stupid to an outsider, but hey. I didn't know what part of the doughnut worked the magic. Did you?

I broke off a piece of doughnut and aimed at a zombie lying on its back in the goop, moaning. I shot that crumb like Lebron James right into his mouth. It went right in. Hazzah! NBA Live pays off again! My confidence swelled. I broke off another piece, and another and tossed one into every open zombie mouth. Sure. Some Larry whips knocked a few out of the way. And yes, I missed and hit a few cheeks, but I kept going until that doughnut was nothing but crumbs. It wasn't that hard because zombie mouths were always open. Always. Seriously. They never stopped groaning.

DeeDee rummaged around in the cabinet, but she didn't have to worry. I had totally saved the day. I couldn't wait to see the look on her face.

Okay.

Any second now.

The zombies shuffled and moaned. Mouths still agape, closing in.

Wait for it! Here we go. Anytime guys.

Uuuuuuuuuuuuuuuh. Aaaaaaaaaaaar. Uuuuuuuuuuuhhhh.

My heart kicked my ribs. Why wasn't it working? Where was the magic doughnut portal that was gonna crunch these guys down into jewelry?

Uuuuuuuuuuuuuuuh. Aaaaaaaaaaaar. Uuuuuuuuuuuhhhh.

They kept on shuffling. No portal opened. Oh crap. Was the doughnut expired or something?

Angel eight ball rolled out from under a bag of Conn's wavy. "Don't quote me on this, but I think the doughnut only works if you swallow it."

"But they did!"

"They didn't swallow. These guys are carnivores. Look."

An arrow pointed to a smattering of doughnut bits—whole, dry, unchewed—accumulating on the floor around the zombies' feet. I got them in their mouths all right, but those bits had dropped right on out, unchewed. I watched as one fell right out of a zombie mouth as it moaned.

Aaaaaaaaaaaar. Uuuuuuuuuuuhhhh.

All hope drained out of me, leaving only dark, ice cold fear. And a hot flame of determination. I was not gonna die by zombie. No way.

"Got it!" DeeDee yelled.

Great. Just in time. I held out my hand, waiting for DeeDee to hand me a crossbow, gun, chainsaw, baseball bat or some other manner of appropriately brain-neutralizing zombie slayer. She handed me a long black stick with some sort of grabber on the end. "What the hell is this?"

"If one comes at you, loop the end around his neck and hold him until I can get the collar back on."

"Are you kidding?" How was I gonna kick undead ass with this? I had trained for this. Left 4 Dead. Resident Evil. Call of Duty Black Ops zombie mode. Last of Us. Plants vs Zombies. Walking Dead. I had played—and beaten—them ALL. I was an expert level zombie killer. Well. Digitally. And not once did I use the same grabber my Great Aunt Edna used to snatch cans of green beans off the top shelf in the pantry as a weapon.

And we needed weapons. Stat. One zombie had finally managed to run the gauntlet of gourds, acid whips, and zombies splayed on the floor, stuck in goop, wiggling and trying to get up. He lunged at us. DeeDee karate kicked him in the ribs. He stumbled and thunked face first into the B in the icy font spelling out "Beer Cave."

"Standard zombie rules apply. A shot to the brain will kill them, but it's the very last resort," she said. "We're contractually obligated to attempt containment first. They're too rare and valuable to destroy. So brain shot is emergency only. Got it?"

"WHAT?" Did you hear that? Did she just tell me we weren't *allowed* to kill the zombies?

"Do you understand the plan?"

"Do you understand? Hello! Zombies!"

"I'll deal with Larry and fix the collars, you distract these guys. Buy me some time. Now, go!" DeeDee rolled, silent and fast like a ninja, right past the pack of moaning zombies. They didn't give her so much as a second sniff as she slid across the linoleum, scooping up containment collars and garden knives. Maybe because Big Larry was kicking undead ass. The movement was involuntary, but dude. Those whips spun those zombies around like records and that goop was like super glue.

I took a deep breath. Okay. The plan. Distract them. Buy DeeDee time so she could ultimately save the day. Which means I have to lure them away from her. I had to be the bait. The delicious, fat, slow moving overweight bait. Shit. I didn't like this plan. Not one bit. But, I was the dumb one in the room, and even I was smart enough to know I should defer to the smart person's plan.

Okay then. Let's do this.

Some of the zombies had picked up on DeeDee's scent. Gulp. It was now or never. I yelled, "Hey. Death breath. Over here!"

That snapped them to. They all turned toward the sound of my voice. "Yeah. You. Over here. Come this way!"

And boom. The zombies shuffled toward me. Kind of. These guys definitely weren't Type A, goal oriented guys on a straight path to success. They took the long way to their destination. But it was good enough. If I could lure them to the other side of the store and keep them together, that should buy DeeDee enough time.

Aaaaaaaaaaaar. Uuuuuuuuuuhhhh.

Due to lack of any other inspiration under pressure, I started singing those stupid Zebra songs Kevin had lasered into my brain, to keep the zombies in step behind me. DeeDee chuckled and asked me if she could request Dio. Then I ran. Slowly, to keep the zombies close enough that they wanted to follow me, but far enough out of reach to be safe. Man. It was tough, because every bit of me wanted to Jesse Owens my fat ass right out of the store and never look back.

The ghouls moaned and shuffled behind me. I skipped and hummed down the row of glass cooler doors. Bubby's TV hung at the very end. Huh. Ding. I had an idea. I filched the remote off the rack as I hummed and skipped by. Geesh. Zebra saves the day. Good thing Kevin is out of it. If he saw this, I'd never hear the end of it.

Uuuuuuuuuuh. Uuuuuuuh.

The zombies followed me into the last aisle. When they were all in, I flipped on the TV and turned the volume all the way up.

Uuuuuh?

They all turned to see. A hillbilly with a bad two-tone mullet pranced across the screen. What the fuck is this? Oh yeah. Tiger King.

The zombies were transfixed. They couldn't look away. Honestly, neither could I. Talk about a train wreck! But I had bigger fish to fry, like waltzing over to help DeeDee with those containment collars. Because my zombie distraction was a success. A warm rush of happiness welled in me. Hello! I totes rocked the plan! It wasn't so bad after all. It was easy!

I turned to go. Shit.

A swarm of pixies hovered at the end of the aisle, blocking my way. Angel may have been right. That bug spray had really ticked them off because this time, they came at me armed. Each one of them carried a red slushy straw. They pointed them at me like spears and attacked.

CHAPTER 21

You wouldn't think that getting stabbed with the scoop end of a slushy straw would hurt, but dude. You get poked with two dozen of those over and over again and tell me it tickles.

I swatted those pixies like mosquitoes, but they kept on coming. I waved that stupid grabber around, but nope. Useless. They dove at me, poking and stabbing my face. I swear they were trying to scoop out my eyeballs.

Darn it. That's it. Mission: Find something to fend off these stupid pixies!

Thwap. Thwack. A streak of red cut through the air. I jumped out of the way. An acid whip hit the shelf, sending pine tree car air fresheners and bottles of fuel injector cleaner cascading to the floor. The pixies looked away for a second, watching to see where the whip was gonna land next. Ha! My chance! I crouched down and duck walked through the aisle looking for a weapon.

Angel eight ball was on the bottom shelf, wedged between two bottles of motor oil. "Wow. It really sucks to be you right now."

"Ya think?"

The acid whip crashed down on top of the rack, scattering pixies to the wind and knocking all the Fix-A-Flat to the floor.

I didn't have much time, so I grabbed the first thing that rolled past my foot. Bacon scented automobile air freshener and odor eliminator. WTF? Who buys this crap? Well. It'll have to do.

Angel eight ball shook. "Is that poison? Remember, thou shalt *not* kill! If you commit a mortal sin while I'm your angel, I lose my wings. I will rain fire down on you. Got it? You have no idea how humiliating it is to *walk* around Heaven."

"I don't care."

I popped the cap, stood up, and came eye to eye with a patch of blazing red pubes. *Blech. No!*

The pixies rose before me in their naked ginger glory. Some of them had ditched the straws. They held a rubber bouncy ball under one arm and a metal jack in their hand. Aw, man. They must have filched those from the toy section. By the looks of it, they'd opened at least a dozen packages, and I know for damn sure they left the wrappers on the floor. "You guys are gonna clean that up!"

I hit the nozzle and waved the bottle around, coating the pixies in a fine bacon-scented cloud. A few of them coughed and flew away, but the rest held steady as the tiny Ed McMahon tittered and barked, his dinger bopping around for the whole world to see.

"Come on, man. Put on some pants!" I waved that air freshener around, filling the air with meaty mist.

Tiny Ed yelled, and the pixies dropped their bouncy balls and jacks and backed away.

Ha! I win! I BEAT YOU! "That's right. Go on. Get!"

I decided my best bet was to use the bacon mist to corral them to the front door and shoo them out. I took one step, and my foot landed directly on a bouncy ball. Oof. I nearly fell over. I stopped spraying while I got my balance. And that's when the pixies got me. They flew right into my chest, all of them, all at once, and hit me so hard the wind went out of me. My shoe rolled out from under me—stupid ball!—and my arms flailed as I tried to grab on to something, anything, to keep from falling. I stepped on another rubber ball and another, until I fell straight down on my butt. I landed on a pile of metal jacks. I howled. OMG. That hurt even worse than stepping on a Lego. Even. Worse.

The little jerks high fived and hugged above me, celebrating like they'd just David and Goliathed this shit. I rolled onto my side and started plucking jacks out of my butt cheeks. *Plink. Ouch. Plink. Ouch.*

A pixie man fluttered down and landed on my knee. He looked right at me and popped a squat like a dog on a nice green lawn. Oh. Hell. No. He was not gonna—oh wait. Yes. Yes, he was. He locked eyes with me and honked out a brown snake. Oh, it's on, brother. It's on! Kevin was right. Pixies are disgusting!

I thwapped that pixie right into next week. He hit the oil funnels so hard they practically exploded off the shelf. I picked one up and clubbed him with it.

Angel eight ball rolled over. "Thou shalt not—"

"Thou shalt NOT poop on my pants!"

The pixie squeaked with every hit, and I would have kept going if angel eight ball hadn't dropped on top of him to shield him. "Do NOT kill him." His triangle turned. "All you have to do is shoo them outside. How hard is that?"

"Outside, huh? Okay." I grabbed the pooping pixie by the wings. He was a little droopy from the ass kicking I'd just handed him. I held him out so the others could see. Of course, they immediately sported their best cute innocent little sad eyes, begging me to let him go. I mean, I think. I don't speak pixie, but hand wringing and sobs are pretty much universal. "I'm not falling for it!"

The pixies shot me the evil eye, then swarmed, looping up and down in circles around me, wings buzzing like angry hornets. But I was not giving in. I did not drop the pixie.

Chink. Chink. Zzzzzzt.

Uh oh. That didn't sound good. I turned around. A handful of pixies fluttered in the air where Bubby's television used to be. One of them held a screwdriver, tag still on it, that he'd filched out of the hardware section. The TV was face down on the floor, in pieces. In the middle of a pack of zombies, who were now disappointed and confused because they would never know how Tiger King ends. The only entertainment left was to eat me.

Fuck. I dropped the pixie. Time to run.

Yes. Running was a great plan. Yes. It would have worked. Except that tiny naked Ed McMahon had just led four zombies into the other end of the aisle. They plugged up the aisle, following that hairy, precancerous mole like it was an unwrapped Hershey's Kiss.

My guts hit my shoe. That pixie had won. He'd put me in the one place you did not want to be in the zombie apocalypse: surrounded on all sides by zombies.

"Hurry, DeeDee!" I yelled across the store. "I don't want to die—i—i-eee. Herp herp ha herp."

I kept that second part on the down low. No need to die with DeeDee thinking I was a coward.

But yeah. I totally blubbered, okay? There were eleven flesh-eating zombies closing in on me and all I had to fend them off was a grandma can grabber and some bacon-scented car spray. Which had spilled all over my pants. Great. Just great. Ten bucks says you wouldn't be able to Rick Grimes your way out of this either.

"I'm working on it!" DeeDee yelled back.

The desire to survive was strong, so I wiped my tears away. I had three options: Fight them off, let them eat me, or climb over the rack into the next aisle. Oh. Yeah. I could totally do that.

I dropped the grabber and knocked all the weird gas tank additives off the top shelf. I gripped the back of it and used the bottom shelf as a step stool. Or tried to. It collapsed the second I stepped on it, sending bottles of motor oil rolling. Really universe? I wasn't *that* fat!

Uuuuuuuuuuuh. Uuuuhrrrrrrrrr.

Zombies. Closing in.

I had no choice but to double down and pull myself over that rack. I held on tight and pulled as hard as I could. My biceps—and plenty of muscles I couldn't identify—burned and flexed. Almost there.

Oh, who was I kidding? I barely moved. The metal edge of the top shelf dug into my armpits, so sharp I was pretty sure it was about to slice my nipples off. I wasn't more than six inches higher than when I started. Wowza. I really needed to work on my upper body strength.

I kicked my legs and managed to plant one knee on the second shelf. Hazzah! Leverage! Then it collapsed. There was a crash, and everything fell to the floor.

Angel rolled through aisle five and stopped in front of me. "If you worked out, you'd be in aisle five already."

"Shut up!"

Still. He had a point. This was totes not working. Time to abandon the plan. My fat ass was not gonna make it across. Okay. Plan B. Get through the four zombies loitering by the unicorn stuffies and glitter scrunchies end cap. (Remind me again why we sell this stuff?) I mean, it had to be easier to get through four zombies than it was to get through seven. Right?

Right?

I didn't have much time. Both groups had shuffled considerably closer during the shelf climbing incident. Which we will never speak of again because it was too humiliating.

Uuuuuuuuuuuuuuuuh. Aaaaaaaaaaaar. Uuuuuuuuuuuuuuuh.

I felt a little wobbly. I didn't know if it was the fear or the strain of attempting a shelf climb, but my legs turned to noodles, and my heart kicked my ribs. This was my worst nightmare. Zombies. Behind those cheap black sunglasses were milky dead eyes and an insatiable appetite for human flesh. My flesh. Their stiff arms reached out for me.

If I was gonna do this. I'd need a weapon. But what? All I had were random bottles of automotive supplies. Which was great because some of the zombies were tripping on them and stumbling. But bad because hello. I'd never once seen or heard of anyone killing a zombie with a bottle of bacon air freshener. Which, now that I'm thinking about it, probably wasn't the best thing to spray in an aisle full of meat-eating zombies.

Aaaaaaaaaaaar. Uuuuuuuuuuuuuuuh.

I grabbed the closest thing. A can of Turtle Wax. Yep. I'm gonna die. Oh well. No time to whine about it. I leaned in like a linebacker and charged at the leader of the unicorn end cap gang. Plan: Hit him like the one pin, and he'll bowl the other three over.

Except I was neither a linebacker nor a bowling ball. In fact, I'd never played football. Not even at recess. And I sucked at bowling, like lucky to break a hundred.

I charged and landed a shoulder in his chest. *Thunk. Ha. Direct hit. Yes!*

Uuuuuuuh? He moaned.

I hit him hard, but he barely budged. It was like hitting a cold rock wall.

He grabbed me. I pushed back, but then stepped onto a rubber bouncy ball and fell. He landed on top of me. I was even worse off than I was when I started.

His glasses fell off, revealing the milky white eyes underneath. He opened his mouth, wide. To eat me. No!!!! The guy who falls down never survives. NEVER!

I panicked and beat his temple with the can of Turtle Wax. I grabbed him by the hair, holding his bitey rotten mouth just far enough away.

Thunk Thunk Thunk. I whacked that Turtle Wax against that zombie skull like an otter beats an oyster shell at lunch time. *Thunk Thunk. Thunk.*

Jesus. How thick is his skull that I haven't hit brain by now?

Thunk. Thunk. Thunk.

OMG. My arm is so tired. Die already. Die!

Thunk. Shplack.

A yellowish liquid, like nuclear pond water, leaked out of his temple. Ugh. Disgusting! But it's working. So yay. *Shplack Shplack. Shplack. Crunch.*

That last hit was a winner. He went slack, mouth open, inches from my nose. Holy crap. I did it! That's right. Lloyd Lamb Wallace. Zombie slayer! Ha! Containment can eat my butt.

Unfortunately, he wasn't the only zombie. The faces of the dead guy's two other friends appeared over me. They bared their rotten black teeth and fell on top of us.

"Aaaaaaaaaaah!" I rolled side to side, using the dead zombie as a shield against the others, but I knew I couldn't keep this up forever. The weight of all three of them was too much.

Uuuuuuuuuuuuuuuh. Aaaaaaaaaaaaar. Uuuuuuuuuuuuuuuh.

"Don't move!" DeeDee screamed. A black and blue blur flashed behind the zombie puppy pile. Then I heard the most disgusting sound I had ever heard, like a pencil poking in and out of Jello. *Shhhppppppppplllllllllllllllllr.*

The zombies flailed and looked around, mouths open, growling.

Something round, sharp, and black emerged from the shoulder of

the zombie directly on top of me, pushing out, longer and more. *Shhhpppppppplllllllllllllllllr.*
It went straight through his coveralls and hit the linoleum next to me.

"The grabbers are multipurpose, you know." DeeDee stood behind the zombies, holding tight to the end of a long black metal rod. Huh. She'd popped the grabber off and jabbed the stick part through all three of the zombies, skewering them like freaking kabobs. Genius! She turned it to the left and the three of them peeled back like wiggling fat pancakes spatulaed off the griddle. "Hurry up, Lloyd. More are coming."

She didn't have to tell me twice. I scooted on out of there, toot suite. She let go of the rod and pulled me up, right as the rest of the zombies fell on the spot where I was lying a moment before.

Uuuuuur? Urrr? Huuuurrrhhh?

They seemed a bit confused that dinner had suddenly disappeared.

She yanked me out of that aisle in a split second, past that fourth zombie, which she had roped around the neck with another grabber. He was trying to scratch it off like a dog in a neck cone.

"Never fall down. Never let them get on top of you. Never let them surround you." Her voice was calm, but forceful, like she was scolding a toddler. She marched me right back to the weapons safe. "Bad news: The collars can't be fixed. We don't have any spares. Help isn't coming, so it's up to us to contain this."

Wow. That was a lot of bad news to process all at once. Did your knees just turn to pudding? No? Just me?

Uuuuuuuuuuuuuuuh. Aaaaaaaaaaaaar. Uuuuuuuuuuuuuuuh.

"Aaaaaah!" Too late. Too late. Too late!

The two zombie kabobs lurched into the space between the beer cave door and the end cap, dragging their limp and lifeless—for realsies this time—comrade along with them. Lucky for us, the pole got stuck, one end in a beer cooler door handle, the other in the nacho cheese dip end cap.

Uuuuuuuuuuuuuuuh. Uuuuuuuhhhh.

Run! I tugged DeeDee's sleeve but she was too busy rooting around in the cabinet. Gotta run!

Uh, no. The rest of them rounded the corner between us and the front door. They had us surrounded. Again.

Big Larry, baby free and recovering from child birth—Well, whatever you call it—had his giant pumpkin head sprawled out on the hot dog station. "Help us. Eat them!" I screamed and pointed at the shuffling herd.

Larry lifted a few leaves and shrugged. Shrugged!

Dude. "I know you eats zombies!" He couldn't do me a solid and eat one or two right now? I screamed at the baby Larries, lined up and snug in their pots. "What about you?"

One curled up a tendril and showed me his open, yet toothless mouth. "You guys are useless!"

DeeDee handed me another can grabber. "Are you fucking kidding me?"

Yeah. I admit I was salty.

"Containment, remember? We can't kill them, or we'll be short staffed forever. Besides, there's no danger. Well, not to the world, as long as we keep them inside, away from the general public," she said. "Relax. We'll lure them into their cooler and lock the door. Easy peasy. Huh. Do you smell bacon?"

Don't even get me started on the smell. This was just my luck. I couldn't grab a normal air freshener in the apocalypse, like pina colada or something. Nope. Not me. I had to be trapped with zombies smelling like a big strip of Lloyd bacon.

"Well, anyway, here's the plan," DeeDee said. "You hold the stockroom door open, I'll lead them into the cooler. Okay?"

Scrreeeeeeeeeeeeeeee.

The piercing sound of scraping metal echoed around the store. "What's that?" DeeDee looked up and around.

But it didn't take long to figure out where the sound came from. The metal storm shutters slid slowly up up and off the window.

Uh, that wasn't part of the plan.

Kevin stood on the control panel. He stared at us with wide blank eyes, one leg still on the red button.

"Kevin!" DeeDee yelled. "How did you get out?"

But I already knew. A handful of pixies hovered in midair, carrying the glass dome. They looked right at me, dropped it on the floor, and flipped me the bird as glass shards flew everywhere.

The zombie cleaning crew, lurching toward us, arms outstretched, preparing to eat us was no longer our biggest problem. There, pressed against every inch of glass—the doors, the windows—were people. And not just any people. People with eyes so wide they were circles, staring blankly, moaning. People who acted like zombies, but were alive. And they were trying to get in.

They were Monster Burger customers. The over-inflated runner who ate too many Dolly's doughnuts? He'd found another cheat food. He clutched an empty Monster Burger bag in his fist. Big Juicy, the guy in the overalls and the red hat who stared at a six-pack of beer for an hour? He was nearly flat up against the glass as a throng of bodies pressed in behind him. Big Juicy stared blankly at me and moaned, "huuuuuuuuunnnnnngggggeeeeeee. Eeeeeeeeeeaaaaat."

CHAPTER 22

"We better hurry. We can't let the zombies anywhere near these people, or the world will be halfway to Dawn of the Dead by morning."

A zombie—a dead one, just so we're clear—lunged for us. DeeDee didn't miss a beat. She roped it with her grabber and held him out and away, turning him this way and that, using his body as a shield to hold the other zombies back.

The people outside grew more agitated by the minute. In their bid to get in, they pressed so hard the poor guys up front were practically steam rollered to the glass. They pawed at the windows and the door.

"What do they want?" I squeaked.

"I don't know. I've never seen anything like this. But we have to keep those people outside, no matter what."

So wouldn't you know it, that's when that spiteful old pixie landed right on the knob and unlocked the door. I raised my fist and yelled, "Damn you, Ed McMahoooooooon!"

Seriously. I had a zombie kabob on my left, a zombie horde held at bay by a grandma can grabber in front of me, and this guy unlocks the door? Haven't we suffered enough?

Thankfully, the door opened out, not in—we have fire codes, you know—so that clump of people didn't spill in through the door like The Blob. Well, at least not right away. They'd have to back up first. Or rip the doors off the hinges. Yeah. Probably that. The metal edges heaved under the weight of all those bodies. Those doors wouldn't hold forever.

"Maybe they just want some chips?" *Hehr herp ha herp.* Yeah. I was desperation sobbing again. On the inside. Not out loud. No way would I let DeeDee see that.

Chink. Chink. Chink. The door glass split into tiny crystal snowflakes under the force of so many bodies.

"Hungeeeee. Eeeeeeet." They moaned. All of them.

I felt something press on my toes. It was Kevin, chewing the tip of my Puma. He moaned, joining the chorus of creeps outside, "hunnnnnngreeeee. Eeeeeeeet."

Okay, then. They were definitely not here for the chips. Great. Who else wanted to eat us tonight? Raise your hands!

The undead zombies had noticed the living ones on the other side of the door, and half of them had turned toward the pile of potential meat steaks on the other side of the glass.

Yep. This would definitely end well. What could go wrong?

Morty stepped out of the beer cave and waltzed up to us. He looked at the zombies—dead and alive—flipped his butterfly collar, said, "Nope," then walked right back into the beer cave and back through the portal.

Gee, Morty. Thanks for the assist.

"New plan." DeeDee handed me the grabber with the undead zombie on the other end. "Kevin's incapacitated, so I'm in charge. I'm calling it. This situation presents too much risk to the public. Kill the zombies. Well, the dead ones. Only the dead ones. Remember, aim for the head."

She rifled around in the weapons cabinet for a minute, then handed me a big red axe. An axe? No way. You had to get close to use one of these. "I want a gun!"

She looked at me. "We don't have guns. Too dangerous."

Too dangerous? Was Demon Mart totally kidding me right now? We've got zombies on the payroll, but a *gun* is too dangerous?

"This is a great weapon. See?" She took my axe.

She jumped in the air, raised that axe over her head and brought it down smack in the middle of a zombie head. The grabber yanked right out of my hand as that zombie dropped like a stone. His skull split like a cantaloupe. A putrid yellow liquid splurped everywhere as she planted a boot in his shoulder and heaved the axe out. She raised that axe again, twirled it around her head, and chopped a second zombie's head clean off his shoulders.

Holee. Shit.

She handed me the axe. "You take the triplets. I'll get the rest."

She was smiling. Smiling! Why is she smiling? This isn't fun!

"Steve will just have to get over it," she said as she dug around in the weapons safe again.

Uuuuuuuuuh. A zombie lunged for her. DeeDee, without hesitation, picked up her stool and jammed it right in that zombie's face. Which for most people would not be a kill shot, but she sunk one of the legs right into that guy's eyeball, and he dropped like a stone. Well. Not quite. Because the leg was still stuck in his eye socket, so he just dangled there. She shook it a few times—the dude was stuck on there pretty good—before she dropped the stool and started looking for a real weapon. She noticed me staring at her, jaw on the floor. "What? I've been training for this since the day I found out Night of the Living Dead was a documentary."

She filched something out of the weapons safe and tucked and rolled right at a gaggle of zombies.

Alrighty then. So we're doing this. This is happening.

Uuuuuuuuuuuh.

I turned around. The zombie kabobs were closing in. Okay. Not really. They grabbed at me, but they couldn't really move forward, because one end of that metal rod was still stuck in the chip rack and the other stuck on the cooler door handle. And they were dragging along a whole man's worth of extra dead weight. And they kept bumping into each other, hampering their efforts to lurch. They were kind of like a zombie three stooges.

I stepped closer, gripped the axe, and took aim at the one in the middle. It was the short fat dude who was theoretically lounging on a beach in Heaven. I raised my axe. And nearly dropped it on my head. Jesus, this thing is heavy! How was DeeDee swinging it around like that? She's half my size!

"Thou shalt not take the Lord's name in vain." Angel eight ball rolled right through some zombie legs. "And, this would be easier if you'd even once bicep curled something heavier than a potato chip."

Clunk. I dropped the axe right on beach bum zombie's head. And it went halfway through. Okay. That was too generous. The tip stopped about an inch in. His head didn't split like a melon. His face didn't cut in half. Not at all. It was kind of a letdown. And he was still moving. Alive? Well, this was awkward.

"You have to swing it with actual force," angel eight ball said.

"Shut up!"

DeeDee grunted and yelled behind me. "You want a piece of this? Do you? Huh? Bring it!"

Yep. She was kicking way more ass than me. This was embarrassing. I needed to step it up. I tugged my axe handle as hard as I could, trying to yank the blade out of this guy's head, but it didn't budge. His head moved forward with every pull. His milky white eyes stared at me while I tried to dislodge the axe. Man. I'd gotten it in there pretty good.

Unfortunately, the third zombie kabob grabbed my arm and pulled himself down the rod, closer to me. He opened his mouth to take a chomp of forearm. I tried to buck him off, but the beach bum lurched, the axe handle hit me in the shoulder, and I ended up flat on my butt. Ow! Jesus. That hurt.

Then a zombie came from behind and tried to eat me while I was down. He ran at me, and I put my legs up. My feet planted in his hips and for a second there, he looked like Superman flying valiantly in mid-air, as I kicked him over my head and straight into the zombie kabobs.

Wow. That was an epic move. Too bad it unstuck the kabobs from the cooler door.

At that point, with the kabobs and their plus one on the loose, something inside of me snapped. I clicked into some sort of Chuck Norris instinct mode. I charged the loose zombie and used his body to push the kabob guys back back back, to the other side of the store. Until they tripped on Bubby's TV and fell flat on the floor. I jumped on top of them. I had three zombie kabobs facing me, two of them still undead and writhing on the floor, and I had the fourth, loose zombie pinned face down on top of them.

That same kabob zombie once again slid down the rod in a bid to bite my arm. But nope. No way. Not today. I snatched a screwdriver off the floor. The one the pixies used to unbolt the TV and had just dropped there because pixies were fucking slobs who didn't clean up after themselves ever.

"Now you know how your mom feels." Angel eight ball rolled past.

I lifted that screwdriver above my head, then stabbed the bitey kabob guy right in the eye. Yellow liquid shot out as his eyeball exploded. It hit me right in the face.

Blech! Spppplltl. Spllltt. Splttt. Yeah. That was me spitting. A lot. Like, a lot a lot. You'd spit too if there was so much as a one percent chance a single drop of zombie goo could land in your mouth.

I dislodged the screwdriver, then sunk it deep into the back of zombie number four's skull. It crunched in, making a little skull volcano crater around the shaft. Man, this is gory.

He went limp. Take that! Lloyd Wallace, ultimate zombie killer!

One left. Except the screwdriver was stuck. I couldn't get a grip on the handle. Too slippery. Shoot.

Splllllllurrrrrrrp. Oh Jesus. That poor dead fat dude on heaven's beach? The one with my axe half in his head? He wanted to eat me so badly, he had nearly pulled himself off of the metal rod. The hard way. Up not out. The rod got hung up on his clavicle.

I didn't have time to waste. I grabbed the closest thing. A yellow oil funnel. Shit. Really? We needed to stock deadlier items in the hardware section.

He looked at me like "Uh oh" as I brought the oil funnel straight down into his eyeball. It exploded, funneling optical mush the wrong way UP through the spout and into my face with one unholy *spluuuuuuuuuuuup.*

Vlurp. Oh my God. So gross. But it worked. He stopped moving. He was *dead* dead.

"Lloyd! I lost one. Watch out!" DeeDee screamed across the store. I could see her, axe held tight at the ready, looking...down?

Huh. Oh. Wait. Never mind. Mystery solved. A zombie rounded the unicorns and scrunchies display and came crawling down the aisle straight at me. Crawling was generous. More like dragging himself. See, in order to crawl, you have to have legs. And this dude was half a man. Literally. He'd been chopped off at the belly button. He had nothing but a gray, rotten bag of intestines dragging along the floor where his legs should be.

Oh my God. Totally gonna barf. So gross.

But nope. I swallowed that bile down. I didn't have time to barf.

That zombie moved fast for half a dead dude. He slid across the polished linoleum, pushing cans and bottles aside, gliding along like a freaking Olympic speed skater. Except dead. With black teeth, growling because he wanted to eat me.

I didn't even have time to grab a weapon. I only had time to stand up, lift my foot and crunch down on his zombie face as he opened his mouth like a boa constrictor, ready to swallow my foot whole.

I stomped, and I stomped.

Raaaaaahrrrr.

Huh. The jerk isn't dead. So I stomped some more.

Raaaaaahrrrr. Stomp. *Uuuuuurh.* Stomp. *Uuuur.* Stomp.

Jesus. Die already! Stomp. Stomp. Stomp.

Raaaaaahrrrr.

He bit into the end of my Puma like a rabid dog, mouth foaming. He wouldn't let go. I could feel the pressure of his teeth through the fabric. Now I knew why DeeDee wore boots. Pumas weren't built to save the world. I had to get him off me before he bit my toes off.

I did a quick scan. The closest thing? A single bottle of bacon scented air freshener lay by this guy's temple. Really? Fuck me. I grabbed it and sprayed the air around the foot-chomping zombie.

Raaaaaahrrrr?

He opened his mouth. I slid my shoe out, and he started biting at the air. Huh. Who would have guessed? I spritzed the air a few more times to keep him busy while I found a more suitable weapon. Which wasn't easy. Because everything was on the floor. Even parts of the shelf. But we will never speak of that again, remember? Only one thing was left on an actual hanger in this aisle. An emergency road flare kit. Huh. Well, worth a shot!

I spritzed more bacon spray in the air to keep the half zombie busy while I opened the pack and scanned the instructions. I took one out, popped the cap and struck the tip like a match. A bright red flame kicked to life, and molten bits of chemical ick jumped out the end. Well. Here goes nothing.

I jammed it straight into his ear, lit side down. Oof. Good thing he's dead, because some of that burning goo landed on his face and burned right through his skin. I pounded the flare in like I was hammering a nail.

"Die! Die! Die!"

Yes. You heard that. A switch had flipped in my brain, turning me into a desperation-fueled killer. I mean, come on. If I lived through this, I would not be able to show my face around here ever again if I couldn't even kill *half* a zombie. The math was already emasculating enough. DeeDee had killed way more zombies than me, and mine had mostly been incapacitated.

The zombie stopped biting. His mouth went slack and his eyes twitched, darting back and forth in their dead sockets. His milky eyes glowed red for a split second, then popped like overripe zits. Liquid that I could only guess was hot brains oozed out. It flashed pink every now and again. Because holy shit. That flare was still lit.

His green, dead fingers finally stopped wiggling. I stomped on the flare one more time, just to be sure. "Have fun on the beach in heaven, asshole!"

"No. I'm pretty sure this guy went downstairs, if you know what I mean," angel eight ball said.

Didn't matter. Because I was a zombie killing machine. I had done it. And not on Xbox. For real! Because I am totes awesome.

Or not. Nope. Never mind. I rounded the corner only to see DeeDee standing in the middle of a pile of headless, no-longer-living dead bodies, soaking wet with whatever unholy liquid was inside of them. One lumbering zombie remained. He moaned and came at her, tripping over the bodies of his comrades. As he fell, reaching for her, her axe cut through him like butter, separating the top of his head from the bottom, right at the jaw. The force of the blow sent the top half flying. Right at me. Face first. Like a demon bowling ball. His dead milky eyes stared at me, still shocked, as he zoomed past my head and smacked into the beer cave door.

"Hit the shutters will you?" She picked a piece of guts off her face. "That door isn't gonna hold much longer."

CHAPTER 23

That was an understatement. The front door looked like thin ice that someone had tap-danced on in moon boots. Cracked. All over.

Hungeeeeeee. Eeeeeeeeet. Hungeeeeeee. Eeeeeeeeet. Hungeeeeeee. Eeeeeeeeet.

They said it over and over. Moaning. And moaning. And moaning some more. Okay. We get it already. You want to eat us!

I hit the red button on the console.

Screeeeeeeeeeeeee.

Yes! The metal shutters slid down.

Screeeeee...oooooop.

Shit. The shutters slid back up as soon as they tapped the top of Big Juicy's head. It must have a safety sensor like a garage door. And yes, like a dumbass, I hit the button a couple more times hoping it would magically roll down and stay down.

Click. DeeDee leaned hard against the push bars and turned the lock. She looked at me and shrugged. Yeah. The door hinges were creaking from all the pressure and the glass was gonna give out any second. We both knew locking it wouldn't do much good, but it couldn't hurt to put lipstick on turds at this point.

"Help me." DeeDee ran to the hot dog station. "We can use this to block the door."

Big Larry was gracious enough to move off the top and lie down on the floor directly under the slushy machines, mouth open. One giant leaf worked the levers, splurping a sugary midnight snack straight into his gaping maw.

We pushed as hard as we could. *Scrruuuuu.* It moved maybe an inch. Jesus. Did we really need a thousand pound stand to hold a couple of hot dog rollers? Speaking of. One more sad push sent all the hot dogs plopping off the heat rollers, straight into Big Larry's mouth. He spit them out. Huh. Guess he didn't like hot dogs.

Wait a minute. He was big, strong, and from hell. "Can you give us a hand?"

Big Larry huffed at me, then reared up and hit the hot dog stand with his giant pumpkin head. Judging from the look he was giving me, he only did it to get me to shut up and leave him alone. It shot across the room and chinked right into the door. The glass cracked more. And the next hand that pounded on it nearly broke all the way through.

"Well, that's not good, but thanks, Larry," DeeDee said. "Can I ask you another favor? Can you sit on top of it? It'll buy us more time."

Big Larry looked put upon, but relented.

"I know, buddy. I wouldn't ask if it weren't important." She patted him on the melon. "Lloyd, help me move him."

DeeDee and I draped a couple of big leaves over our shoulders and heaved, helping him to the door. His white wiggling roots spilled out and around the pot, pushing him along like creepy toes. Jesus, he was heavy. Moving Larry fifteen feet felt about as easy as that Hercules plane pull in the World's Strongest Man Contest. I mean, I'm guessing. I've never personally done it, but I saw it on YouTube once.

But we made it. Big Larry laid his head on the hot dog station and collapsed, exhausted. He unfurled his leaves and tendrils, which covered most of the door.

"Thanks, Larry. I know it's hard, but we need to keep those bad people outside. They could hurt the babies." She glanced at the baby Larries, then at the clock. "Oh shoot. It's dinnertime. Lloyd. Can you look for Kevin while I feed them?"

Um, okay?

Against a nearly non-stop soundtrack of "hungeeeeeeee eeeeeeeeeet," I stepped slowly through the pile of zombie bodies looking for Kevin. If there was one silver lining, it's that he was way bigger and fatter than usual. Because I'd never find a regular size roach in this haystack of guts and gore and upended shelves.

DeeDee disappeared into the beer cave. She emerged a few minutes later rolling a dolly stacked with forties. She handed each baby Larry two forties of Schlitz malt liquor—the kind with the blue bull on the label. She popped the caps, put what looked like a nipple on the bottle, and patted each one of them on the head. They clugged and jugged and sucked those forties like human babies with a bottle of milk. Their spiky teeth were already growing back in, and they'd all doubled in size already.

DeeDee then went back into the cooler and came back out with a big silver beer keg, which she rolled up next to Big Larry. She unfurled a clear plastic tube and Larry put it in his mouth like it was a twisty straw.

I did eventually find Kevin. He was behind the counter, mindlessly circling his Monster Burger takeout bag. "Hungeeeee. Eeeeeeeet."

"Yeah yeah. We know." I scooped up Kevin and the bag, then retreated to the employee lounge. DeeDee came in behind me, locking and securing all the doors.

Gulp. The employee lounge. Posh, like a Vegas nightclub. Filled with any kind of food or drink you could ever want. Heaven right? Nope. It's hell, because there's always a catch. Like dead people cooking your food. I hadn't been in here since I found out Chef was a—

"Uuuuuuuuuuh," he said.

Yeah. That.

He stood in his usual spot behind the grill in his crisp white uniform, chef's hat perky and spotless, sniffing the air. I craned my neck, trying to get a good look at his collar. Green lights. Phew. Still on.

"Normally I would never suggest coming back here in a zombie outbreak. Holing up where they can corner you should always be the last resort." DeeDee double checked the locks on the door. "But at least we can see what we're up against."

She pulled a chair over to the row of employee lockers tucked in the corner at the end of the drink coolers. She stepped up on the chair, put a boot in the high shelf of her locker and foisted herself up. She sat on top, messing with a black rectangle on the wall. It looked like the cover of an electrical box, until DeeDee opened it up, and there was a window behind it. Huh. Who knew?

She looked through it for a long time before she said anything. "Okay, so there are thirty of them outside the pawn shop and another twenty outside of Henrietta's. And we've got thirty, forty...about a hundred right outside. Do you want the good news or the bad news?"

Uh. Good news. Only good news. Please let there be good news.

"These people are basically zombies, but they're alive. Which is good. For them. Not so good or us. If they were dead, we could chop their heads off and be done with it. But these people are alive, so store policy is de-possess. No casualties. We can't kill or injure any of them. The bad news is I don't know how to de-possess them, because I don't know anything about the magic spell that made them this way in the first place."

"What's the good news?" I didn't remember hearing any good news, did you?

"They're alive. That was the good news."

Oh. Great.

Suddenly, I felt a tiny sharp pain on my neck, like a mosquito bite. I put my hand up to it and found Kevin. "Ow! He tried to eat me! Stop it!"

I grabbed his portly body and pulled him off of me. His legs wiggled. His eyes were wide circles, nearly round. He looked like one of those cartoon hypnotism victims, with the swirling black and white eyes.

He moaned, "hunnnnnnnnngeeeeeeeee."

"Well, don't bite me. I'm not lunch!"

Then he chomped down on my knuckle. That's it! I flicked him onto the nearest table and tipped his Monster Burger bag upside down, showering him with fries. "Eat this."

He immediately bit down into the closest fry.

Mmm. It did smell good. It couldn't hurt to carb load before the next round of zombie slaying, right? I popped a fry in my mouth. Blech! Healthy sucks! "Sorry, Kevin. I know you don't like it, but dude. Fries *need* salt."

I grabbed the shaker out of the tabletop caddy and went to town. I let that salt rain like it was monsoon season. I salted the fries, the burger, even lifted the bun to get it all over the patty. Tiny white salt grains bipped and bopped and bounced around in a cascade of deliciousness. I mean, I drowned that food in salt. Probably three times as much as I would have usually sprinkled on, but I had to make up for what Earl wasn't allowed to put in it anymore. I grabbed a fry, dumped more salt on it, and ate it. OMG. So good! Now *that* tastes like Monster Burger.

"Nommmmm. Mooommm. Mummmmm." Kevin put two whole fries in his mouth and swallowed them. Wow. He must really be out of it if the salt didn't stop him.

I stuffed a handful of fries in my mouth. That's when I noticed DeeDee had been talking this whole time. Oops. I nodded and pretended I had followed the entire conversation.

"...I'm sure the Monster Burger zombie curse is on the food. Why else would they give it away for free?"

I immediately spit out all the fries. Curse? On the food? Fuck me.

"Oh, what was that? The evil magic curse was IN THE JUNK FOOD? THAT I TOLD YOU NOT TO EAT?" Angel eight ball rolled into the pile of fries, like he was standing on the bodies of his slain enemies. "See? You should listen to me. Mysterious ways indeed."

Great. He was right. And he'll never let me forget it.

DeeDee looked at me. I still had a french fry in my hand. She looked at the fries on the table, and at Kevin, munching away. "Oh no. How much did you eat?"

"Just a couple?" This time. A pit opened up in my stomach. I had eaten Monster Burger, not as much as Kevin, but still. Did that mean I was gonna be one of them? Shit. I was gonna turn, wasn't I? I'd played the games. All it took was one bite. Okay. Usually something or someone biting you, not you biting something, but still.

Tink. Tink. The sound of breaking glass echoed through the store.

"We're out of time. We need a plan," she said. "It won't be long until they're all inside. We can't stay back here. We'll be trapped."

Or would we? The window was a rectangle about the same width as a pizza box. A medium pizza. I wouldn't fit through it, but DeeDee could. I mean, her boobs might get stuck. Unless maybe she could fold them or tuck them under her arms. Can chicks do that? Do boobs smoosh in an emergency? I wasn't exactly clear on how boobs worked, but in my experience they were both versatile and amazing, a wonder of nature, so anything was possible.

My voice shook. I was about to be a hero. I was about to sacrifice myself for true love. DeeDee must live. "I'll stay. You should go."

"You should stop staring at her tits already, pervert. Jesus, you're as bad as Morty." Kevin stood with two legs on his hips tisking me and two legs rubbing his temples. "Man. My head feels like Larry Bird's been tap dancing on my eyebrows. I haven't felt this bad since that necromancer roofied me back in ninety-seven."

We looked at Kevin. Kevin looked at us. "What are you two dumbasses staring at? Holy shit! What did you do to me? Why am I fat?"

He ran his legs over his carapace. Yep. Roach muffin tops all around.

"Kevin. It's you!" DeeDee slid down off the window ledge and practically hurdled everything between the lockers and the table to get to him.

"Of course it's me. Who else would it be? What? Did y'all suddenly get stupid? What time is it? Who's watching the store? Why are we all back here? Is this like an employee meeting or something? Where's Faust?"

"Kevin," DeeDee said. "What's the last thing you remember?"

"Waking up in this pile of shitty salt-covered fries. I'm looking at you, dipshit." He moved his fingers back and forth from his eyes to mine. "I know you ruined my food with your damn hippie ocean pellets. You trying to kill me? I have high blood pressure, you know. I'm on a low-sodium diet for a reason!"

"Before that," DeeDee said.

Tink. Tink. Crash. More broken glass out front. The moans were getting louder.

"What the hell was that? Did some asshole just break into my store? Oh, hell no. Go get me the taser. I'll show those bastards."

DeeDee paced and tapped her lip, muttering to herself like she was thinking. "Serpent and the Rainbow. The Magic Island. White Zombie. Aha! I think I've got it."

"No way." Kevin huffed. "We aren't listening to nineties industrial bands on my shift. You listen to that crap on your own time. Now let's go show that robber who's boss."

"Not the band. Kevin. I'm talking about voodoo zombies. I hate to tell you this, but you were turned into a living walking zombie controlled by some outside force. But the spell broke."

"Voodoo? Did Doc mess up again? I tell ya, he's slipping since he got that fat, sassy girlfriend. Guy's a chubby chaser, for sure. Wait. What zombies? What are you talking about?"

Man. Kevin really had been out of it.

"Uh. There are like a hundred fat guys trying to break in the front door to eat all of us right now," I said. Hey. Might as well pull the Band-Aid off, right?

"Great. Just great. We're open two weeks, and the place goes to shit again. I just moved my whole record collection here because I caught my stupid broke dickhead roommate pawning them for cash. Whatever you do tonight, you stay away from my records, do you understand? My Dio and Zebra are mint. Original labels!" Kevin paced—okay, waddled— agitated at the thought of it. "Go grab me a water, kid. I gotta wash all this damn salt out of my mouth. Mmm. It's as drier than the butt end of Nevada in there."

DeeDee's perfectly tweezed eyebrows furrowed. "That's it! Lloyd. You're a genius!"

"Wait a minute. Did I wake up in Bizarro world?" Kevin thumbed an arm at me. "Did you just call this one a genius?"

"Chef. Make us french fries. All of them. Every single one you've got," DeeDee said. "Lloyd, Kevin. You guys gather up as much cooking spray, salt, and paper clips as you can find. Meet me back here in five minutes. I have a plan."

160

CHAPTER 24

Ten minutes later Kevin, DeeDee, and I stood between the counter and aisle four, heavily salted. I was armed with two five-gallon buckets of fries, one by each foot, and two old-lady can grabbers, one in each hand.

All the Larries locked vines. We had lined their pots up in a row that gently curved from the front door, parallel to the counter, blocking the entrances to all the aisles. We'd essentially made a chute, a bottleneck, so the burger zombies only had one way to go and could only move in two or three at a time. Unfortunately, that chute led directly to me.

Maybe I should back up and explain.

While Chef deep fried every potato in the building, we'd changed into some extra coveralls from the zombie utility closet. We sprayed the fabric down with cooking oil and generously salted it. Then, DeeDee used a dozen packs' worth of paper clips to hook single french fries like worms on a fishing lure. We dipped each fry in salt and hung them all over the suits, front and back. We looked like cheap Christmas trees covered in potato ornaments.

"Explain the plan to me one more time." I tried hard to keep my knees from trembling.

"Salt breaks the spell. Use the grabber to drop french fries in their mouths. They eat the fry, they're neutralized. They bite the suit? It's salted. They're neutralized." She recounted the plan as she strapped a shaker of Morton's to each of my hips like they were six guns in holsters. "We've got a pretty good coating on us, so it should be enough. But this will only work if we keep them in the bottleneck. We're outnumbered, so we have to play this like the Spartans at Thermopylae."

"Ther-what?" I looked around, wondering if that was another weapon I was supposed to use. She didn't notice.

"If too many get in at once, they could trample us to death or rip us apart before we salt them all. Stay on your feet this time. Don't fall down."

"Are you sure this is gonna work?" Gulp. Nope. Totally not gonna work. We're doomed. "I mean, it's just salt."

"Caroline's mystery partner removed the salt from the recipes the minute they bought the restaurant. You salted your Monster Burger before you ate it, and you didn't change. Kevin hates salt. He ate the food. He changed. You salted Kevin's food. He turned back. A lot of ancient cultures believed salt was magic. Doc uses it all the time. There has to be something to it. Kevin! Stop. Spit it out! We need every last one of those. Don't you think you've had enough?"

He was neck deep in one of my buckets, chowing down. The fry level had dropped at least an inch. "Hey. A man's gotta eat. I'm starving!"

"How can you possibly be hungry?" DeeDee asked. "You've eaten nonstop for two weeks!"

"I don't know. Maybe I'm going through a growth spurt or something. Why are you complaining? More of me to love. Heh. Heh." He shoved another fry, whole, right into his mouth. "Mmmmm. Nummm. Num. Mum."

This plan was definitely not going to work.

"Okay. Places everyone." DeeDee clapped her hands and inspected the row of baby Larries like a drill sergeant.

They interlocked vines, creating a hopefully impenetrable spiky red wall of vegetation. If you're wondering how a bunch of newborn plants could make an effective line of defense, yeah. I wondered that, too. But normal earth rules don't apply to hell creatures. The babies had grown. They were nearly as tall as me now. Because they'd had a midnight snack. While we were holed up in the back, they'd nommed that pile of cleaning crew zombies down to nothing. (And killed a dolly stacked with Schlitz.) One of the baby Larries still had a leg, from the knee down, work boot still on it, hanging out of his mouth. It moved up and down as he chewed. Because this was Hades' hedge of nightmares. And, you know, they couldn't eat those zombies when they were chasing *me*. Not that I'm angry about that. (I totally am.)

DeeDee jumped up on the counter and stood by the register, grabbers in hand, flanked by her own buckets of salty potatoes. Kevin crawled up the wall and across the ceiling, a row of picnic sized salt shakers strapped around his waist like grenades. He hunkered down on an acoustic tile, upside down, ready to sprinkle salt on any unsuspecting open mouth that passed underneath.

"All right," she declared. "Let them in. Slowly."

Big Larry, looking moderately livelier and currently sucking on the tail end of his third full keg of beer, pushed the hot dog station back two feet, peeled his leaves away from the front door, and dragged his pot behind the wall of Baby Larries. His job was to pull the recently de-possessed people onto the other side of the hedge, out of the line of fire.

As soon as he moved, the throngs broke through the glass. It shattered, sending chunks crashing and sliding all over the floor. People pushed in around the hot dog station, squeezing like toothpaste out of a tube. The Larries stiffened. I loaded my grabbers with fries.

Go time.

Huuuuuunggggggeeeee. Eeeeeeeet. Eeeeeeeet. Eeeeeeeet. Eeeeeeeet.

It turned from moan to chant as soon as they saw us. They came, quick and lots of them. But the lane was narrow and the baby Larries strong, so they immediately squeezed into a tight line of wriggling bodies, bouncing between the Larries and the counter.

DeeDee was the first line of defense. Despite our best attempts to slow the inflow, she was quickly surrounded by moaning zombies grabbing and biting at her legs. Unruffled, she swung her grabber around, dropping fries into open mouths then sinking those grabbers into buckets, reloading lightning fast.

Big Larry was on top of his game. He spread his leaves and vines across the ceiling, and he dipped down and grabbed people the second a fry dropped in their mouth. The bastards were still chewing as they flew up and over the Baby Larries into the candy aisle, which we were using as a holding pen while we figured out if this was actually gonna work.

Kevin was the second line of defense. As soon as a burger zombie made it past DeeDee, Kevin swooped in. Literally. I watched with horror as he dropped down off the ceiling straight into the open mouth of a Lululemon soccer mom. He waved his freshly salted behind around in her mouth yelling, "you like that, huh?" as she tried to eat him.

Holy shit. Any second now, she's gonna crunch down and roach guts were gonna squirt straight into her tonsils. Or not. She stopped chewing, stopped moaning, and stared into space, confused. Then she spit Kevin out, right onto the next guy's shoulder. A second later, Larry grabbed that soccer mom by her ankle, flipped her upside down and dropped her in the candy aisle.

I was the third line of defense. Anyone who got past DeeDee and Kevin came to me. DeeDee was so fast on the draw, there weren't many stragglers. Five minutes in, I'd only dropped one grabber's worth of fries into three or four mouths.

Hellz yeah. We were totally rocking the plan.

We salted and fried, and salted and fried. Big Larry snatched and dragged. The candy aisle filled up with very confused, out of it people. DeeDee had nailed it. As soon as those people swallowed, their moans changed. Their arms stopped reaching, and they stopped trying to bite us and eat us. It was totes working. Except they were still hungry. We had about thirty people blocked into the candy aisle, ripping open candy bags and pouring Skittles, gummy bears, M& M's, you name it, straight into their mouths.

Screee. Tink. Tink. Tink.

Uh oh.

That sound was bending metal and breaking glass. A wave of bodies pushed through the front door. The force of them pushed the hot dog stand completely clear of the frame and shattered all the glass.

The little Larries held tight, but couldn't hold the line with the force of all of those people pouring in at once. A few of them fell over, pots rolling as the burger zombies rushed past them. Big Larry stopped snatching newly salted customers, opting to protect his babies instead.

Huuuuuungeeeee. Eeeeeeeet. Eeeeeeet. Eeeeeeeeet.

The moans were loud, angry. The burger zombies spilled into the area between the slushies and the beer cave, and a swell of them rolled into what was left of the chute. I had to give the baby Larries props. The ones that were still standing tried hard to hold the wall.

"Look out, kid!" Kevin screamed. He was upside down. Shaker furiously shaking. "Incoming!"

Big Juicy ran straight at me. You couldn't miss him, in those overalls and that stupid red hat. He popped at me like a champagne cork, propelled forward by the desire to eat me. *Oh. Shit.* I lunged and parried, fry and grabber out, like I was a freaking musketeer. I aimed straight for his mouth, and I hit him. Right in the eye. But before I could slide that fry down into his gaping maw, he snatched my grabber and twisted it so hard, it flipped out of my hand, up and away, curlicuing through the air. It landed on the other side of the Larries, who struggled to contain the swell of people running in behind him.

Big Juicy tackled me. As the two of us fell, the world seemed to move in slow motion. The fry buckets tipped, spuds spewed all over me and the floor.

Kevin screamed "Banzai!" and dropped off the ceiling, right onto the face of the lady who'd coasted in on Big Juicy's wake. I couldn't see DeeDee for the crowd leaning across the counter, arms out, chanting "Eeeeeeeet. Eeeeeeet. Eeeeeeeeet."

I hit the floor. Big Juicy landed squarely on top of me. *Pffft. Uuuuuuh.*

Yep. He was a big one. He squeezed all the air right out of me. Big Juicy opened his mouth and tried to bite me. It took all my strength to hold his face away. I bucked and squirmed, but dude. This guy didn't budge. Big Juicy was a really, really big boy.

"Eeeeeeeet. Eeeeeeeeeeeeeeeeeet." He snapped his teeth.

He opened wide. He put his weight into it, and he sunk his teeth into me. Into my sleeve. At the elbow. Because I was a total chicken and had covered my face. His wide eyes looked even more confused when he realized my elbow was so deep in his mouth, he couldn't move his jaw up and down to chew. Ha! Take that!

I slid my other hand across the floor, gathering as many fries as I could, and I was just about to smoosh some into the corner of Big Juicy's mouth when the faces appeared. A dozen people, eyes wide and vacant, leaned down over me and moaned. "Eeeeeeeeeeeet"

Oh. Shit.

They had me surrounded. They were on me in a split second, biting into my coveralls, clawing at me. Oh God, Oh God, Oh God. They're gonna rip me open! *Dear Baby Jesus, please don't let them eat my guts!*

Yep. I was gonna die.

Eaten by a giant hillbilly. And a bald guy in a tweed blazer. And a chick with a bright red beehive and rhinestone glasses. And a bubba in a camo baseball hat. Then the beefy jogger addicted to doughnuts stepped up to the Lloyd buffet. Shit. If I had sold him the doughnut, he wouldn't be trying to eat me right now!

The store filled with moans. And screams. DeeDee's screams. Tears welled up in my eyes. My heart felt like a lead weight. And not just because a four hundred pound hillbilly was steam rolling me. This was the worst feeling ever. I was being eaten, sure, but worse: I'd let DeeDee down. I couldn't save her. I wasn't a hero. I couldn't be *her* hero. I would die as I had lived: A failure. I should have pushed her out that tiny window and done this alone. At least she would have survived.

This was destined to end badly from the start. How many people actually get to save the world twice?

CHAPTER 25

Lying there, trapped underneath a four hundred pound man who'd clamped his teeth around my elbow like an alligator, I made a decision. I was not going to give up. Sure. It seemed hopeless. I had a dozen people chewing on my legs, trying to eat me, and a dozen more waiting behind them to slurp up the scraps, but there was still hope, right? I was going to fight. I had no other choice. I had to save DeeDee—and the world—or die trying.

I scrambled, trying desperately to grab the Morton's off my holster, but Big juicy had rolled onto my one free hand. I couldn't get it out from under him. I was trapped.

Mouths pressed into my body. I felt the sharp edges of their teeth, the pressure of their lips and jaws as they bit me, but I didn't see any blood or feel my guts spilling out. Not yet. It's like they couldn't get their incisors all the way through the coveralls. The fabric was too thick.

I grunted and wiggled, and my breath formed a white cloud. The temperature had seriously dropped in here. Kevin's dickhead roommate probably messed with the thermostat again. My teeth were chattering it was so cold, but that sure didn't stop Big Juicy. He chewed on my elbow like it was his job.

They all kept chewing. "Mmmmmm. Nummmm. Ummmmm. Nummmm. Mmmmm."

And more burger zombies joined them, gathering around me like I was the prime rib station at the Golden Corral. Faces—so many faces—looked down at me. "Hungeeeee. Eeeeeeeeet."

I had no way to fight them off. I was pinned. Gulp. This was it. This was the end.

A shadow blocked out the light above me. The faces closed in, eyes wide and hypnotized. They moaned. "Eeeeeet. Eeeeet. Eeeet."

I closed my eyes and braced to be eaten to death.

Crunk. Thunk. Thud.

Any minute now. Wait for it. But no new teeth bit into me. I opened one eye, just to scope out the situation, but the faces were gone, replaced by another face. Bright. Translucent. Blue. With eight white eyes and giant pincers.

Bubby, the two story tall jelly centipede from hell stood where the zombie faces used to be. He had knocked them away. He looked confused by the whole situation. He wore an impossibly large yellow and green flower print Hawaiian shirt and held at least eight margaritas with salted rims in his claw arms. Oh. He must be fresh back from Jamaica.

Bloop blup. Click?

"Help me."

He looped his claw arm through Big Juicy's overalls and lifted him off me. He dangled there in the air, teeth still biting, wiggling around. He was so big even Bubby had a hard time holding him up.

"Salt," I sucked in air, finally able to breathe. "Feed him salt."

I sat up and grabbed the Morton's out of my holster. I was about to shake it on Big Juicy, but Bubby had taken care of it. Big Juicy sucked on the salted rim of one of Bubby's margaritas, looking a bit confused about how he'd ended up speared on the claw of a giant hell centipede for cocktail hour. And, just my luck, *that's* the moment Big Juicy spit out a paper clip, fry eaten, spell broken.

So I turned the shaker on the dudes chewing on my legs. I shook that thing, and the salt rained down like snowflakes at Christmas.

The beefy jogger stopped chewing on me and sat up. He had half a french fry hanging out of his mouth. Then the guy in the camo hat stopped, sunk his finger into his mouth, and pulled out a paper clip. He dropped it and chewed up whatever was left in there.

The bald guy in tweed was more determined. He lunged at me, and I shoved a handful of fries straight into his mouth. Dude. Those had totally been on the floor, but he didn't seem to mind. He crunched them down to nothing in less than a minute. Then looked at me like, "Who are you?"

None of my assailant were trying to eat me any more. They sat, looking around as if they were stunned. DeeDee stood on the counter, pouring salt into the open mouths of the crowd around her. Big Larry had righted his fallen babies, taken their place in the hell hedge, and tried once again to separate the possessed from the de-possessed.

"Hungeee. Eeeeeeet." The moans came from behind me. I turned around, salt shaker in one hand, wad of mooshy floor french fries in the other. All the zombies Bubby had knocked away from me lay in a pile at the end of aisle five, confused and moaning on top of the broken shelves and bottles of motor oil. I sprung into action. Well, okay. I scrambled. I am chubby with a history of minimal thigh work outs. I don't really spring. But I was over those fiends, shaking my salt shakers into their mouths like I was shaking maracas in Gloria Estefan's back-up band, in under a minute.

"Good work, kid!" Kevin crawled across the chubby red-headed lady's face, knocking her rhinestone glasses right off. He dutifully shook his salt shaker into her mouth. Until he caught a glimpse down her V-neck sweater. "Wow. This one's got a face like a foot but she's smuggling watermelons. Check out these cans, kid."

"Are you serious? Zombies!"

"Yeah yeah." Kevin shrugged. He hopped onto the back of another guy's head, a dad jeans dude who reached out for me and kicked his legs, obviously still determined to eat me. Kevin scuttled down the side of his face, picked a french fry off his back and shoved it in the dude's mouth. "Larry! We got more over here!"

Bubby had dropped Big Juicy on the floor. He lay there, beached like a whale. He stared at me—face blank as a sheet of paper—as a red vine wrapped around him and dragged him backward. Satan's hedge parted, Larry yanked Big Juicy through, and the hedge closed up again.

One by one the fiends stopped clawing at us. They stood around, staring blankly, confused. One by one, the Larries' vine-fence parted, pulling them into the VIP de-possessed section in the candy aisle.

The store was absolutely packed with people, but they'd stopped moaning and they'd stopped trying to eat us. For the most part they milled around, looking confused. The place was wrecked, of course. The front door had broken out completely, frame and all. Aisle six was toppled. And the recently de-possessed had nearly eaten the candy aisle bare. They were ankle deep in empty wrappers. It seems like we'd only broken half the curse. They were still hungry, just not for human meat.

I spotted Big Juicy stuffing a whole pack of beef jerky in his mouth. And I mean stuffing. With his fists. They were all still eating. A grandma in a powder blue cardigan pounded bottle after bottle of Strawberry Quik. And the beefy jogger with the lifetime doughnut ban? He was on his knees in front of the doughnut case when a Larry vine got hold of his leg. He shoved two devil's food cake chocolate frosted in his mouth, double-fisted, as Larry dragged him across the floor.

But we'd done it. We'd made it through.

DeeDee marched around the store barking orders, in crisis management mode. "Kevin. I'm going in back to get more rotten meat for the baby Larries."

Kevin stood on an end cap, directing the Larries like one of those runway traffic guys with the orange light cones at the airport, while sipping one of Bubby's margaritas. Bubby helped Kevin sort through the remaining people to figure out who still needed de-possessed.

My nerves were frayed, on high alert, but my body felt like it'd been trampled by buffalo. My coveralls were soaked with saliva, and most of the french fry lures had bent or been pulled off. Only a few dangling, smooshed fries remained. But we had to finish this. So I wandered through the store, salt shakers ready, trying to be useful.

When Bubby blurped down the housewares aisle, I found a guy under his tail, lying on his stomach, wiggling.

"Uh, you okay, dude?"

"Eeeeeeeeeeeeet! Eeeeeeeeeeeeeet!" The jerk chomped down on my ankle.

"Aaaaaaahhh! Zombie!" I popped that shaker into action and salted my leg like it was a pretzel. But that grizzly zombie kept right on chewing, I tried to pull my leg away, but he had a death grip on me. He scooched right along with me.

"Mmmmm. Mmmmmm. Mmmmmmmmmmmmmmmmmmm."

Aw, man. He wasn't biting me, was he? Nope. No, he wasn't. This was kind of worse. His mouth was wide open, and he rubbed his tongue around on my ankle, licking up salt. Jesus. He was french-kissing my ankle bone.

"That's the most action you've had in a while, isn't it kid?" Kevin stood next to me. "Larry. We got another one over here!"

Larry dragged the lascivious licker away, and he finally let go of my leg.

Kunk. Kunk. Kunk. The door to the stockroom kicked open and Chef stomped out, metal mecha-braces scraping through leftover zombie parts and Big Larry afterbirth. He pushed a cart heaped with rotten meat, and scooped out portions to each open hungry mouth in the row of tired, slightly wilted baby Larries.

DeeDee stepped out of the door behind him. She looked at me and smiled. My heart skipped a beat. She was a vision, a Venus in french fry-baited coveralls. She walked over to me and said, "Are you all right?"

I nodded, and was just about to say something romantic, like "I will be all right as long as you are safe and alive, my beloved!"

When she began spraying my coveralls with cooking oil and shaking a can of salt over me and said, "Good. Take a bucket of fries and go save Doc and Henrietta."

CHAPTER 26

There is no creepier experience than being outside, alone, at night, when the only sounds are zombie moans and the rattling of glass as their fists pound on windows, trying to break in so they can eat you. Nothing. Creepier.

If there was a silver lining to this turd of an evening, it was that there weren't many zombies left outside. Apparently, almost all of them had chosen to descend on Demon Mart, so they'd already been salted and potatoed into submission. Maybe whoever created them hated me and DeeDee more. Or, maybe we were more appetizing than a really buff, gruff Pawn shop owner with a vaguely Caribbean accent and a teeny eighty-year-old woman who hawked dashboard Jesuses all day. Who can say?

There were maybe fifteen burger zombies in front of Doc's shop. They all had their hands up, like they were doing the wave at a high school basketball game. It took me a minute to figure out they were reaching for Doc, who stood on the edge of his flat roof with a bright green T-shirt cannon that said "Canton Crocodiles" on the side.

"Hello, New man!" He called to me. "How was your night?"

He had to be kidding, right?

"Do you need help?" I raised my bucket of french fries and immediately felt stupid.

"You are funny, new man." He laughed. And when I say laugh, I mean bellowed, deep and loud, from the bottom of his belly. "Ha. Ha. Ha. Fatty boom boom, help me. Priceless. Now go. I will save the old woman. Jesus Saves shares a roof!"

My cheeks went hot. He just called me fat. And laughed in my face. And embarrassed me in front of all these people.

"Don't be too upset. They're zombified. They won't remember." Angel eight ball was triangle up in my bucket of fries. "But look at those biceps. You should ask Doc where he works out. If you were stronger, you could have rolled that fat guy off you."

"Where the hell have you been? You hung me out to dry back there."

"What was I supposed to do? I work from home!"

Doc fired his Canton Crocodiles cannon. Sparkling yellow crystals showered down all over the people trying to break into the pawn shop. One by one, the crowd lowered their hands and looked around, confused. Doc moved to the corner, shooting crystals off the other side of the building above the Jesus Saves Discount Religious Supply Store.

Huh. He really did have it covered. Nothing for me to do out here. I turned around, and three little old ladies with white cotton ball hair and pastel embroidered sweatshirts grabbed me.

"Eeeeeeeet."

What? Oh shit! I dropped the bucket.

One granny opened wide and sunk her teeth into my collarbone. Because that's about as high up as she could reach. The other two dug right in. One bit the nearest love handle, the other sunk her dentures right into my butt cheek. "Aaaaaaaaah!"

It hurts! It hurts! I pushed, but couldn't get them off me. I would have punched them, but dude. They were someone's grandma! I spun, but the grannies spun right around with me. They clamped those teeth down harder and held on for dear life. Man. Poligrip really works!

Ow ow ow ow ow! OMG, they had me. Death by grandmas. And I didn't even see it coming.

Rip.

Uh oh. The coveralls. My only defense. The collarbone grandma stumbled backward. A strip of fabric hung from her mouth. She straightened up, locked eyes with me, sucked that fabric in between her sparkling white dentures, chewed it up and swallowed it. She stared at me, blinked a few times, then said, "Oh dear. What did I just eat? Something isn't agreeing with me." She rubbed her belly. "Gloria? Edna? Do you have any Tums in your purse?"

One set of teeth, then another, eased up. Then I felt a tiny squeeze on my butt cheek.

"Ooh. Nice tushy. Call me sometime, handsome." Edna winked at me. She smiled and the ring of salt on her lips glistened in the red glow of the Demon Mart sign.

The love handle biter just looked around, confused.

Okay, then. Awkward. But the salt worked!

"Sorry dear," Gloria patted my arm and the three of them waddled off into the darkness, arguing about where they parked the car.

Well then.

"Number seven! Number seven." A shout came from behind me.

I turned around. Earl staggered across the Demon Mart parking lot, his tracksuit smudged with dirt and ripped at one knee. He held one arm across his belly as he moved, like he was injured.

"Earl! Are you all right?" He had no idea how relieved I was to see him. "I thought you were dead!"

Or worse.

Earl panted, trying to catch his breath. "Why do you have a whole bucket of french fries?"

"Long story. What happened? The phone went dead."

"The new guys went nuts! They attacked me. It sounds crazy, but it's like they were trying to eat me or something. I barely got out of there. It has to be drugs, man. The dudes never slept, never took breaks, never stopped working. You can only do that with a little chemical assistance, know what I mean? They must have had too much. Street drugs are crazy these days. Remember that guy in the news that ate a dude's face? I was afraid I was gonna be that dude!"

I didn't have the heart to tell him he almost was that dude. I gave him a quick once over, looking for bites. I didn't see any blood. Phew.

"The zom—the new guys. Where are they now?"

He pointed at Monster Burger. "Still inside. I snuck out the back and locked them in. They work hard, but they aren't too bright. Look at 'em, banging on the glass. They haven't even tried the knobs."

I made the mistake of looking. Gulp. His undead coworkers? Yeah. They were pounding on the front door, trying to get out. And they were the kind of zombies you couldn't cure with salt.

Lightning cracked above the restaurant.

"That's weird, right?" Earl watched the sky flash green, yellow, then blue. "I called the electric company, but they said it was fine on their end."

Um, no. Definitely not fine. None of this was fine. "We better get inside."

Just then, a very expensive European sports car squealed out of the Monster Burger parking lot and sped down the street. Nearly plowing down the newly de-zombied customers. "Slow down! You almost hit those people!" Earl shook his fist. "That's the new boss lady. She doesn't give two craps about anyone. Not like Mr. Jimmy. I miss him so much."

New boss? It wasn't Caroline. It was a brunette. I didn't recognize the car.

I had bigger problems than Caroline Ford Vanderbilt. I had a wrecked Demon Mart and some for-real zombies trying to claw their way out of Monster Burger. "Come on, man. Let's go."

This wasn't over.

I put my arm under Earl and helped him to the door. I wasn't quite sure how to explain what he was going to see inside. A giant blue hell centipede sipping margaritas. A bunch of meat-eating ambulatory plants who'd drained five kegs between them. Upended shelves and recently de-possessed living zombies? But I had no choice. He was injured. I couldn't leave him outside.

When we stepped back in, DeeDee was working the cash register like a fiend, barely keeping up with the rush. The Monster Burger customers had formed a line snaking all through the store, their arms piled high with Slim Jims and King Dons, Cheetos and Honey Buns. Seriously. Armloads. Each and every one of them.

On the plus side, the Monster Burger customers seemed to be completely de-zombified. No one tried to eat me or french kiss my leg. But clearly we didn't manage to cure their underlying hunger.

The baby Larries had moved to their usual spot by the Spanish fly slushy machine, and tried their best to hold stone still, not moving so much as a root, now that the store was filled with reasonably sentient customers. Big Larry and Bubby stood in the back corner, swaying slightly, sipping margaritas when the humans weren't looking. And sharing a keg. Dude. Each one of them had a clear plastic tube curling into their mouths like twisty straws. Well, at least someone was having fun.

"Wow. Your Halloween decorations are still up? They're off the hook. Those animated inflatables look *real.*" Earl's eyes went round as silver dollars as he sized up Bubby and Big Larry. Then he grabbed me and whispered, "Listen man. I gotta tell you something. This is gonna sound crazy, but I saw Ed McMahon in the restaurant. He was tiny, but it was definitely him. I don't know how he shrunk down that small, or came back from the grave, but he sicked my buddies on me. He told them to attack me. You gotta believe me."

Oh. I believed him all right. I glanced up at the heat vent over the front door. Sure enough, a row of tiny hands hung through the grate, shooting me middle fingers, planning their next attack. "God, I hate pixies."

"What did you say?"

"Nothing."

The little Larries had blocked the door to the back, so I had no choice but to sit Earl down behind the counter next to the magazine rack. He flipped through the car magazines. "Look at this crap. They haven't made a good sports car since The IROC-Z."

"What's he doing here? We got enough problems!" Kevin pushed his tiny broom around on the floor behind DeeDee, sweeping up french fries. "Look at this place! I ain't got time for loafers. You two got time to lean, you got time to clean. If you hadn't noticed, the cleaning crew's permanently out to lunch!"

I pretended to be fishing around for something under the counter, blocking Kevin from Earl's view, so I could lean over and whisper, "the pixies freed the Monster Burger zombies. They tried to eat Earl."

Kevin stopped sweeping and stared at Earl. "Great. Just great. Did he get bit? Get the axe and cut his head off. We ain't taking chances. I'm *not* going zombie, you hear?"

I looked at him. He looked at me. "That last time didn't count."

"We're not cutting his head off. He's fine!"

Kevin looked Earl up and down, then shot me some side eye. "He gets the cold sweats, he's headless, got it? Are the zombies at the restaurant contained?"

"He locked them in, but they're trying really, really hard to get out."

He sighed, then scuttled up the cabinet, pulled out his tiny binoculars, and peered out the window for a good long time. "Well, shit. Looks like I gotta man up."

"But you're a roach."

He shook his head and scuttled off.

"What are we gonna do?" I yelled after him. "Anything I can do to help?"

"If you have a big Band-Aid back here, I could use it," Earl said.

"What?" I spun around. Silly me. Earl thought I was talking to him. "Oh yeah. Right."

I rooted around until I found the first aid kit, a little white box with a red cross on it. Dude. You'd think we'd have a bigger box working in a place like this.

"Can you give me a hand with this?" Earl rolled up the greasy sleeve of his tracksuit. There was an angry red wound on his wrist.

My guts sunk. Oh, no. Earl. Was that?

"One of the jerks bit me. Crazy, right? If you want to settle a beef, fine. Use your fists. What kinda weirdo bites another man?"

Earl filched an alcohol swab pack out of the box, but struggled to open it.

"Here. Let me help you." And I did. My heart sank as I patted his wound as gently as I could. Earl flinched. It had to hurt. I could see the teeth marks, and the start of the raging purple infection snaking out from the edges. Not. Good. Jesus Christ. Poor Earl. What were we gonna do?

"Thanks, man."

"Of course." I tried really hard to keep calm as I put a big swab of cotton over the bite and bandaged it as best as I could. I put the kit away and spotted a handful of mini bottles of Wild Turkey under the counter. Kevin's stash. "It's been a crazy night. Do you want a drink? Do you like whiskey?"

Earl's eyes lit up. "You know it."

I cracked one open and handed it to Earl. He drained it in one swallow. I mustered a fake smile. Because that's what you do, right? Help the dying. Calmly, with a kind word. And booze. Lots of booze.

"Are you kidding me right now? Is that mine? Hell no." Kevin crawled out from under the counter. He had a dozen Bic lighters taped to his body, all in a row like they were grenades.

"What are you doing?"

"You're buying me more whiskey, kid. Why's the first aid kit out? Has Earl been bitten? Where's the axe? Kill him now."

"He's fine, and I'll buy you a big bottle, okay? He's had a rough night."

"Whatever, kid. I've had a rough night. You've had a rough night. This guy's been walking in a field of daisies."

"Why are you covered in lighters?" Come on. I'm dying to know, aren't you?

"Ask Earl if the grills at Monster Burger are still gas."

I did. Earl looked confused. "Uh, yeah. Why?"

"No reason." I turned back to Kevin and whispered, "What are you doing?"

He looked me right in the eye, knotted a black rag around his head, and said, "Live for nothing or die for something, am I right?"

Then he scuttled up and across the counter, grabbed a pack of cheap smokes off the carousel, and left through the front door.

CHAPTER 27

An hour later, Demon Mart was finally empty again, apart from the usual suspects.

Bubby and Big Larry swayed in the corner, claw arms and vines around each other's shoulder, smiling as they drained another keg. This one wasn't for nutrition, it was for fun. Apparently, it was hell beast happy hour.

Chef kunk kunked back and forth, refilling all the baby Larries' Spanish Fly slushies, because they were eating machines. Seriously. The rotten beef cart had been licked clean. And all that was left of the cleaning crew was a pile of boots and some empty coveralls. The baby Larries had squeezed the zombies out of them like they were Gogurts.

I stood by the hole where the front door used to be, sweeping up glass while I kept one eye on Earl—who sat at the end of the counter casually inspecting his second issue of Hustler, oblivious to the hell beasts around him—and one on Monster Burger, where zombies were *still* pawing at the glass, trying to get out of the restaurant.

DeeDee walked up with a mop in her hand. It was dripping with— nope. Don't want to know. "Have you seen Kevin? I'm worried about him." She looked down and around on the floor.

I was worried, too. A roach didn't just crawl out the front door with a bunch of Bic lighters strapped to him for fun.

"I hope he isn't curled up somewhere eating again," she said. "I still don't know why the salt didn't curb his appetite."

"Aaah!! There! There! Do you see him?" Earl screamed and pointed. Oof. His arm didn't look good. His bandage was red, soaked through with blood. "It's Ed McMahon!"

Earl wavered and dropped like a stone to the floor. He must have passed out from all the excitement. Or maybe it was the blood loss.

"Oh no." DeeDee huffed. "Not again!"

I was sure DeeDee was about to grab an axe and decapitate Earl. Instead, she pointed to the candy aisle. A gaggle of pixies hovered in the air, holding tight to the corners of a pack of cotton candy, struggling to carry it up into a heat vent with an unhinged grate.

Gah! Stupid pixies.

"Kevin's right. Cruelty free is a dumb idea." DeeDee sighed. "If they get that cotton candy into the air duct, they'll have food for weeks. We'll never get rid of them."

A few seconds later, DeeDee stood in the candy aisle, swinging her mop through the swarm of pixies, fwapping nudists like she was playing Whac-a-mole. That cotton candy went splat on the floor.

Big mistake. Cue pixie revenge, round two.

While she dealt the pixies a crushing blow, I checked on Earl. I found him splayed out on the floor behind the counter, lying in a pile of nudie and car mags. "Earl? Earl?"

I shook him. Oh God. Please don't die. Please don't turn. I didn't think I could chop the head off of the man who'd made me the best burgers I had ever eaten for the past seven years. I shook harder. His mouth opened, and his head lolled. "Earl! Earl!"

"Uuuuuuuuh."

Oh God. He's a zombie. I grabbed the closest thing and raised it up, ready to crush in his skull. Sure, it was a weird magical gourd with a long twisted stem, but it'd have to do in a pinch.

"Uuuuuuuuuh," Earl moaned. His eyes rolled back. His mouth fell open.

"Uuuuuuuuuh. Oooooo. Weeee!" He opened his eyes. "Wow. That whiskey went straight to my head. I swear I just saw Ed McMahon flying around with a bunch of naked Solid Gold dancers."

Phew. Still human.

He looked up at me, holding a curly red gourd over my head. "What are you doing?"

"Nothing." I lowered it. "How about we get you a new Band-Aid?"

He looked at his wrist and seemed surprised by all the blood. "Oh. Yeah. Okay."

I helped him sit up, then peeled the bandage back. Sweet Jesus, it smelled! Like dead raccoon frying on hot pavement. Not good. The bite mark looked even worse. Weepy with lots of pus. Deep purple veins feathered out, longer, angrier. "Maybe we should take you to the hospital. Get this looked at?"

"What? No way, man. For one bite? I'll be fine. Just squeeze some of that antibacterial stuff on it. It's all good."

I nodded, and I did it. Because the more I thought about it, the less the hospital seemed like a good idea. The ER staff probably wasn't ready to chop a guy's head off over a hand injury. The zombie apocalypse wasn't even on their radar. It was fiction. But we knew better. And if it came down to it and Earl changed? Well, if I couldn't do it, DeeDee would.

I ruffled around in the first aid kid. I squeezed out an entire tube of bacitracin on a clean cotton bandage, covered up the bite, and taped it up.

"Uuum. I'm so....hungry. But I don't know what for. Mmmmmm." Earl rubbed his belly. "You know what sounds good?"

Brains? Please don't be brains.

"Funyuns. You mind if I snag a pack? Wait. Never mind. I left my wallet at the restaurant."

Funyuns? Not brains? Yay! "It's on me," I said. "Be right back."

DeeDee stood in the candy aisle waving a pair of rusty scissors and a net at the errant pixies, who had retreated inside the vent.

I went to the chip rack and dug through the bags the burger zombies had left behind, which wasn't much. I gathered up all the Funyuns, about three bags, and nabbed a few PBR tallboys, too. Earl may as well go out with a bang, right?

"Dinner is served!" I piled it up around him and put on my best fake smile.

"Wow. Thanks man." His eyes lit up.

And my smile slid off. He was sweating a lot, and he was pale. Maybe I should tell him. He deserved to know, didn't he? Then at least he'd have the chance to make peace with the higher power of his choice. I'd want to know. Well, okay. Maybe I wouldn't want to know. But I wasn't Earl.

"Earl. I—"

"You saw him, right? Ed McMahon?" He popped the tab on a PBR and looked up at me with the most sad, desperate eyes. He looked like a golden retriever in time out.

"I sure did. And you're right. He is a jerk." In that moment, I changed my mind. I couldn't tell him he was gonna be a zombie. I just couldn't, but I could try to make the end of his life as good as it could be. "You were robbed. You should have been on Star Search. Your caterpillar is the best I've ever seen."

"Lloyd, help! I've got them cornered!" DeeDee screamed.

"We're gonna take care of Ed for you. Right now. We'll show him." I winked at Earl. He smiled.

All right. Time to go kick that pixie's ass for good.

BOOM! The store shook like an earthquake.

"Aaaaaaaaaah!" I screamed. And ducked. And covered my head. What the hell was that?

BOOM! The windows blew out, and glass rained down all over us. The store shook, and a bright orange light filled the store. I rose, slowly, and poked my head just far enough above the cabinet to peek outside. Holy. Shit.

The front half of Monster Burger had blown off. It lay in pieces in the grass and in the street. The rest of it was engulfed in flames. A plume of fire that looked like an erupting volcano tore through the roof. "Oh. My. God."

"What is it, b-boy?" Earl moved up beside me. "Noooooo! That restaurant was my life!"

Earl descended into tears as the two of us stared through the hole where the window used to be.

BOOM!

Another fireball blew the bun right out of the neon Frankenstein's hand and sent it crashing into the parking lot. The remains of the restaurant crumbled into a heap of molten brick. The heat of it singed my eyebrows.

"Everyone get down!" DeeDee rolled up out of nowhere and pushed us both down to the floor. She crouched down next to us. "Do you smell gas? There might be a leak in the lines. The whole block could blow. I need to get to the shut-off valve. I'll be right back."

She started to go, but I stopped her.

"No. That's not it." Gulp. My insides were jelly. It all made sense now. The cigarettes. The lighters. The gas grills? "I think Kevin blew up the Monster Burger. Because of the zombies."

"What?"

I filled her in, but I whispered so Earl wouldn't hear. The zombie staff pawing at the front window. Kevin covered in lighters and cigarettes.

"Kevin? No. No way. Nothing could survive that blast. Not even a roach." Tears welled in her eyes. "You're wrong. He's not in there. He would have said something."

"He said 'Live for nothing or die for something.'"

She howled. "Noooooo!"

And sobbed. Tears flew. Her mouth twisted up.

Holy crap. I'd never seen her cry. She was always so...together.

I put my arm around her, and tried to come up with something profound to say that would make her feel better, but nothing came to mind. I just held on to her for a while. Her body heaved as she sobbed.

"I'm sure Kevin's all right?" Maybe? We could feel the heat from the fire all the way over here.

"No. He's. Not." She sobbed. "He only quotes Rambo when he thinks he might not make it. It was a suicide mission."

"But—" Suicide mission? My bottom lip shook, and my vision went blurry. I blinked. Really hard. Like really, really hard. Might not make it. She was kidding, right? A wave of feelings crashed down over me. Kevin can't be dead. He just can't. Sure he ogled my Mom and bossed me around, but he'd grown on me. Deep down, he had become my friend.

"Uuuuuuuuuuuuuuh," Earl moaned.

Oh, no. He'd turned. I wiped my tears away. Weapon. Quick! This time, the closest thing to me was that weird bottle of curse breaker floor wash Henrietta had left me. The explosions knocked it off the shelf. I raised the bottle and aimed it straight at Earl's brain.

"Uuuuuuuuuuuuh," Earl moaned. "Uuuuh. Those Funyuns didn't agree with me."

Pffffft. Yep. He farted. Then he pointed. "Look! Ed McMahon!"

The good news? Earl was very much alive. The bad news? Chef stood at the end of the counter, blocking the way. A tiny, naked Ed McMahon stood on his shoulder. He flipped us all the bird. Then he kicked Chef right in the neck.

Tink. Clunk.

Chef's containment collar fell to the floor and broke into pieces.

CHAPTER 28

Long story short: We're screwed. We're trapped behind the counter by a zombie Chef in a mech suit, and one of us has been bitten. There's only one way this story can go: South.

Chef growled and closed in. *Kunk. Kunk. Kunk.*

Shit! Shit! Shit! My heart jumped into my throat. "Move!"

I hopped up, grabbed Earl by the tracksuit, and pulled him to his feet. "DeeDee, get up!"

She looked up at Chef, at his grabby hands and bared teeth and said, "Chef. No. Not you."

Tears streaked down her cheeks, but don't be fooled. Any minute now, she was gonna flip into ultimate zombie killer mode. She'd jump up, chop Chef's head off, and his body would join his soul, singing front row center in the choir invisible for all eternity. Amen.

Kunk. Kunk. Kunk. He staggered closer.

"Uuuuuuuuuuuuuh."

And no. That wasn't Earl. Earl had gone completely stiff from sheer terror.

Chef lunged. I kicked him in the ribs, and he fell headfirst into some speakers. While Chef ran his hands around knocking things over, trying to right himself, I pushed Earl past him and yelled "Run, Earl. Run!"

I whirled around. DeeDee was still on the floor. "Get up! Let's go!"

I put my butt on the counter and was about to swing my legs across and jump out of there, when I realized DeeDee hadn't moved. She didn't hop up, didn't grab a weapon, and didn't look even remotely interested in chopping Chef's head off. She just sat there, blank staring. It's like she had shut down.

Chef, once again standing, hungry, and sniffing the air like hell's rabid bunny rabbit, kunk kunked right past me, straight for DeeDee. She looked up at him and whispered, "No. Not you. Not you, too."

Chef fell on her. He had her pinned, mouth open, ready to bite, but DeeDee didn't fight. Why wasn't she fighting? Holy shit, she's not gonna fight!

So I kicked Chef in the shoulder with both feet. He moved, but not much. The mech suit was heavy, and he was hungry.

Chef growled "Grrrrrrrrrrrrraaaaaaaaaaaaaaa."

DeeDee looked at him, eyes filled with tears, and still didn't whip out any sweet ninja moves.

Chef opened wide.

"DeeDee. No!" I jumped on his back, put him in a headlock, and put my hand in front of his open mouth.

He bit down.

Right around the bottle of curse break floor wash in my hand. He opened so wide, his mouth slid down completely around the end of it, and it got stuck there. I mean, that thing was so deep the cap had to be tickling his tonsils. Apparently, zombies didn't have a gag reflex.

He pawed at his face, confused, while I grabbed his Chef's jacket, planted a foot on a shelf, and tried to pull him off of her. Man. He was so heavy. Stupid metal! "Run! Run!"

But DeeDee didn't roll away. Or run. Or fight. Or anything. She sat there staring wide eyed at me, then at Chef, who was gluck glucking, trying to hack that glass bottle out of his mouth.

I pulled on Chef, but I wasn't strong enough to move him off. He didn't budge. "Earl. Help me!"

"His face. He's." Earl stuttered behind me. "Oh, geez."

I glanced back at him. Earl was full-on cold sweating and Popsicle stiff with fear, like he was reliving the trauma of his own zombie battle. "Oh God. Is he? Not again."

Earl looked at me, at Chef, then his eyes rolled back and he passed out, splayed across the floor.

Well. Shit.

Crink. Crunk. Slurp. Chef tried his best to spit out that glass bottle. It was in there deep, but it wasn't gonna hold forever. And neither could I. I pulled and pulled on him, and he pawed and pawed at DeeDee. She held her hands up, more so she couldn't see his face than to defend herself.

"DeeDee, run!" I was losing my grip on Chef's jacket, but she didn't run. I held on as long as I could. My arms, my legs, every muscle everywhere burned from the strain. This wasn't working.

I let go, then kicked down hard on Chef's shoulder. He face planted into the floor, his growly mouth barely missing DeeDee, who thankfully —finally—took the opportunity to slide out from under him. He flailed, but he wasn't down for long.

Kunk. Kunk. Kunk. He stood up and sniffed the air, looking for me.

I looked for anything vaguely resembling a weapon.

Chef turned back to DeeDee.

No. No way. I couldn't let him get her. "Chef! Here! Here!"

He stopped lurching for a minute, listening. He heard me, all right. But he appeared to be considering his options—the fat dude or the chick who was already on the floor. He turned back to DeeDee. She was the easier meal.

Gulp. I yelled and poked him in the back with my finger. "Over here! Don't take her, take me! She's too skinny. Not enough to eat. Look at me! I'm fat and delicious, like a Christmas ham. Mmmm. Look at me! Eat meeeeeeeeeee!"

I rubbed my fat belly and grunted yummy noises until I convinced Chef that I would be more filling. The irony. The guy who fed me was gonna be the guy who ate me. The diner becomes the dinner.

Chef came at me. I backed up, and he followed me. Behind him, I could see her slowly snapping to. She stood up and looked around. Yes! Yes! Run, DeeDee. Be freeeeeeee!

Chef kunk kunk kunked at me, arms out ready to grab. Woah boy. Boss battle. Lloyd vs zombie in a mech suit. Shit. How was I gonna get out of this mess? I thrust my leg out and kicked Chef right in the nuts. Well, that part of his man brain still worked because he hunched over, cupped his nuts and looked stunned for a minute. He looked at me like, "how could you? Nuts!"

Oooooh. "Sorry, dude."

He did not accept my apology. He looked extra mad. He started chewing. *Crunk. Crunk. Crunk. Tink.* He crunched that glass bottle down to nothing, then swallowed the shards. Ouch. Milky green curse breaker dribbled down his chin, soaking his Chef's coat.

Huh. Well, that stuff didn't work. Still cursed!

He came at me. I planted one hand on each counter, swung my legs up and kicked him right in the face. He reared back and fell into the stereo. Speakers and turntables and albums flew in all directions. I watched in slow motion as Kevin's Zebra album arced through the air, slid out of the sleeve, and onto the floor. Chef stepped right on it, and it broke into pieces.

Oof. It was a small mercy that Kevin didn't live to see that.

But that vinyl must have been slippery, because as soon as Chef stepped on that record his foot when out from under him. His arms waved as he tried to catch his balance.

Ha! Take that! I started to jump out of his way, but Chef landed hard on me and the two of us slid down to the floor. *Shit! Shit! Shit!*

I clawed, but there wasn't anything to dig into. The new doughnut case was Plexiglas and bolted to the counter. My hands slipped right off.

I grabbed everything I could on the way down, hoping to come across at least one potentially skull-crushing object. Magic rocks. Nope. Mason jars of sticks and leaves. Nope. Weirdo magic trumpet? Seriously? Y'all couldn't put a knife or a baseball bat back here?

I hit the floor. Ow.

"Uuuuuuuuuhhhhhhhhhhhhhhhhhhhh." Chef moaned, excited for dinnertime.

The weight of his metal braces pressed down on my gut. The pressure made my head feel like a gigantic zit about the pop.

"Grrrrrrrrrrrrrrrrrraaaaaaaaaaaaaaaaaaaaaaaaaarrrrrrrrrrrrr."

He opened wide and went for my cheek. I scrambled, running my hands along the floor for something, anything to defend myself. Angel rolled across my face, screaming, "Nooooo! Lloyd can't die a loser!"

Chef bit down hard on the plastic eight ball.

Crack.

Red fluid splurped out. Chef shook his head and ka-kacked, shaking angel loose, and came at me again. My hand came up clutching a shard of Zebra. The record, not the striped African horse. Chef's teeth snapped shut, barely missing my neck, as I sunk that bit of Zebra right into his eye. He bared his teeth and moved in for another bite. I clutched that piece of vinyl like it was a knife, and as he moved in for the kill, pushed it deeper into his eye socket.

Spluuuuuuuuuuuuuuurpp.

Chef must have been really rotten, because dude. That record cut his eye socket like butter. It was squishy as a black banana. Yellowish fluid squirted out all over my face.

So gross. Definitely gonna barf this time.

"Uuuuuuuuh?" Chef said, then collapsed on top of me. Dead. Like dead dead. For real this time.

Yay. We did it! But, gross. Because he was dripping eyeballs and brains all over me. I wiggled and bucked and kicked, trying to get out from under him, but he was just too heavy.

Angel eight ball rolled around on the floor, hemorrhaging red.

"Help me! I'm stuck," I said.

"Help you? Help me! Plug me up before I bleed out." His triangle turned. And yes, his fluid was running low. "I told HR they needed to upgrade me to an app on your iPhone, but no, they didn't listen."

Suddenly, the weight of Chef lifted off of me, no thanks to angel eight ball. Bubby's face appeared above me. He held Chef aloft on the tip of a claw arm.

"Gee. How nice of you to take a break from cocktail hour to help me!"

Bubby's eyes turned to angry slits. He dropped Chef. Right on top of me. Eow. "I'm sorry! I'm sorry! But Chef almost ate me!"

Bubby picked him up again, lifted him over the counter, and dropped him head first into Big Larry's open mouth. That plant glup glup slow slurped Chef in like a boa constrictor sucking in a pig. Until he got to the metal braces. Then he had to stop. The bottom half of Chef dangled unceremoniously out of his mouth while he and Bubby had a whole conversation in blurps and clicks—I mean, I'm guessing here—about how to eat around metal.

I sat up. DeeDee wrapped her arms around me.

"Are you all right?" She kept on squeezing me. Hello. Shorts tingling. You feel me? Although, this would be way better if we weren't covered in salt and zombie goop. "I'm so sorry. I froze, and it almost got us both killed. I'm so, so sorry."

Okay. She was squeezing me super tight now. Like, ouch. Girl had some muscles. "You saved my life. You're my hero."

Angel eight ball shot me one last message—"mysterious ways" with a thumb's up—before enough liquid leaked out that his triangle wouldn't turn anymore.

"If you died, I would have never forgiven myself." Her body shook. She was crying. "I couldn't carry on if I lost you and Kevin and Chef all in one night."

Kevin. I looked around at the shattered remains of his record collection. Zebra, shattered. That Stargazer album? Out of the sleeve, cracked, with a zombie boot print on it. His stupid rock-and-roll hour saved my life. I owed that roach. Big time. And now I'd never be able to pay him back.

DeeDee eventually let go and looked at me with sad gray eyes. Her eyeliner had streaked down her cheeks. She was even more beautiful. I rubbed some away with my thumb. She grabbed my hand and pressed it hard into her cheek. She was silent for a long moment, then said, "I vote we close the store and go home early. We're calling in sick tomorrow, too. Movies and pizza at my house instead. Sound like a plan?"

"Hell. Yeah." Could anything sound better?

She stood up. I took her hands, and she pulled me up. Earl walked up behind her.

"Aaaah!" I screamed.

"Relax. He's fine," she said. "I checked him. He's still breathing."

Phew. Okay. "Hey man," I said to Earl. "You need some more Funyuns? Another PBR?"

"Uuuuuuuuuuuuuuh," Earl said. Man, he was indecisive.

"I'll take that as a yes. I'll be right back."

"Uuuuuuuuuuuuuuh."

I patted him on the shoulder, and he tried to bite my hand. That "uuuuuuuh" was an "uh oh." Because that wasn't the moan of indecision. That was the moan of the recently zombified. Earl's eyes had gone milky. Dead. His skin was white as paper. His nose sniffed the air aggressively.

Poor Earl. He didn't deserve this.

"My bad," DeeDee said. "He's not fine."

And wouldn't you know it, while poor Earl stood there, sniffing around, adjusting to his new afterlife as a man-eating zombie, that tiny naked Ed McMahon fluttered down out of the heat vent and landed on his shoulder. He looked right at DeeDee and flipped her two birds.

"What's he mad about this time?" She planted her hands on her hips.

"The cotton candy." Here we go again.

Ed McMahon tittered at us, then reached elbow deep into the collar of Earl's track suit. Ed looked confused. He held open the collar and fluttered in a circle around Earl's neck, titters growing louder and more irritated. Oh. I get it. He's looking for Earl's zombie containment collar, so he can screw us over. Again.

Earl sniffed the air around that tiny naked pixie as he fluttered around, digging in the tracksuit, looking for a collar that wasn't there. Which was all fine until he accidentally sat his butt crack directly on Earl's nose. In a flash, Earl's hand moved. He snatched that naked pixie by the wings. Tiny Ed kicked and yanked, trying to get away, but Earl grabbed his feet and held him out longways like a corn on the cob.

Earl opened wide and...

Crunch.

Holy. Hell.

Crunch. Crunch. Crunch.

Earl ate little Ed McMahon. Seriously. He crunched that pixie down bite by bite like he was eating corn on the cob, typewriter style.

DeeDee and I couldn't look away. It was that horrible. I had never seen anything so gory.

When Earl finished, all that was left was a pink skinless skeleton thing that looked like a Popeye's fried chicken leg. *After* Big Dan had had his way with it. Eek.

The only recognizable bit left was an uneaten section of belly. The mole. Still intact, billy goat hair still sticking out of it. Earl dropped it and moaned, like "mmmmmm."

Wow. Guess Ed hit the spot.

"Uuuuuuuuuuh."

Nope. Still hungry. Earl lunged at DeeDee, trying to bite her shoulder. I hit him with a left hook. His neck snapped, and he stumbled, but he wasn't down for long. He found his footing, turned to us and moaned. "Uuuuuuuuuuuuuuuuh."

A black blur flashed before us.

Click.

Something snapped around Earl's neck. Green lights blinked, and he immediately went from "aaaaaarrrrrrgh" to "huuuuuuuuuuuuuuh?"

I was just as confused. Earl now had a containment collar. It was on the end of a long black rod. A grabber, like the one DeeDee had given me earlier. And holding the other end of that grabber was a middle-aged white dude who looked at us like we were the stupidest people on earth.

"Do naht tell me you idjits let that dang plant eat my cleaning crew!" He jabbed his thumb at Big Larry, who still hadn't figured out how to suck Chef's legs out of his metal braces, and who for the record looked like he felt a little guilty about it. "Haw many times do I gotta tell yinz? Zahmbies dahn't grow ahn trees! Nah where's Kevin? That jagoff left me so many voice mails, he broke my phone!"

CHAPTER 29

That middle-aged white dude was Steve. Yes. *That* Steve. From the plant. He had a clipboard packed with wrinkled, coffee-stained papers, and he flipped through them angrily as he outlined our shortcomings.

It was a long list.

"We just did a total rebuild a this store, and you idjits blew it up! AGAIN! Yinz couldn't keep the place together for two weeks? Twelve zahmbies destroyed. Breach of human interaction protocahl, a hunderd and seven times? That's a record. Violation of the Hades endangered species feeding guidelines, *and* ya let these two jagoffs drink half the stock in the beer cave. They're so drunk, they're pickled! Do they look like they can handle another rahnd?"

He pointed at Bubby, who girl-drink-drunk swayed as he poured eight bags of Smart Pop directly into his open mouth. Big Larry had tapped another keg. He sucked on the tube like it was a bendy straw, but he froze when Steve singled him out.

"We haven't gotten to the big one. Unauthorized zahmbie creation. Forty years without an incident. Forty years! Until you morons show up. I clearly got two tweedle dumbs." He jabbed his clipboard at us, then at Earl. "But who's tweedle dee here?"

Earl stood next to us moaning softly, looking up and around, bewildered by his new and unexpected life after death. Poor Earl didn't know if he should eat us or do the robot.

"He's the cook from Monster Burger," I squeaked.

"A cook, huh? Well, I hope you like him because he's yours nah. Yinz luckcd into a new Chef. Of course, nah I gotta to take him in, get him juiced up, and bring him all the way back here. 'Til then, you two idjits are making your own damn lunches." He flipped another paper on his clipboard. "Christ almighty! You had a work order to neutralize a patch a hungry grass in front a Monster Burger, and yinz didn't do it! You coulda prevented this whole thing. I dahn't know this moron." He pointed at me. Man, he was pointy. "But I expect better from you."

He pointed at DeeDee, and her cheeks flushed. She stared at the floor in shame.

"Hungry grass?" I whispered.

"Oh man. I should have known," she said. "That explains a few things."

"It does?"

Steve looked through the holes where the windows used to be at the smoldering wreckage of Monster Burger. "Well, the fire probably took care a the grass, but do it anyway, just to be sure. Yinz messed up enough for one night. It's about time you did something right. You still have your work order?"

He flipped through his clipboard. "Never mind. Take my copy and dahn't lose it."

He ripped a piece of purple paper off the clipboard and thrust it at DeeDee. It had a Ziploc baggy containing a white mini bottle of holy water and a can of Murphy's Irish Stout taped to it. And...that's when an angry naked pixie chick plopped straight out of the heat vent, landed in Steve's hair, and started pulling on it like it was her job. Dude. That pixie did not read the room.

"What the? Pixies. Still? You let this go on for two weeks?" Steve yanked the pixie—and a handful of his own hair—off his head and smacked away the other pixies who were stupid enough to flutter around him. "Geesy Pete! This place is a zoo! I oughta send you two to employee boot camp."

He flipped another page on the clipboard and huffed. "It says right here Henrietta Getley ordered yinz some pixie bait, and Dolly's delivered it. But you idjits didn't use it. What are we paying ya for? I'll be right back."

Steve stomped through the shattered remains of the front door and over to a white utility van parked neatly in the spot on the far end of the two handicapped ones. Of course. Because this dude followed rules, even if the lot was empty. He opened the van door, pulled something out, then stomped inside carrying a—Barbie Dream House?

Well, this night just keeps getting weirder. It was just like the one my sister had when we were little, two stories of pink and teal plastic. It had lacy curtains and plastic molded furniture in a rainbow of optimistic colors. Steve sat it on the counter. Then, he carefully opened all the little doors and windows and rearranged the furniture.

Uh. Okay?

He opened the doughnut case and tonged out a pumpkin spice fritter. He broke a hunk off and crumbled it into pieces, which he sprinkled into the little bowls on the pink plastic dining room table. He dropped the rest of it whole and untouched in what could best be described as the house's living room. The pixies hovered around him, eyeballing that Barbie Dream house and that pumpkin spice fritter with a focused intensity, equal parts desire and determination. They wanted both. Bad. They tittered to each other, sizing up Steve and the house and me, as if they were debating.

When he was finished, Steve shook his head at us and stomped off to spew his ire all over Big Larry and a still visibly intoxicated Bubby. I mean, that jelly centipede was so drunk, he held onto the wall like he was gonna spin off the earth.

The second Steve stepped away, a pixie zoomed in close to the Barbie Dream House. A lady one. She peered in the window, caught sight of the closet full of Barbie clothes, and lost it. I mean, she went full on feeding frenzy. She dove into that closet and tore through it, yipping like a chihuahua on meth. Tiny pink silk dresses fluttered all around, glitter sparkling, until that naked pixie chick emerged, victorious, wearing only tiny pink plastic cha-cha heels, a pageant sash and a rhinestone tiara. No pants. At all. Okay, then.

She twirled around, and that was it. The rest of the pixies zoomed straight into that house. Some of them dug through the Barbie clothes, fighting with each other and grunting as they assembled their own equally weird outfits. None of them with underpants. Those pubes were loud and proud. Jesus. It's like they wanted the whole world to see their junk.

The rest of them dug into that doughnut like they hadn't eaten in a month.

Only one pixie had doubts. I'm pretty sure it was the jerk who tried to poke out my eyes with spicy Bugles. He flew circles around the house, flitting up and down, examining every inch of that plastic mansion. He must have decided it was safe, because he eventually flipped me the bird and flew in. All the doors and windows immediately snapped shut and locked, trapping the pixies inside. A couple of them pounded on the plastic window 'glass', but the rest didn't seem to mind. They were too busy playing dress up, testing out the mattress in the master bedroom (ahem), and chowing down on that doughnut.

Oh, man. We really were idjits. The doughnut was the pixie bait. Henrietta had ordered it for us. Duh.

"Works every time. Pixies love pumpkin spice. Dolly's delivered them for a reason, ya morons." Steve shouted at us from across the room. "Nah get to work."

Well, shit. I had a deep, sinking feeling that we could have avoided near death at the hands of our zombie cleaning crew if only Kevin didn't hate pumpkin spice. If we'd fed the pixies, maybe they wouldn't have been so mean. That's probably how Henrietta lured them into her purse.

DeeDee seemed unburdened by second-guessing. She examined her work order while scratching her head. "Hungry grass. I'm so stupid. It was obvious. Mr. Jimmy died on the grass under the Monster Burger sign, didn't he?"

Yes. Yes, he did. I nodded.

"That must have done it. See?" She showed me the paper.

It said, "Hungry grass has been detected in your sector. Please neutralize this threat immediately. DO NOT walk across the grass. It is magically contaminated. Symptoms of infection include insatiable hunger and unchecked desire for food."

There was a drawing underneath of a beautiful meadow of tall grass with red flowers on the end. Wait. Those weren't flowers. Those were tiny mouths lined with spiky teeth. It was just like the picture in the Dante's Guide. Great. More hell plants. Right here on earth. What next? Possessed parsnips in the produce aisle?

"I may have this wrong, but I think any grass can become hungry grass if someone dies horribly on it. Or if there's a body buried under it that didn't get last rites. So, either Mr. Jimmy's death cursed it, or the grass was always cursed and he was keeping it contained somehow? We'll probably never know."

Okay then.

"Either way, hungry grass must be why the salt didn't cure the hunger. The new owner closed the drive-thru, so customers had no choice but to walk over the hungry grass. It was double magic. A spell on the food to control whoever ate it, and the hungry grass to keep them coming back for more so the spell didn't break."

DeeDee looked out the window hole. "No salt? Hungry grass? Zombies? Whoever bought Monster Burger knew what they were doing. Caroline Ford Vanderbilt is definitely in over her head."

"Yinz get moving." Steve snapped his fingers at us. "This is your mess. Clean it up!"

He already had all the baby Larries in a line, directing them back into the beer cave like hell's school crossing guard. They used their leaves to pick up their pots, white roots poking through the drainage holes in the bottom as they tiptoed into the beer cave.

DeeDee examined the contents of the Ziploc and the diagram on her work order. "I'll right back. Good luck with Steve."

She moved and her boot bumped angel eight ball, who lay motionless in a pool of red liquid that looked suspiciously like blood. "Oh. He doesn't look so good. You might want to patch him up."

I picked angel up. The triangle, red and crusty, lay silent in a dry ball. If he hadn't hopped into Chef's mouth, I might be halfway to zombie by now.

"Hey. Idjit. Stop patty caking and get a mop!" Steve barked at me. He pointed at the pile of boots on the floor—feet still in them—and to the sticky puddle of Larry goop and zombie guts in front of the slushy machines.

Great. Guess I get the fun job. DeeDee was already out the door, halfway across the parking lot on her way to Monster Burger.

"And you. Fatty thousand legs." Steve pointed at Bubby, who was in the pharmacy section eating whole bottles of aspirin, trying to stave off a hangover. "Make yer giant meat body useful and help me poosh this pumpkin through the door."

That giant pumpkin was Big Larry.

"What in the Sam Hill? Is this yours? Why am I tripping over limes?" Steve held up a discarded margarita glass. A sad, crumpled umbrella clung to the side for dear life.

It was the last reminder of Bubby's vacation. Poor Bubby had come back to this? Talk about relaxation erased! Bubby slumped, then blubbed to the beer cave to help push Big Larry through. He looked at me with eight sad white eyes.

"I feel ya, dude."

"No commentary. This isn't a Stillers game. Get the mop!" Yep. He was yelling at me. "Geesh. I should have this whole block shut dahn!"

Steve pulled on a pair of thick yellow rubber gloves and dipped his hands into a bucket. He emerged holding two giant runny globs of what looked like Vaseline, which he then rubbed on the sides of Big Larry's head. "Your head always get this big? Gonna be a tight fit! You got moss for brains? Don't just stand dere. Get rubbing!"

Big Larry sunk his vines into the bucket and starting smearing petroleum jelly on his fat pumpkin head, and boy he did not look happy about it. Of all the things he'd eaten and excreted, apparently lube was the thing that grossed him out. Who would have guessed? Big Larry drooped.

"Dahn't give me that look," Steve said. "Not my fault yer head's so fat!"

The line of baby Larries hadn't moved an inch. They bunched up, blocking the entrance to the beer cave. Steve stopped lubing Big Larry and stomped on over to the littles. "What's the hold up? What do ya mean the gate won't open? It's working just fine. What? Did Kevin tell you to say that? No. I ran a diagnostic. It passed inspection. The gate isn't broken. It's user error. See?"

Steve pushed that baby Larry in through the door, but there were so many other plants still in there, that he shot back out like a pinball. His pot hit the door frame with such force that a chunk of metal trim popped off. Something small and blue fell out of the wall, arced through the air and bonked Steve right on the head. "Ow!"

It plinked to the floor. Steve picked it up. It looked like a blue glass bottle. "What the hell is this?"

He opened it, and out dropped a tiny white scroll and some random sticks and flowers and other weird junk. Steve unrolled the teeny paper and huffed. "Great. Just great. Nah wonder your gate's on the fritz. You." He pointed at me. "When your lazy butt finally gets that mop I been asking for, you better add a whole bottle of Curse Breaker Floor Wash to the water. I dahn't know who you pissed off, but someone put a hex on the store!"

CHAPTER 30

Well, this is awkward. I don't know if you remember, but I fed our only bottle of curse breaker floor wash to Chef. When he tried to eat us. Come on. I didn't know I was gonna need it. It didn't come with instructions!

So here I was, standing by the slushy machines next to a mop bucket of fresh hot water. Steve stared at me and shook his head whispering, "idjit" as he poured one of his own bottles of Quita Maldicion Curse Breaker Floor Wash into the bucket for me.

"Do ya have two brain cells to rub together? You shoulda mopped the floor with this as soon as Henrietta gave it to you," he said. "If it says floor warsh on the label, that means use it to warsh the damn floor. I dahn't know how ya messed that up."

DeeDee tromped through the muck, dropping the last of the zombie cleaning crew's boots—and yes, the feet were still inside them—into a black trash bag. All the Larries, big and small, stood impatiently in and around the beer cave, waiting for me to mop. Which would somehow break the curse and fix the gate so they could go home. Because yeah. That's the world I live in, people. Where your choice of cleaning products could open the gate to hell.

Bubby held what looked like a giant shoe horn, which Steve had given him along with instructions on how to lever Big Larry's lubed up head through the beer cave door once the babies were out. Kevin was, well, not here, and every second he was gone meant the odds that he was really, truly gone increased exponentially.

Steve shook the bottle, and the last few drops plipped into the mop water, turning it milky neon lime green. I swished the mop around, put it in the squeeze wringer, then plopped it right in the middle of an orange puddle of Big Larry afterbirth and zombie juice. I mopped in circles, cutting through the goop.

So wouldn't you know it, as soon as that mop hit linoleum, a whirling purple portal opened directly above me, and something big and black dropped straight out, right on top of me. "Aaaaaaaaaaah!" GIANT

MAN-EATING SHRIMP!

I screamed. I ain't proud. And wriggled and writhed because I was about to be eaten or killed or ripped apart by nasty hell beast. I thought this stuff was supposed to break curses!

Horrible death pending. Any minute now. Wait for it. Huh.

I opened my eyes and saw a disheveled Faust stand up, smooth himself out and button his blazer, which was ripped in several places and coated with mud. "My my. I do apologize," he said to me. "I have reason to believe that I was kidnapped and imprisoned by magic. I was sitting in my office then I'd suddenly been transported to a rather strange, unpleasant dimension filled with very angry creatures. I fear someone intends to hurt us. I do hope that I have returned in time to thwart the evildoer. Did you have any trouble while I was away?"

Dude. The store was wrecked, capital W. Was he blind?

Steve looked at his empty bottle of Curse Breaker Floor Wash, then said, "Wow. This must be an extra strong batch. Too bad you two morons didn't use it earlier."

Faust leaned down and picked something up. It was my broken angel eight ball. His fall must have knocked it out of my pocket. "Tisk tisk. Those poor angels. So behind on their technology. It's a shame really, but we do get all the good start-ups." He held it out to me. "Is this one yours?"

I took angel eight ball, and Faust finally noticed the toppled racks, the zombie goop and the gaggle of baby Larries spilling out of the beer cave. "Oh, my."

I swear I saw his skin flash full devil red for a split second. "I must speak to Kevin immediately. Where is he?" Faust looked at me. His skin had returned to his normal swoon-worthy olive, but his eyes burned red.

"He's...He didn't make it."

"Oh." He let my meaning settle in. Then smiled and patted me on the shoulder. "Take heart. This isn't the first time."

Wait. What?

"Ah right. We're done with the feelings circle. We need to talk. Friend of yours?" Steve held up a little wax figure. A man in a suit, carved to look exactly like Faust. "Your store is cursed, and it's personal. Listen up."

Steve unrolled the tiny scroll from that blue bottle and read it to us:

This place I curse and all within.
May thee be devoured by the accursed,
thy heart be splintered,
thy body drowned under the tide,

Thy soul cast into the gate.
Death shall call this store its home.
By my hand, a terrible end will befall you all.
Hell Hath No Fury Like a Woman Scorned.
Love, Katia
P.S. You said you'd call me. Why didn't you call me? Please call me!

"Oh, dear." Faust swallowed hard and tugged nervously at his collar. "If you'll excuse me, I have some matters to attend to."

He walked through the stockroom door, eyes wide with terror, like a freaking robot. Great. If the devil—oh excuse me, "a" devil not "the" devil—is spooked...

"That can't be good." I thought it, but DeeDee said it out loud.

"Woo. Katia. Didn't see that coming." Steve pulled a second bottle of curse breaker out of his utility belt and poured it into my bucket. "Extra extra strength. You're gonna need it."

"Who's Katia?"

"Faust's ex girlfriend. She doesn't play arahnd." Steve clapped me on the shoulder. "Wouldn't wanna be you."

Oh. Great. Just great.

I had a lot of time to think about Faust's bitter break up as I mopped. Because I mopped like I have never mopped before. Splinters? Drowning? Terrible ends? DEATH? Hello! I had to break that curse, stat. I mopped and swabbed that floor like it was my job. Okay, technically it was my job, but this time I did it like my life depended on it. Because I had a sinking feeling that it did.

I refilled that mop bucket with clean water three times and each time Steve circled back to slip an extra bottle of curse breaker into the bucket. We were up to five extra bottles of curse breaker per bucket at this point. He didn't say anything, he just shook his head and looked at me like I was on my way to the guillotine.

I mopped my way through that goop and through the store, front to back. DeeDee and I worked as a team. She picked up and swept everything in the upturned aisles, and I mopped up behind her. While she wrestled Bubby's busted television into a big garbage can, Faust emerged from the back in a brand new suit. Hair coiffed. Okay. All of him was coiffed. No one would never guess by looking at him that he'd just been chewed up and spit out through another dimension.

"Young mister, Lloyd. It seems we have a problem." He stepped to me in his thousand dollar shoes. He seemed to glide through the store, unsullied by the mess, like he was magically Scotchgarded head to toe.

"A problem?" Gulp. Yep. Okay. I had fucked up. Hungry grass, pumpkin spice fritter, pixies, Earl? Henrietta and the floor wash? I didn't know!

He put his hand on my shoulder and inserted himself between me and DeeDee. "I have done a thorough soul search, but it seems you have no desires that I can fulfill. I'm not sure how to reward you."

"Reward?" Was he kidding?

"Your performance bonus?"

I blank stared at him.

"Young man, you must know you saved the world tonight for the second time. I've never had such an accomplished graveyard shift crew. Modern civilization is indebted to you. You see, the undead are wonderful, useful entities when contained, but if even one was ever let loose on the world, it would be the end. They reproduce exponentially, you know. One becomes two becomes four until there are no living left. Didn't you see that wonderful documentary? What was it called, 'Night of the Living Dead?' Thankfully, Mr. Romero and his crew were able to contain that outbreak."

Holy shit. It was a documentary. "DeeDee wasn't kidding."

"Yes. DeeDee. We must speak about that." Faust glanced over at her. "You did have two desires in your file, but I cannot provide either of them. You see, I can only fulfill your tangible, material desires. My own personal rule. I'm sure you've heard the stories about devils granting wishes. Those wishes tend to go horribly awry. That's why I no longer partake in such activities."

Uh, no longer?

"As such, I cannot grant you the love of a particular woman or the body of a Hemsworth." Faust glanced down at my beer belly. "You must earn fitness and love through traditional means, without my intervention, I'm afraid. But a free gym membership is one benefit we provide."

"OMG. How embarrassing. The devil thinks you're fat." Angel eight ball rolled through aisle five. Rolling is generous. More like wobbled. Maybe I forgot to mention it, but I'd refilled him with sink water and wrapped him in duct tape when I refilled the mop bucket. Because I felt bad for him. Apparently, this was my reward for getting sentimental.

Oh, wait. Faust was still talking. Oops.

"...and maybe with time, your pure heart and bravery will win over the fair maiden." He winked. "In the meantime, please do consider any tangible need that I could fulfill. I will write you a blank check. Use it wisely."

Shlooooooooooploop.

Yeah. That was Big Larry's head finally squeezing all the way through the beer cave door, thanks to Bubby's clever use of a giant shoe horn and Steve's swift boot kick to his pot. The frame dripped with petroleum jelly. "You're next, fatty." Steve put his hand on Bubby's backside and ushered him through the door.

"Well, now that the way is clear, I will take over." Faust took the mop out of my hand. "I will personally release the curse nearest the gate. It's best if we don't take chances. Why don't you take a break? This evening has been long and difficult for you, I'm sure."

He didn't have to tell me twice. I walked outside and sat my not-Hemsworthy fat ass down on the sidewalk.

The air was thick with smoke. Heat pulsed from the glowing orange remains of Monster Burger. The parking lot was littered with bricks. The force of the explosion had shot them all the way across the intersection. One even hit the ice machine, breaking a big round hole in the glass.

DeeDee came out and sat down next to me, carrying a bottle of Wild Turkey. Not a mini, either. This one was so big it had a handle. There was a red ribbon wrapped around the stem.

We both sat there looking at Monster Burger. We didn't speak. I knew what she was thinking, because I was thinking it, too. Kevin. This victory was bittersweet. It didn't feel like a victory at all. It felt like survival. And loss.

After a while, she put her hand in mine and squeezed. She looked at me, and through a sad smile said, "Who would ever guess we'd save the world twice? I only wish Kevin were here to see it."

A tear streaked down her cheek.

"Yeah. Me, too."

I didn't know how it happened, but that little asshole had become my friend.

"I planned to give him this for his birthday, but..." She cracked the seal on the Wild Turkey bottle and took a swig. She handed it to me. "For Kevin."

"For Kevin." I took a sip, and it burned. Jesus. How did he drink this stuff? Roaches really could survive anything. "So, do you know Faust's ex-girlfriend? The one who cursed us?"

I whispered that last part, because speaking about it felt suspiciously like tempting fate.

"Nope. Never met her. But now we know who Caroline Ford Vanderbilt's mystery partner is. I mean it said HHNF on the card."

"Uh, what?"

"HHNF? Hell hath no fury? Clearly, Katia is the woman scorned."

Oh yeah. Duh.

"Poor Caroline." DeeDee shook her head. "Speak of the devil."

Sure enough, a stretch Hummer limo pulled up in front of the pile of charred bricks that was once Monster Burger. The giant chauffeur guy stepped out of the driver's seat, lurched to the passenger door, and opened it. Caroline Ford Vanderbilt clip clopped out on her designer crutches, dressed head to toe in fur. "Why are we stopping? I told you to drive me straight home after the cocktail mixer!"

It didn't take her long to figure out why. She stared at the smoking ruins in shock, jaw practically on the ground. The giant chauffeur slipped into the driver's seat, closed the door and started to drive off. She yelled after him, "Stop! What do you think you're doing? You can't leave me out here with these vagrants. This is a terrible neighborhood!"

She waved her hand in a big gesture toward Demon Mart and the pawn shop. Yep. We're the vagrants.

The Hummer stopped and backed up. "That's right. You do what I tell you. We don't pay you to think," she barked, charming as always. "The help these days. You need to learn your place."

The driver's side window rolled down. The chauffeur threw her purse out the window, then peeled out of there like he was stunt driving in a Fast & Furious sequel. That purse hit her right in the face, triggering a stream of expletives that shot out of her like demon barf. It didn't matter. That stretch limo sped down the street and off into the sunrise, never to return again.

"Looks like Caroline just got dumped," DeeDee said.

Caroline, in a tizzy, turned around and caught sight of us. "What are you two low-class minimum wage losers looking at, huh? Did you do this? Did you burn down my restaurant? This is your fault, isn't it? I'll get you!"

Gee. Caroline wants revenge? Get in line, lady.

"I think I'd rather be inside than out here with her," DeeDee said. "Come on. If we're feeling charitable, maybe we'll call her a cab."

We both stood up and started inside.

"Uuuuuuuuuh."

We both froze, solid as ice.

"Uuuuuuuuuuuuuuuh."

DeeDee and I locked eyes. You heard that, right? That sound could only mean one thing: Zombie. DeeDee slowly tightened the cap on the Wild Turkey, then turned the bottle upside down, wielding it like a club.

"Uuuuuuuuuuuh."

I pointed to the ice machine. The sound came from inside. Weird, right? I looked at DeeDee like, "how did a zombie get in there?"

And she looked at me like, "I don't know!" as we tiptoed closer to the machine.

She motioned for me to open the door as she prepared to club whatever was in there. I opened it, slowly, so as not to alarm our soon to be skull-crushed target.

"Uuuuuuuuuuuh."

The sound echoed around inside. It came from a dark shadow on top of all the bags. Huh. Too small to be a whole zombie. Maybe it was just the head? I mean, they could still moan and bite and stuff if they were decapitated, right?

DeeDee raised the bottle over her head and moved in.

"Uuuuuuuuuh. Uuuuuh. Oooooh. My head."

Oh my God.

"Pour me some of that whiskey," a tiny voice said. "I need something to take the edge off."

DeeDee dropped the Wild Turkey. From shock. The bottle broke on the sidewalk.

"Are you a pack of dumb asses? Did you spill the booze?"

"Kevin?" Sure enough. When my eyes adjusted to the darkness, I could see Kevin on his back, legs wiggling, stuck in the crack between two bags of ice. It looked like it had melted briefly, then refrozen as a solid block around his backside.

DeeDee chipped him out with her fist. When she fished him out of the machine, he was pitch black, covered in soot, and his belt of Bic lighters had melted down to nubs.

Holy shit. That little jerk made it out alive. Guess that explosion didn't shoot a brick straight into the ice machine. It had shot a Kevin.

DeeDee burst into tears, kissed Kevin all over, and hugged him so tight I thought his legs might pop off.

"Gee, Kevin," I said, disguising that I was totally amped to see him. "That's the most action you've had in a while."

"Jealous?" Kevin shot me four thumbs up—well, you get the idea— as DeeDee rained kisses on him. "Don't just stand there, dipshit. Pour me a drink. I've had a hell of a night."

It took longer than usual to ride home. Apparently, when a hundred people who have been turned into mindless zombies by the local hamburger stand trample your bike, the frame and wheels bend. And bust the gears. And the chain falls off. Like ten times. On one ride home.

When I stepped in the front door, Mom was in the kitchen getting ready for work. She stood comatose by the coffee machine, as usual, until she saw me. Then she perked up. "Oh my goodness, honey? Are you okay? What happened?"

"I had a rough night." And I looked it, too. Yeah. I still had salt, embalming fluid, and Larry slime all over me. Did I forget to mention that the employee shower was cursed? It sprayed acid, not water. No magic shower for me. Faust was spritzing it with curse breaker as we speak.

Mom started crying. "You tell me right now what you do all night. I know something is up. Look at you. And all that money? What's going on?"

Angel eight ball hit my foot, leaking red. "Remember, lying to your parents is a sin."

Yeah, yeah. I know. Thanks for the assist.

While my Mom cried and checked me over for injuries, my brain spun. What the hell was I going to tell her?

Something stiff appeared under my shirt. (Not that. Get your mind out of the gutter.) I sunk my hand under the hem and pulled out a manila envelope. The label read, "Loan agreement between Asmodius Faust and Lloyd Lamb Wallace."

Oh. This must be my blank check. My reward.

I thought about it. Huh. A loan. That was a great excuse. A logical, easy answer for Mom. It would explain the money.

"It's a lie, though," angel said. "From a devil."

I looked at Mom. Her sad eyes, her tears, the worry wrinkle, and my mind reeled.

After a minute or two, I said, "Look. Working at Dairy Mart is dangerous. All kinds of crazy people wander in. Stuff's always exploding or breaking. Mr. Faust, my boss, pays me well *because* it's dangerous. He can't find good people to work there, so he'll do anything to keep me. He says I'm doing a good job."

"But—" Mom had stopped crying, but that worry wrinkle was still super duper deep.

"The money? My boss knew I was in debt. I was looking for other jobs because I needed money. He helped me out. He paid my bills."

The manila envelope? The writing disappeared, and so did the thick stack of papers inside. It was empty. I didn't cash my blank check. As crazy as it sounds, lying to my Mom just felt too bad.

"Oh, honey." She hugged me. Big mistake. She was definitely gonna need another shower before work. "I'm so sorry I doubted you. I'm so proud of you. My baby boy."

Angel eight ball hit my shoe. "Holy crap. You pulled it off. You didn't lie. Sure, you equivocated a little, but you that's not *technically* lying."

Ugh. Shut up. I kicked him away.

Mom eventually let me out of her death grip hug and left for work. I took a very long shower, extra soap. Seriously, like two whole bars. Then

I crawled into bed. I sunk into a pile of nice warm covers, exhausted. Gertrude snuggled up next to me and purred—alive, totally not smited by God—and for the first time in a long time, I felt like maybe, just maybe, the worst was behind me. Everything was going to be all right.

So of course, that's when a tiny green portal opened right above my head. Kevin dove out. He landed on my chest and started waving around a triangle of black plastic. "Do you wanna explain to me exactly what happened to my Zebra record? You had one job, kid. One!"

Grrrrrrrrrrrrrrrrrrrrrr.

"What the hell was that?" Kevin dropped the sad remains of his Zebra album and put his fists up, karate style.

I sat up. Gertrude hissed.

Grrrrrrrrrrrrrrrrrrrrrr.

We all turned to the closet. My employee manual emerged from underneath a pile of ugly wool sweaters my Great Aunt Edna had knitted me for Christmas. It growled at us, then snapped up one of my dirty french fry and zombie guts soaked socks and dragged it back to its closet hobo lair.

"Jesus Christ! Don't tell me." Kevin shook his head. "You still haven't read your employee manual, have you?"

The End

Thank you so so much for reading 24/7 Demon Mart.

Visit www.dmguay.com or follow me on Bookbub if you'd like to be alerted when new books in this series are released!

Coming next: Angel Trouble!

BOOK SAUSAGE

Here we are again at the end of another book, and finally, the fun part. It's book sausage time! This is where I pull back the curtain so you can see how I killed, chopped, molded, and stuffed all of my embarrassing/ funny/ sad/ romantic/ <insert chosen emotion here> life tidbits into the proverbial sausage casing to make the book you hold in your hands right now.

Hi, guys! Welcome to the end of yet another 24/7 Demon Mart book. I am SO amped that you're here. Seriously, it means the world to me. It's May 22, 2020, and a lot has happened since *The Graveyard Shift* was released last October. (I did NOT see Pandemic 2020 coming, did you?)

First, Podium Audio will be producing the audiobook editions of the 24/7 Demon Mart series, and they have hired voice actor Todd Haberkorn to narrate. I am over the moon. He's been part of so many shows that I love: Ben 10, One Piece, Attack on Titan, One Punch Man, Tokyo Ghoul, AND the World of Warcraft, Destiny 2, and Resident Evil 2 and 3 video games. Yeah. He rocks, and I can't wait to hear him bring Kevin, Bubby, Lloyd, and the rest of the gang to life.

And, because of you, dear readers, we've been able to donate $1,587 to the Kidney Cancer Research Alliance since March 2019, and $910 to food banks in Ohio in 2020, since this stupid C virus popped onto the scene, causing demand for food assistance to rise. So thank you for supporting me. I donate part of my book sales to charity every month. I'm not a Stephen King-level big money author with millions to spare by any stretch, but hey. We all have to do what we can. Be the good in a hard world, right?

As if all this good news isn't enough, I am also in remission. I have stage 4 kidney cancer. It totally sucks, long story. But, by some miracle, I have made it into the eight percent of patients who have a "complete response" to immunotherapy, meaning there are no visible tumors on my scans. I'm incredibly grateful. Of course, I don't know how long it will last. Three months, ten years, forever? Whatever it is, I'll take it. Because life is beautiful and I want MORE!

I never dreamed the Demon Mart series would receive so much love. I didn't even think I'd live long enough to write these books, but here we are. Holy cow. We made it people, and it's been a wild ride!

Now, let's talk about zombies.

The first zombie movie I ever saw was Return of the Living Dead. It played on endless repeat on cable TV in the late 1980s, and young, rural country bumpkin me was hooked. OMG. I'd never seen anything like it. I tuned in to watch every single time it was on. This movie was a magical combination for me. It was scary. It was funny. And the soundtrack? Amazing. I mean, The Cramps? Hello! I can't point to this movie as the reason I became punk rock and dyed my hair pink, purple or blue—I blame that squarely on the Missing Person's "Words" video—but I do still love The Cramps. And zombies. And horror comedy. And this movie, like so hard.

(Let's agree not to talk about the sequels. Return of the Living Dead 2? Groan. I don't even know what was up with that Tar man. Seriously. Couldn't they just use the same suit from the first movie? Shoot. Now we're talking about the sequels, aren't we? Crap. All right. You got me. The only one I liked was No. 3, the one with the punk rock chick with the piercings. Moving on.)

Now, when I was making Monster Burger, I tried really hard to include all of my favorite bits and pieces of the zombie fiction formula. Like the trope about how humans pretty much always act like zombies, at least a little bit, all the time. Which is why they wander the mall after they die in Dawn of the Dead, and why the main characters never notice that the zombie apocalypse has begun until it's too late. Waaaaay too late. (My favorite use of this trope is in Shaun of the Dead, when Shaun walks past a dozen zombies on his way to the store and doesn't even notice.)

But I also tried to dig deeper. I love a snarling legit dead zombie as much as the next guy, but those weren't your standard zombie until Night of the Living Dead lurched onto the scene in 1968. Before that, most movie zombies were created by magic—usually voodoo—and were living, enslaved people beholden to their magical creator. Bela Lugosi's 1932 White Zombie created the mold for the genre, by featuring Lugosi as magical master enslaving the living via clever use of magic and pharmaceuticals. (Along with your standard offensive stereotypes of island residents. Ahem. Moving on...) It really wasn't until George Romero came along that zombies turned primarily into walking, flesh-eating dead people.

Don't get me wrong. I love all the Romero films and was totally stoked to run into his Dawn of the Dead and Creepshow DP, Mike Gornick, at a horror movie festival last October. Yes, I geeked hard and got an autograph!

But I hope that my burger zombies paid appropriate homage to all the magic zombies that came before George transformed the genre. My magic zombie inspiration came from old 1930s and 40s voodoo zombie movies, as well as the books DeeDee mentions—*The Magic Island* and *The Serpent and the Rainbow*. They are real books about Haitian voodoo and include legends of living people turned into zombie slaves. *The Magic Island* by William Seabrook debuted in 1929 and was the inspiration for White Zombie and all the zombie films that followed. It's a dated book, but it's also the reason zombies are a thing at all in pop culture.

And if you're wondering about my use of salt as the cure: That isn't made up. There is a link to salt and zombification in real life. Stories suggest that people were drugged into a zombie-like state so they could be used as slave labor on large island plantations. In some accounts, food fed to the living zombies contained no salt. The working theory is the food was drugged, and not salting it alerted the zombies' handlers just in case they ate out of the wrong pot at lunch time. According to Alfred Metraux's 1959 book *Voodoo in Haiti*, the folk belief is that salt ends zombification. So yeah. I took that whole salt idea and ran with it.

I totes stole the idea for the zombie containment collars as well. They were inspired by the horror comedy movie Fido, which in my humble opinion, is an overlooked gem. I have included a short list of my favorite overlooked zombie films below.

We also have some special guest stars in Monster Burger. Gertrude was inspired by a cat my family adopted when I was in the third grade. She was fat, gray and had three-legs. (She'd been caught in an animal trap, and no one wanted to adopt her. I did a 4H veterinary medicine project about three-legged cats that won a rosette ribbon at the county fair. Yes, I'm bragging. I still have the ribbon.) She lived to the ripe old age of twenty, and at the end was blind, mostly deaf and liked to pee all over everything.

Steve from the plant is a not even disguised version of my friend Steve. Who is from Pittsburgh, frequently refers to people as idjits, jagoffs and morons—mostly during Steelers games—and has a serious Pittsburghese accent. Like seriously. He talks just like Pittsburgh Dad. (Check him out on Youtube.) God bless him. He's got a gruff exterior, but he's all sweet genuine kindness and gold on the inside. I have no doubt that if the zombie plant in Monroeville were real, Steve would be running it and he wouldn't be putting up with any patty cake hands nonsense from any of us.

As for Kevin's Zebra album. Music is huge in my life. I love listening to music and going to shows. I once saw a Journey cover band in a Louisiana dive bar located on a bayou sandbar that you could only get to by boat. I once stood around the Ponchatoula Strawberry Festival in the sweltering heat for hours waiting for Zebra to play. I'm dedicated. I lived in New Orleans for a decade, and Zebra is one of our many hometown rock stars.

Kevin's love of both Dio and Zebra are a nod to my long-time bestie Lee Williams, a true fan who is able to articulate exactly why they are awesome and why you should love them, too. We have many conversations about this. When he was a kid, Lee rode his bike to the record store to buy Zebra's album the day it was released. Sadly, he lost that copy when Hurricane Katrina flooded his house. Alas, there's no replacing it, just like there's no replacing Kevin's copy, but the music and the love lives on. (Yes, I own the album on vinyl.)

Maybe I shouldn't be telling so many stories, because they tend to come back to bite me. If you remember, in *The Graveyard Shift's* Book Sausage, I told you about my Mom, who passed her love of horror onto me, and about my six-month stint working the graveyard shift in a convenience store in Portland, Oregon, in the mid 1990s, for the princely sum of $4.50 an hour.

Well, I don't know how many of you read these ramblings, but my Mom did. She stepped in my front door clutching her paperback copy of *The Graveyard Shift* to the embroidered snowman on her sweater and said, "You never told me you were robbed at gunpoint!" Cue the sobs.

Yeah. I may have left out some of the more unseemly details of my life as they were happening, because I was young, female, and two thousand miles from home. Why worry your mom?

Now for the movies. We all know Return of the Living Dead, Shaun of the Dead, Night of the Living Dead plus sequels, 28 Days Later, etcetera etcetera. But there are so many more awesome zombie movies out there. Here's a very short list of some of my forgotten favorites!

Denise's favorite underrated and overlooked zombie movies

Cemetery Man (aka Dellamorte Dellamore. 1994). This is an Italian film about an outcast cemetery caretaker and his hunchbacked, Igor-like assistant who watch over the cemetery and kill the recently risen dead. In this town, some people rise from the dead as man-eating zombies seven days after they die. No one knows why, they just know it's a thing. Add in romance, great effects, and artful filming, and you've got a really well done movie that is a rare combination: equal parts horror, comedy, and art.

Fido. This is a 2006 movie about a post-zombie apocalypse world that looks suspiciously like 1950s America. Colorful, perfectly manicured towns are surrounded by fences to keep the zombie hoards out, while the affluent use collar-controlled zombies as maids and butlers. The questionably ethical corporation Zomcom runs the show, and anyone who steps out of line risks being cast out of town, left to fend for themselves on the other side of the gate, which is a barren wasteland. Naturally, things go south.

Chopper Chicks in Zombie Town (1989). When an all-female motorcycle gang looking for a good time rolls into a sleepy town in the middle of nowhere—which just happens to have a mortician/mad scientist conducting zombie experiments and an abandoned mine—what could go wrong? Someone slipped this gem to me on VHS tape back in the 1990s, and I was hooked. MTV VJ Martha Quinn, Billy Bob Thornton, and Don Calfa, who played Ernie the undertaker in Return of the Living Dead, are all in it!

Zombies of Sugar Hill. I totes love this 1974 blaxploitation zombie film, not quite as much as I love Blacula, but pretty close. When Sugar Hill's boyfriend is murdered by mob thugs, she does what any grieving woman would do. She summons the voodoo loa Baron Samedi and his army of zombies, so she can kill them all spectacularly. Duh. Thugs beware: Never take a cab out to a pigpen in the middle of nowhere. Oh, and watch out for alligators and quicksand!

BrainDead (aka Dead Alive in the US. 1992). Did you know Peter Jackson of Lord of the Rings fame made a zombie film before he traveled to middle earth? Oh yes, he did, and it is fantastic. When a rabid Sumatran rat monkey at the Wellington Zoo bites Lionel's incredibly domineering and unpleasant elderly mother, she turns zombie. And boy, she does it spectacularly, in a slow burn gross out that builds to what might be one of the bloodiest and most fun zombie slaying scenes ever. I first saw this movie at its U.S. Premiere at a 24-hour horror movie marathon, and I have been in love with it since.

Night of the Creeps. (1989) Night of the Creeps is an overlooked comedy mish mash of both sci-fi and horror comedy. Its fun. It's tacky. It doesn't take itself too seriously, and that's why it's such a fun movie. When a canister of extra terrestrial brain eating space slugs crash lands on earth, well, nothing good happens. The cryogenics lab gets wrecked, and you can forget about the spring formal. You can't resist a movie where Tom Atkins of The Fog and Creepshow fame gets to deliver this epic line: "The good news is your dates are here, the bad news is, they're dead."

That's all for now. Stay tuned for the next 24/7 Demon Mart books, "Angel Trouble" and "Critters from the Poo Lagoon." Coming soon! Until next time.

WHO THE HECK IS DM GUAY?

D. M. Guay writes about the intersection of real life with the supernatural. She's an award-winning journalist living in Ohio, a hobby urban farmer (you can't beat her beets!), a painter, and a retired roller derby player. Her favorite things—besides books— are tiki bars, liquid eyeliner, the 1968 Camaro, 24-hour horror movie festivals, art by Picasso, rock concerts, and most of all, people who make art, despite adversity, no matter what life throws at them.

She's had to put that in action herself. She has stage 4 kidney cancer and is still alive and kicking two years months *after* her oncologist said she would be dead. Thanks for reading. Visit her at www.dmguay.com, follow her on Bookbub, or visit her at twitter.com/dmguay.

Printed in Great Britain
by Amazon